RUSSIA

Chasing Chinatown Trilogy Book 1

(Abby Kane FBI Thriller)

Ty Hutchinson

This book is a work of fiction. Names, characters, places, and incidents are the product of the author's imagination or are used fictitiously. Any resemblance to actual persons, living or dead, is coincidental.

All rights reserved. No part of this book may be reproduced, stored in a retrieval system, or transmitted in any form or by any means (electronic, mechanical, photocopying, recording, or otherwise) without the prior written permission of the author, Ty Hutchinson.

Published by Ty Hutchinson
Copyright © 2013 by Ty Hutchinson
Cover Design: Kay Hutchison

For my fans. Enjoy.

RUSSIAN HILL

Chasing Chinatown Trilogy Book 1

(Abby Kane FBI Thriller)

Chapter 1

Jerry and Vicki burst through the door of their hotel room in a fit of giggles. She led; he followed. She dropped her purse, then removed her brown wig before spinning once like a ballerina and falling back onto the king-size bed.

"I had such a wonderful time today." Vicki let out a breath and smiled. "Isn't San Francisco the best city ever?"

"Charming and quite loveable," said her husband as he collapsed onto the bed next to her. He buried the side of his face in the soft pillow, causing his cheek to squish upwards and clamp his eye shut.

"The day unfolded perfectly. It couldn't have happened any better."

He lifted his head. "There was a little planning involved."

She jabbed a finger into his ribs. "You know what I mean, silly."

"Boy, I'm beat." He cuddled the pillow and turned his face away from her.

"Me, too, but we have dinner reservations at Top of the Mark and I'm looking forward to it."

Jerry didn't need to look at his wife to know she had

pouty lips. Her voice conveyed her stance. He also knew that, if he looked at her, she'd hit him with fluttering eyelashes. He never could say no to that. "Okay, we'll rest for a bit," he mumbled.

The comfy pillow top sucked the couple into its dreamy grasp, slowing their breaths and muting the knock of their heartbeats. *Just for a few seconds...*

In fear of losing the night to an early bedtime, Vicki reached over and pushed her husband's arm until he rocked back and forth.

"I'm up, dear."

She continued.

"I'm up," he said louder.

"We have to motivate, or we'll both fall asleep." She swung her legs off the bed first. "Come on; get up. I'll shower while you get the pictures ready."

By now, Jerry had eased himself into a sitting position on the edge of the bed, his eyes still closed. She walked over to his side, grabbed both his hands and pulled him to his feet.

"My camera is in my purse." Vicki gestured toward the desk.

She disappeared into the bathroom, ignored the tub, and stepped into the shower stall. She fiddled with the hot and cold knobs until the water temperature was perfect. She stood still, letting the drops massage her neck and back as she recounted the day in her head. Those thoughts produced a smile. She lathered bath gel across her arms and belly but stopped at her breasts. There, she traced a straight line across her chest a number of times before snapping out of her trance. She continued showering and washed away whatever remaining desire she might have had for sleep. She then wrapped her short, black hair in a fluffy white towel and slipped on an equally soft robe before exiting the bathroom.

"I feel so much better," Vicki announced as she approached Jerry from behind.

He sat at the desk, browsing through a photo organizer on his laptop. He had plucked photos one by one and dragged them to a desktop folder titled Piper.

She leaned down and let her arms rest on his shoulders. "What pictures are you thinking of using?"

"There are a bunch of good ones, but I'll show you the ones I think are the best."

He clicked on the folder, and it sprang open. "This first one is of you and Piper on the ferry."

"Oh, yeah, that's a good one. We look like we're having fun."

"Here are the two of you eating cotton candy at the pier. It really shows off Piper's beautiful, hazel eyes."

"Indeed."

"This one is from our hike in Muir Woods. You two were trying to stretch your arms around a redwood tree. Remember that?" he asked, twisting his head around.

"Those trees were so tall."

"But I think what will really seal the deal here is the video."

"I'm glad you recorded this time around."

A black rectangle popped up on the screen, and a moment later footage of a young woman with a ponytail began to play. She walked on a trail while looking up at the trees around her. Every now and then, she would playfully look back at the camera. "Why are you filming me? You should be filming your wife in all this beauty."

"Oh, it's just that we're both having such a wonderful time with you," said a male voice off camera. "I want this for memories. Isn't that right, dear?"

"Absolutely." Another woman's voice could be heard outside the frame. She stepped into view and hooked arms with the young woman. "Trust me, Piper; he has a ton of pictures of me. It's nice not having to be the focus of his lens."

"You both look great," said the male voice.

The young woman let go an innocent laugh. She appeared unaware of her beautiful Mediterranean looks. Her long locks started with dark roots until right above her shoulder, where they began to lighten into perfect, washed-out surfer strands at the tips. She stood tall at six feet even and sported long, graceful limbs. The cut-off denim shorts and gray, San Francisco Giants T-shirt she wore complemented her naturally olive complexion, and her cross-trainers perfectly highlighted her slender calves.

The three had left the paved path of the park, where most visitors spent their time, and ventured on to one of the many trails that crisscrossed the surrounding forest. Forty minutes later, and without passing a single other hiker, they reached a beautiful clearing and rested. Birds could be heard talking to each other while the leaves rustled every so often from the gentle breeze—a calmness foreign to most city dwellers.

"This reminds me of growing up in Ohio," Piper said from the screen. "It was so quiet there—only the sounds of nature. Nothing more."

"This is the part we've been waiting for," said the man as he poked his finger at the volume button on his laptop, maxing it out.

Piper had been looking straight up toward the trees while slowly spinning around. As she turned toward the camera, the older woman entered the frame with her right arm cocked back. She firmly planted both feet before swinging her arm around in a wide arc as hard and as fast as she could, driving a small hatchet directly into Piper's chest. *Thunk*. The force nearly toppled the young woman, but the older woman grabbed her shirt and steadied her before backing out of the frame.

Piper's eyes widened as she looked down at the instrument buried deep in her chest. Her bottom lip trembled as a dark, red stain spread from the hatchet and across her shirt. She took a few quick breaths, looking straight into the camera. A moment later, she dropped to her knees. The camera followed. Still, she focused on the lens, unable to speak and barely breathing.

She reached out with one arm, her only way to convey the two words her mouth no longer could: *Help me.*

And then she fell.

The camera followed as she hit the ground on her left side, her eyes still gazing at the lens.

One breath. Then another. Then nothing.

Jerry closed the video window and looked up at his wife.

"Bravo! Excellent work, my dear," Vicki cheered. "I love how you followed her to the ground. Brilliant."

"I couldn't have done it without you. You have a great arm. And that disguise—I love you with longer hair." He stood up, grabbed his wife by the waist, and gave her a kiss. "But Piper is the real star, a wonderful participant."

"Shall we upload before dinner?" Vicki asked.

"Yes, of course. I'm very excited about this one."

Jerry sat back down and clicked on his Games folder, then on a dragon icon. The screen went black before a gold and red, animated dragon appeared, snorting a few breaths of fire before morphing into a logo with the title "Chasing Chinatown."

He entered a password, and a few seconds later, a map of the world appeared with a waypoint in Toronto and San

Francisco connected by an arced line. Two cartoon turtle avatars dressed in nautical outfits appeared in the upper right-hand corner over the words "Team Carlson."

"Just think; six months ago we were bored and looking for adventure. Now we've logged five thousand miles and left our mark in two major cities, all thanks to this little program."

There were five links to the left of the map: Attractions One through Five. Jerry clicked on the third and started uploading photos. Within a few seconds, the transfer was complete. A confirmation message appeared, followed by another stating that their content was under review.

"I hate this part—the waiting." Vicki took a seat on the bed and leaned back on her hands.

The wait seemed like an hour, but only thirty seconds had passed before the screen erupted into fireworks and the word "Congratulations!" appeared. After the light show, the header titled Attraction Four turned from red to green. Jerry clicked on it, and a graphic of a paper scroll appeared. It unraveled, revealing a message: *Good fortune comes in many forms. Find the right one for your next clue.*

Vicki sat up and leaned forward for a closer look. "Good fortune? Could they be any less clear?"

Jerry looked back at his wife. "Don't worry; we'll figure it out. We can talk it through over dinner if you want. But for now, let's enjoy the fact that we completed three Attractions." He stood up and pulled his wife off the bed.

"We're on a roll."

He danced with her, spinning her around before dipping her back, her towel falling off her head and her robe opening, leaving her naughty bits in plain view.

Vicki smiled as he brought her back to a standing position. She planted kisses all over his face before pulling away. "You were so right about this trip. I'm glad we did it."

"Yeah, me, too. I'm having a killer time."

Chapter 2

Dim Sum Sunday.

That's what Ryan and Lucy had come to call it. I had fallen into the habit of taking the family out for brunch every Sunday. We all enjoyed the outing, especially my mother-in-law, Po Po. She had made friends with a few of the shopkeepers in Chinatown and used that time to talk, most of it gossip. She felt the need to converse in her native language. I didn't crave it like she did, but I could understand. The language was a part of her and needed to be expressed. Plus, sometimes a story is funnier in Chinese.

I spoke English most of the time, and so did the kids. But they were learning Cantonese—not Mandarin, the official language of China—because Po Po was determined that they were to learn the language we spoke in Hong Kong. When I wasn't home, she would only communicate with them in Chinese. English wasn't allowed. She was firm on that issue, and I agreed. Being bilingual would give Ryan and Lucy an advantage someday. They didn't seem to mind. Both took it in stride as something normal.

We all loved Chinatown for different reasons. For Po Po and me, it gave us a taste of some of the things we missed: the up-and-down tones of Chinese spoken on the street, the smell of dried everything and anything wafting out of the pharmacies, and the plethora of Chinese restaurants serving up our favorite foods, to name a few. For the kids, it was the usual: toys and sweets.

Lucy, my youngest, was six and a half and had come to develop a mind of her own. Instead of shadowing me like she had in the past, she found other ways to entertain herself. Everything Hello Kitty was her obsession. Whenever we passed by the store that sold those stickers, she would pull me inside, hoping I'd pull out my wallet.

At age nine, Ryan continued to mature and seek his independence. More and more, he spent time with friends and in numerous after-school activities, ranging from Judo to soccer and even taking cultural lessons at the Chinese Youth Center. His Chinatown guilty pleasure was the little boxes of snappers. He would beg and promise me he wouldn't throw them at his sister. The last time I bought him a box, he threw the very first snapper at Lucy's head. I threw the rest into the trash.

I remember telling him, "I told you not to throw them at people."

"But, Abby, you didn't say you would throw them away."

"I expect you to listen to me whether you know the consequences or not." *I may not be his biological mother, but I am still his mother, and I make the rules.*

Ever since then, he would ask, and I would say no. However, that day, my mood was positive, and I felt lenient. He had been punished long enough, so I bought him a box and reminded him of the rule.

We'd finished brunch a half hour earlier and were enjoying a stroll along Grant Avenue when Po Po stopped us in front of the Eastern Bakery. "I go buy rice cake for later."

That was another treat that had become customary.

She disappeared inside while the three of us remained on the sidewalk, hovering on the edge of the Sunday foot traffic. No sooner had I looked away from the kids than I heard a yelp, and Lucy ran behind me.

I looked at Ryan. "Did you just throw a snapper at your sister?"

"She said I could," he said calmly as if he had an airtight defense.

"What did I tell you earlier?"

He raised his shoulders and held his arms out. "But she said it would be okay."

He started to huff and stomp his feet; he knew what was coming.

I held out my hand. He handed over the box, and into the trashcan it went. I looked down at Lucy, who had a devious smile on her face. I reached down and took the package of stickers from her hand.

"Hey, those are mine."

"Not anymore." Into the trash they went. "Next time, don't taunt your brother."

Po Po returned to find two kids moping—frowning at the sidewalk when they weren't glaring at me or each other. Before she could ask what had happened, a loud cracking sound caught my attention. I drew a sharp breath. *A gunshot!* I quickly ushered the kids and Po Po back into the bakery. "Stay here."

Back outside, my eyes scanned the area. To my left, about fifty yards away, I noticed a commotion. I stepped off the sidewalk and took two steps into the street for a better look. That's when I saw him: a male teen pushing his way through the crowd. Behind him, in pursuit, I saw a tall man in a suit. Elderly people were pushed into one another as the teen bumped off them like a pinball. He soon left the sidewalk for the open road. That's when I spotted the gun in his right hand.

I couldn't tell why he was being chased, but as he approached me, I saw that his shirt was torn, and tattoos covered his chest. I'm not saying that made him a criminal, but I was in Chinatown, and I knew the neighborhood had Triads, a Chinese gang.

No sooner had I noticed his ink than he fired another shot at the suit following him. *This kid is nuts.* The sidewalks were packed with people, mostly families. If he kept shooting, the odds were that some innocent bystander would get hit.

I was off duty, but I still had my weapon on me. However, I didn't want to encourage him to fire his gun by pulling out mine. I figured at his speed, I could trip him up. He wasn't tall, but neither was I. A tackle was out of the question. I looked around for something to take his legs out but saw nothing. I worried whether my legs were long enough to tangle with his and if I could keep my balance. He was closing in. Fast. I had to decide.

Right as he was about to pass by, I stepped back into the street and swung my arm up as hard as I could. My forearm and fist caught him at the top of his chest, right below his Adam's apple. The force stopped him and kicked his feet up in front of him, causing him to land flat on his back, hard. He groaned as the gun fell out of his hand, and I kicked it away. The clothesline method triumphed again.

A few seconds later, the man in the suit arrived and flipped the kid over. He wheezed pretty hard as he tried to speak. "I'm a detective. Back away." He put a knee into the kid's back and handcuffed him.

"You shouldn't have interfered. It's dangerous," he said, still working on finding his breath.

My head jerked back, and my brow crinkled. I was expecting a thank you of some sort. "From the looks of it, you needed the help."

"I was catching up," he said between breaths.

He squatted, resting his hands on his thighs for a moment before standing fully upright. That's when I really noticed his height—unusual for an Asian. He had to have been at least six two, though a little on the skinny side. Sweat poured down the sides of his face and seeped into his collar. I watched him loosen his tie.

"You okay? You look like you're about to pass out."

He squinted at me. "I'll have you know I chased this guy up California before turning down Grant. You know how steep California is?"

"Mm-huh," I said as I clucked my tongue.

Just then, another tall man in a suit appeared. He was bald, white, and muscular.

Let me guess, SFPD paired up the two tall guys. "You caught him. Good work," he said with a Russian accent.

I cleared my throat.

Both men looked down at me. I shifted my weight to my left leg and folded my arms across my chest.

"She helped," the Asian one admitted.

A large smile appeared on the other guy's face, followed by a deep laugh. He then bent down and yanked the kid off the ground. He radioed for a squad car to meet him at the corner.

"Why were you chasing him?"

He paused before speaking. "He's a wanted suspect."

"Looks like a gang member with those tattoos on his chest."

"You normally involve yourself in law enforcement matters? What are you, a first-year law student or something?"

The left eyebrow arched. "Only when I help law enforcement *do* their job."

"Like I said, I had him."

By then, Po Po and the kids had returned to my side. "Well, it looks like everything is under control." I patted my stomach. "We just finished a large meal of dim sum. Time to go home and rest." *Zing!*

Clearly irritated and ready to move on, the detective handed me his card. "If you end up seeking medical attention for your arm, call me. I can probably get the department to reimburse you for any expenses."

"Thanks." I snatched the card out of his hand with the arm I had used earlier.

I watched him hurry to catch up with his partner before looking down at the card: Detective Kyle Kang, Personal Crimes Division.

Chapter 3

The next day, I arrived at the Philip Burton Federal Building at my usual time, 9:15 a.m. I had a travel mug full of hot tea in one hand and an onion bagel stuffed with cream cheese and double lox tucked away in my purse. My stomach grumbled during the elevator ride to my floor. I couldn't wait to sit down and devour my breakfast.

The office doors opened to a quiet floor. That week, an unusual number of agents were out in the field working cases, which I loved. A little quiet time coupled with my lox bagel was all right with me. No sooner had I placed my breakfast on my desk than I heard the one thing capable of ruining my morning.

"Abby!"

Dammit! I looked to my left and saw my supervisor, Special Agent Scott Reilly, leaning out of his office and tugging at me with his index finger. Generally he was okay and fair with a sense of humor. But boy did he have the worst timing of anyone I had ever known. I slipped my heels back on, picked up my tea, and made my way over to his office.

"Take a seat." He removed his wire-framed glasses and

wiped his face with his hand before letting out a breath. "How's that case with the attorney coming along?"

"We're close to raining on his parade."

The case I had been investigating involved an attorney who stole the identities of his terminally ill clients to fraudulently obtain millions of dollars from insurance companies. I thought I saw some sick bastards when I hunted serial killers back in Hong Kong, but this guy took it to a whole new level.

He would purchase variable annuities with death benefits and death put bonds and list his clients as co-owners. When they died, the bonds allowed survivor options, meaning the bond could be redeemed years before maturity at face value. Same thing with the annuities he purchased: they provided a guaranteed return of all money invested plus a guaranteed profit upon the death of the person named the annuitant. All he had to do was wait for them to die—which they did. We were days away from raiding his office and making an arrest.

"You're doing a great job. I'm pleased with your performance with the white-collar cases, considering your background."

A compliment. This can't be good. Part of the deal when I came on board with the FBI was that I would work white-collar crime. I had worked on enough cases involving homicide and organized crime and wanted a change of pace. Reilly agreed to it on one condition: if he believed my background would be helpful on a certain case, he would put me on it. So far he hadn't abused his powers, but I felt as if one of those moments were coming.

"The satellite office in Oakland has themselves in a pickle. Over the weekend, we received a tip that the man fingered as the person responsible for mailing arsenic to the office of the Mayor of Oakland was seen camping in the woods near Mount Tamalpais, in Marin County. They coordinated with a couple of rangers from the U.S. Forest Service and did a sweep of the area they believed him to be in."

"They find him?"

"No, but they did find a fresh body: a young woman with an axe sticking out of her chest. Doesn't look like a camping accident either."

"So what's the problem?" I asked, folding my arms across my chest.

"The rangers are arguing that the FBI should take the lead since our agents were the ones who *technically* discovered the body."

"Yeah, but it's their jurisdiction."

"I know. Here's where it gets tricky. The body, and I'm not kidding here, was found on the boundary of State land and the land of the National Parks—Muir Woods to be exact. So that's another agency, the National Park Service, that's involved, and right now, everyone's pointing fingers."

"Talk about splitting hairs. If you want my opinion,

those two agencies should fight it out. Between the two of them, they're responsible for all things wilderness."

Reilly sat quietly, pondering the dilemma. After a few moments, he took a breath and straightened up. "Abby, I want you to take over the case."

I knew that was coming. "Why do you want the case, if you don't mind me asking?"

He shook his head. "I have a bad feeling about this one. If we leave it up to those two agencies, they'll screw it up. And if I pull the case in, you're the best we have."

Reilly handed me a file. Inside were pictures of the crime scene and the victim and reports from both the forest rangers and the agents in our Oakland office. The medical examiner would need a few days to weigh in.

"She's pretty," I said. "She could be a model."

"Such a young girl. She had her whole life ahead of her."

I've never seen much emotion from Reilly, but this girl had a noticeable effect on him. Then it dawned on me. Behind him, on the credenza, was a picture of his daughter. She looked to be the same age. The story was she had just graduated from the UC Berkeley when she vanished. Her car was found abandoned on the 101 near Stinson Beach. No leads. No witnesses. The case went cold fast.

Every year, on the anniversary of her disappearance, he drives up to the location and spends the entire day there. From what I understand, she was all he had. His wife had died four years earlier from breast cancer. I felt sorry for him. I could understand his pain, having lost my own husband to a horrific crime while living in Hong Kong. Not knowing what happened had to be the worst part.

I stood up with the file in hand. "I'm on it."

He barely nodded as he gazed out his office window.

Chapter 4

After finishing my bagel, I spent the rest of the morning poring through the contents of the file Reilly had given me. Piper Taylor was twenty-three years old. According to her parents, she graduated from Ohio State a year ago and had wanted to travel around Europe since the age of seven, when she first saw *The Sound of Music.* "She wanted to twirl on a mountain just like Julie Andrews," they said. "She spent a year waiting tables to save up enough money." They also mentioned that Piper added Los Angeles, San Francisco and New York to her itinerary at the last minute.

My victim sounded like an adventurous one. Her parents referred to her as "free spirited." There wasn't much information from them, which wasn't surprising considering a field office in Cleveland had conducted the interview. The parents kept up on Piper's travels through her blog, which I pulled up. Her postings were infrequent and general in the sense that she put up a few pictures and talked a little about what she did that day. Her parents seemed like genuinely nice people, and I didn't get the impression that Piper had any problems with them.

I knew a couple of agents in the Oakland office, one pretty well: Agent Tracy House. We'd crossed paths a few times and had hit it off. Lucky for me, she was one of the two agents handling the arsenic investigation and was also the one who had stumbled across the young woman.

In her report, she wrote that she discovered the body in a small, hidden clearing. There were no equipment or signs that any camping or picnicking had taken place. The victim's personal belongings consisted of a small backpack that included bottled water, a map of SF, some cosmetics, a small wallet, and a bag of chips. *A short day hike. She could have easily been by herself or with someone she met along the way.* Her wallet, passport and money were still intact as well. *I can cross off robbery as a motive.* I saw no mention of a camera. I thought it odd being she was a tourist. Also, I found no mention of a cell phone. *Did the killer take these items?*

Agent House wrote that there were no immediate signs of sexual abuse, but I figured I'd leave that up the medical examiner to decide. Her parents had confirmed she was staying at a small hostel on Sacramento, between Kearny and Montgomery. *That's right next to Chinatown.* From what I could tell, no one had talked to anyone at the hostel. I wondered if management knew one of their guests had already checked out.

I had intended my next move to be to the coroner's office but decided the hostel had a better chance of telling me more about Piper than her dead body could at the moment.

After a twenty-minute drive, I stood in front of a wooden door adorned with bright red wrought iron. Above it was a tiny sign with Asian font lettering that identified it as the Lucky Buddha Hostel. I rang the doorbell and, a few seconds later, was buzzed in.

Eighteen wooden steps up a narrow and creaky stairwell dumped me into a lobby where two mismatched love seats, separated by an end table, greeted me. Above, written on the wall in white chalk, was a list of hostel FAQs and other information. Against the other wall was a pair of bookshelves stocked with travel books and brochures. A computer touting free Internet access sat on a desk next to it.

As I walked through the lobby, I passed a large bulletin board that had been tacked to death by a plethora of tour advertisements. One promoted a day trip to Muir Woods. *Why didn't Piper sign up for that tour?* Not far past that, I noticed a young woman sitting behind a Dutch door.

"Hello." She brushed her chestnut hair out of her eyes. "Welcome to Lucky Buddha. Do you have a reservation?"

"Sorry, I'm not here to stay." I flashed my identification. "I'm Agent Abby Kane with the FBI. I'd like to ask you a few questions."

Her smile flipped upside down and her posture deflated. "What's wrong? Are you here to arrest someone?"

"No. I need information. May I have your name, please?"

"My name is Katerina Yezhov," she said, straightening up in her chair.

The name matched the accent. "Are you the owner?"

"No. I work part time, and the owner lets me stay for free."

"How long have you been working here?"

She tilted her head towards the side as she gathered her thoughts. "Maybe three or four weeks. In two weeks, I leave for Los Angeles and meet up with some friends."

"So you travel alone?"

"Yes, for almost one year now."

"Isn't it dangerous for a young woman to travel by herself?"

She shook her head, and her hair followed. "No, it's fine. One only needs to be responsible and use common sense."

Gee, which one was Piper lacking? "You have a guest staying here, Piper Taylor."

"Yes, Piper. I know her. She's great fun. She's been here for four days." The receptionist tapped a few keys on the laptop next to her. "She's scheduled to be with us for another two days. Is everything okay?"

"When did you last see her?"

"Saturday morning. She had plans to see the redwood trees in Muir Woods. I tried to sign her up for one of our tours, but she is very independent. She said tours are silly and limiting."

"Did she tell you anything else? Was she planning to meet anyone or travel there with another guest in the hostel?"

Katerina took another moment to think. "No," she said as she shook her head. "She was going alone. It's not that difficult. She planned to take the ferry to Sausalito and visit the town as well—you know, kill two birds with one stick."

"Stone."

"Huh?"

"The saying is, 'kill two birds with one stone.'"

"Ooh. I always mess up these American idioms," she said, her cheeks flushed red. "Agent Abby, all these questions... Did something happen to Piper? Is she hurt?"

No sense beating around the bush. Now she has me saying them. "We found Piper's body near a hiking trail on Mount Tamalpais."

The girl inhaled before slapping her hand across her mouth. "No. It can't be. I just saw her. Are you sure you have the right person?"

I took out my cell phone and pulled up a picture of the victim's face. "Is this the Piper that is staying at your hotel?"

"Yes, that's her."

"I'm assuming her belongings are still in her room."

Katerina still had her eyes locked on the picture when

she nodded. "Yes, of course. I'll take you to it right now." She groped around the desk, searching, until she finally opened a drawer beneath and pulled out a ring of keys.

She led me down the short hall and up two more flights of wooden stairs until we reached a large room with eight bunk beds.

"This is the women's dormitory. Over there," she pointed. "I assigned the lower bunk to Piper."

Under the bed was a built-in locker. "Is her stuff in here?"

"Yes, but that is her lock. We don't have a key."

"What do you do when the occasional person loses their key?"

"I'll be right back."

While she was gone, I poked around. A blue towel had been draped over the framing of the bunk. Other than that, nothing else signified Piper's presence.

A few seconds later, Katerina returned with bolt cutters. "I'm not sure how these work. I've never had to use them before."

I took the cutters from her hand, and in one snip, the lock fell to the floor. "It's that simple."

Inside the locker was a large backpack. I rummaged through it and found no surprises: clothes, toothbrush, a few travel books. Nothing out of the ordinary—except I didn't see a camera or a mobile phone. I did, however, find a laptop.

"Katerina, do you know if Piper had a camera or a cell phone?"

"Yes, she had an iPhone. It was doubling as her camera. You know, two birds."

"Got it. I'll be taking the laptop right now." I wanted to get one of the Information Analysts started on it. "Another agent will stop by to collect the rest of her belongings. Until then, keep them in a safe place. Do you know when the owner will be in?"

"Oh, he almost never comes to the hostel. He talks to the staff by phone. He totally trusts us to run this place. Crazy, huh?"

I guess I can scratch the owner off my list of people to talk to. "Here's my card in case you think of anything else that might help. Call me anytime."

Katerina walked me down the stairs to the entrance. As I turned to walk away, she called out.

"Agent Abby, wait. I remember. Piper mentioned a place in Sausalito. I can't remember the name but she said they made organic cotton candy."

Chapter 5

I was a block away from my favorite dim sum shop; I figured a quick bite before heading across town to the medical examiner's office wouldn't hurt. I huffed it uphill along Sacramento Street to Young's Fresh Dim Sum on Stockton. I knew I had pigged out on this stuff the day before, but I have a serious addiction to dumplings. Plus, Young's wasn't like the sit-down restaurant I took the family to on Sundays where the servers push carts around from table to table. No, this place was a hole in the wall. It had character.

Young's had a simple counter to order from. Behind it were three stacks of bamboo steamers four high. Each one was filled with a different dumpling. There were a few tables to sit at, but mostly the place was designed for takeaway. I didn't feel much like taking this stuff back to the office, and there was a seat open at one of the tables, so I made my selection and sat my butt down in the open chair.

I didn't pay much attention to the gentleman next to me. He appeared busy with his spread of cheap eats. Two bites in and I realized the suit next to me was the Asian detective from the other day. *Of all the dim sum joints in town...* I couldn't believe my luck—stuck at a table next to a guy I never thought I would see again. I couldn't get up and leave; there was no place to go. It was only a matter of time before he recognized me. Wrong.

The guy continued to eat without looking up or taking a breather. He plopped his dumplings, one by one, into the sweet dipping sauce before popping them into his mouth, chewing fast and loudly. When he finished his main course, I thought for sure he would look up and notice me. Nope. He steamrolled right into the rice cake.

I finished my entire meal without being discovered. *What kind of detective is this guy? Clearly he wasn't observant. Sheesh, lucky for the SFPD. Real keeper they got—*

"I remember you," he said without any sort of prompt coming from me.

I looked around, unsure if he had spoken to me. Eventually, he turned his head to me.

"How did you know? You never looked up once."

He motioned with his head to the table in front of us. Sitting on top was a brand new, hot water heater used for tea. I could see both of our reflections in it.

"Oh."

"I'm sure you were thinking I must be some crappy detective for my bad observation."

Busted. "Why would I think that?"

He finished the last of his rice cake and wiped his

hands on a napkin. "Look, I'm really a nice guy. We started off on the wrong foot. Truce." He stuck out a clean hand and followed that up with a large toothy smile.

Realizing how silly the situation was, I gave in. "Truce. My name is Abby Kane."

"Nice to meet you, Abby. I'm Kyle Kang. How's the arm?" he asked as he held onto my hand and turned my arm from side to side as if he could somehow see through my jacket and make some sort of medical observation.

"The arm's fine. Thanks for asking."

"Do you eat here much?"

"Not as much as I would like," I said, wiping my hands with a napkin. "You?"

"Quite often. I work out of the Central Precinct, which isn't far. Plus, we're responsible for Chinatown. You work in the area?"

"No, my office is near City Hall."

He nodded as if he knew what building I worked in. "Oh, yeah, yeah. Do you work at the Asian Art Museum? Are you a docent there?"

Just when I thought we could be friends. "No, but nearby."

He stood up quickly and adjusted his jacket. "It's nice to properly meet you, Abby. I hope to see you around," he said, smiling, completely oblivious to the barb he had thrown my way earlier. I hoped it wasn't intentional.

I politely said goodbye and headed back to my car. It

was time to pay my friend, Dr. Timothy Green, a visit.

Chapter 6

Detective Pete Sokolov sat at his desk with butcher paper spread out. He was busy picking pieces of flesh off an entire dried mackerel.

Kang waved his hand in front of his nose. "I should have known you were the source of that smell."

"I'm Russian. This is my people's food. And anyhow, you eat that fermented fish sauce. It's worse smelling than this."

"Maybe, but I don't eat it every day." Kang leaned back in his chair and watched his partner and best friend since high school tear away at the fish like a lone piranha. "Hey, remember that lady from the other day? The short Asian one?"

"The one that took our guy out? Yeah. She's a looker, that one. Why?"

"I ran into her again at the dim sum shop."

"Maybe she's following you to make sure you don't need help," Sokolov said before letting out a low laugh.

"Yeah, yeah, yeah." Kang waited for the big man sitting across from him to calm down. "I'm serious here. Something's been bothering me since that day, and I finally figured it out after bumping into her again. She reminds me of someone we know."

"You talking about that inspector from a few years ago?"

"That's exactly who I'm talking about. What was her name?"

Sokolov scrunched his eyebrows. "Chu, Chee—"

"Choi! That's her name. Inspector Choi."

"What about her?"

Kang shook his head from side to side. "She just really reminds me of her. I don't know why."

"Maybe it's because she's short, female and Asian."

Kang rolled his eyes. "It's more than that."

Sokolov gripped both flaps along the gut of the fish and tore it open, revealing more of the flesh. "You've seen this woman twice, and you think you know her."

"Eh, it's a hunch. Forget about it. What's new?"

"Cavanaugh wants to know where we're at on those two bodies that popped up last week."

"I think we have to tell him what we're thinking."

"You remember what happened the last time we went that route?" Sokolov spit a bone between his two fingers before brushing his hands together.

"Yeah, and we were right."

"I'm not so sure he remembers it that way, regardless of what ended up happening."

"Are the two of you trying to blow my diet? You know damn well that food is my go-to in stressful situations." Captain Richard Cavanaugh stood there behind his desk with both hands on his hips, his belly hanging over the front of his belt buckle and his face projecting a look of disbelief.

"I'm just saying that findings are pointing this direction and we think we need to start looking at one guy here," Kang answered evenly, not wanting to worsen the situation any further.

"I'm not seeing it. Make it clear for me."

Words sputtered out of Kang's mouth as he sat perched on the edge of the chair, waving his arms like a conductor who was desperate to keep his symphony from straying. "This isn't random," Kang continued. "The killer knows what he's doing." He held up a hand and began a count. "Our male vic had almost all of his gold teeth removed. His other jewelry and money was left untouched. He wasn't beaten. There were no witnesses. He died quickly from a knife across the neck. Our second vic, she had her finger removed—"

"She was robbed. According to her husband, there was a diamond ring on her finger," Cavanaugh blurted.

"Hold on. If that's all the person wanted, why kill her? Why leave a body that could come back to bite them in the butt? A true robber doesn't want that headache."

"Maybe he didn't want to be identified."

"Nah, it's too easy to steal and get away with it. An older white woman like that probably thinks all brown people look alike."

"I'm not buying it, but please, continue," Cavanaugh said.

Kang brought his hand back up and continued to rattle off his reasons. "She had other jewelry on her, all of it left untouched. She was also killed quickly and efficiently with a knife to the neck. I'm telling you, this person knows how to kill. The mutilation of the body is part of the ritual."

"So you're saying this killer is randomly targeting people and mutilating their body afterward in some weird way?"

Kang nodded his head. "Yeah, I am."

"And what about you?" Cavanaugh looked at Sokolov. "You got anything you wanna add, or are you going to sit there and transfer your thoughts to me telepathically?"

Sokolov gritted his teeth. "I agree with everything my partner says."

"Right. Of course."

Cavanaugh couldn't argue with Kang's assessment. It was textbook profiling, and the facts actually made a case for it. He sat down behind his desk, pissed at the idea of another possible serial killer in his neck of the woods.

Kang gave his partner that I-told-you-so look. Right before they entered Cavanaugh's office, he mentioned,

"This will piss him off, but not because innocent people are in danger. He doesn't want the attention the word 'serial' would bring to the case."

He was right. Having a serial killer brought the scrutiny of the higher-ups. Plus they were harder to catch.

"The last time I suggested Chinatown had a serial killer, I was right," Kang said, breaking the silence.

"I remember," Cavanaugh spat. "I also remember that you had help closing the case."

"It would have been easier if you hadn't forced me to work the cases separately for so long," Kang fired back. He held Cavanaugh's gaze.

Sokolov saw that the situation was at a standstill. He stood up and clasped his hands together. "Okay. We continue working the case on our assumption, and you get us some help."

With that said, he turned and walked out of the office.

Chapter 7

Traffic that afternoon wasn't much of a problem. I used Polk Street to cut across town, and it rewarded me with traffic light jackpot. I smiled at the green signals until I reached Market Street. The medical examiner's office was located on Bryant, only a couple stops farther.

I hadn't seen Timothy Green since my last visit regarding a dead DEA agent. I received a couple of follow-up emails from him, and that was it. He was a nice man, however eccentric at times, and I did look forward to seeing him again. On my way over, I called his office to let them know I would be there shortly, hoping to avoid a long stay in their dull waiting room.

When I entered the office, Green was waiting for me with a smile. "Hello, Agent. I'm happy to see you again," he said, a hair above a whisper. He waited until I got closer before extending his hand.

"Good to see you, too, Doctor." His hand was soft but cold.

He looked like I remembered. Shaggy brown hair, Ben Franklin specs, earring in the left ear, and a height that I was fond of: about even with mine. His lab coat still looked two sizes too big—his hand disappeared like a turtle's head when he lowered his arm.

"So you're here about the hiker?"

"I am."

We stood there a bit longer—him smiling, me wondering. "Can I see the body?" I finally asked. *Quirky doesn't even begin to describe this guy.*

"Yes. Follow me, please."

Green led me down the same corridor I remembered from my last visit. As our footsteps echoed in the sterile hallway, he was more interested in hearing about my morning than in talking about the body.

"My day's been okay so far," I said pleasantly. "I have no complaints."

"Well, I hope it stays that way." He stopped and pushed open a door, allowing me to enter first. Before I could even react to the smell, he handed me a bottle of lemon oil.

"I remembered," he said, grinning at me like a golden retriever that had just brought the ball back.

"Thanks." I smiled and dabbed a bit under my nose. He pointed to the first autopsy table, sparing me the walk by the other five tables, each with a corpse.

"Busy day, huh?"

He looked down the row of bodies. "Yes, it's that time of the year."

"What time of the year?"

"Dying time." He smiled at me. "Medical examiner joke," he said as he chuckled to himself.

I chuckled. "What can you tell me about the girl?"

He pulled back the green sheet, revealing a nude woman with a large gash in her chest. "I've only just begun my investigation, so forgive me if I can't yet answer every one of your questions. Now, as you can see, the victim received direct, sharp force trauma to the chest area by a small axe." He looked up at me over his glasses. "You've seen the picture of the weapon?"

"I have."

He pointed at the gaping wound in Piper's chest. "The opening is clean, and I don't mean hygienically. Well, it is clean, because I cleaned it but that's not what I mean. What I'm trying to say is the victim received one blow. You see, repeated blows don't always follow the same course of trajectory; some are off to the left while others are a little off to the right. That can leave a jagged edge around the wound." He took a large forceps and ran it along the edge of the opening. "You see how straight that is?"

"Yeah. So the attacker killed her with one chop?"

"Well, yes. But the amount of damage caused by this one-time blow needed to be enough to kill the victim quickly. Now, it is possible to survive a blow to the chest with an axe. And that reason is because most people don't understand how hard it is to drive an axe this far into the body." He waved his index finger at me. "Don't believe what you see in the movies."

Green picked up a chest spreader, which basically looked like a pair of large, stainless steel, salad tongs, and stuck it into the wound, prying it open.

"Come closer. See how deep it is?"

I leaned over for a better look, my face now inches from Green's. When I didn't hear more observational notes coming from the doctor, I turned my attention to him and found him looking directly into my eyes.

"I hope you don't take this the wrong way," he started, "but you have a most unique green hue to your eyes."

Green had caught me off guard, even more so since we were clearly deep into each other's personal space. I expected an observation about the body, not my eye color. "And the victim? What do you think about her?"

Green smiled sheepishly. "Oh, yes, the entry point. The depth of the trauma is what I find interesting. Here, the axe not only penetrated the sternum, which is no small feat, but it then severed the superior vena cava and the inferior vena cava, the two large veins that move blood into the heart. It continued right through the lower two ventricles of the heart and even cut into the primary bronchus of the right lung. With this sort of damage, the victim died within seconds."

I leaned back, having seen enough. "So what does that mean? That our killer is a guy? A big strong one?"

"No, not necessarily," he said, removing the tongs and allowing the gap to close. "When I said it's possible to survive an axe wound to the chest, I said that because the sternum, or breastbone, normally would have served its purpose and prevented the blade from entering the chest very far. Unlike a pointy object, an axe, even though the blade is quite thin, has a larger surface mass. The larger the object, the more force needed to penetrate."

"I'm not sure I'm getting the point you're trying to make, except that a strong person did this."

"What I'm saying is yes, you need a lot of force, but not a lot of strength. If you, Agent Kane, took an axe, wound up and swung as hard as you could, you would probably do the same damage we see here. The key is knowing you need to wind up."

I smiled at Green, realizing what he was trying to tell me in his puzzling way. "This isn't the first time our killer has swung an axe into a person's chest."

"It's the only way he would know to wind up. A first-timer wouldn't think to."

Green's observation told me one thing: I had a possible serial killer on my hands and my one-off homicide just blew up into a big deal. I thanked Green for his time, and he promised to update me on his findings but said he'd already told me "the juicy stuff, no pun intended."

Before I exited the autopsy room, he stopped me. "Excuse me, Agent Kane."

I looked back. "Yes?"

"Would you mind having dinner with me?"

With a question like that, I sort of expected him to stutter, or look away, or fidget with his pockets or pen, but he didn't. He just stood there, totally relaxed with his eyes holding still on me.

For the second time in one day, Dr. Timothy Green had caught me off guard. He was a nice person but not the type of guy I normally found myself attracted to. *Not that my track record with men is anything to brag about.* I had to admit, though, his boldness impressed me. "Would you accept a cup of coffee instead?"

If I had disappointed him with that answer, he certainly didn't show it. He only smiled and nodded before saying he would be in touch.

Chapter 8

While I had made decent progress that first day, I hadn't anticipated that my victim might be connected to others. I had a lot of work ahead of me but I knew the drill. Boy, did I know the drill.

Initially, I had thought about calling it a day and heading home but decided otherwise after my visit with Green and dropping the laptop off at the bureau. It was nearing four in the afternoon. If I hurried, I could get a jump on the Golden Gate Bridge traffic. With sunset nearing eight, I would still have plenty of daylight to survey the crime scene.

One of the park rangers at Muir Woods had left a detailed map of where the body was found, but I wasn't in the mood to play find-the-location. I put a call in to the ranger, and he said he would meet me at the park office near the entrance.

Forty minutes later, I was removing a duffel bag from the trunk of my vehicle when I heard a voice call out. "Agent!"

My head turned to the left, and a bearded man in a uniform about thirty yards away waved at me. He wore the standard, gray shirt and dark green pants with that all too familiar Smokey hat. He also had a smile that projected a good distance. I waved back and headed toward him. He waited with both hands on his hips.

"Thanks for meeting me." I extended my hand. "I'm Agent Abby Kane."

"It's not a problem," he said, giving me two prompt shakes. "I'm happy to help. I'm Elijah Finch, but you can call me Finch. Everyone around here does."

"How did you know I was the agent?"

"You're the only one wearing a suit. I have to say," he motioned to my feet with his eyes, "I'm a little concerned about your lack of proper foot gear."

I held up my duffel bag. "I always keep a change of clothes in the trunk in case something like this happens. If you have a place I could change quickly, I'd appreciate it."

"Sure thing. You can change at the office and leave your belongings there."

Finch let a couple of eager tourists slip by us on their way to see the tallest living things on earth before moving forward.

"How late is the park open?" I asked as I followed.

"Well, daylight savings just went into effect, so we're open until eight every night."

"Do people normally stay so late?"

"Oh, yeah. The park is very popular. I'd say right now there are about a hundred people hiking along the main trail and thirty or so still on the outer trails." He looked down at his watch. "They have three hours to get out, or they're spending the night."

"Is that allowed?"

"Camping and picnicking in the park aren't allowed, but there are trails that go in and out of the park and lead to a few camping areas. Have you been here before?"

"I have, actually. I've brought my kids a few times, but we've always visited in the morning and only for a few hours."

"That's very typical for most visitors."

He led me into the park's office and pointed out the bathroom. There, I made my quick change into a pair of jeans, a T-shirt, cross trainers, and a hoodie.

"Be sure you use the bathroom while you're in there," I heard him call through the door. "It'll take us about forty-five minutes to get to the location."

Finch wasn't kidding when he said forty-five minutes. The hike wasn't hard, and it was scenic; I can't say I didn't enjoy looking at the tall redwoods. The woods smelled fresh and seemed untouched by mankind. I almost forgot why I was there. We approached a sign stating the trail was unsafe and hikers needed to turn around.

"What's wrong with the trail?" I asked.

"Nothing. We were instructed to keep people from trampling through or near the crime scene during the investigation. We didn't think draping the area with yellow tape was a great idea. An unsafe trail works better as a deterrent; people won't think there's something exciting to look at and sneak in for a peek. The location is up ahead and off to the left."

We walked another thirty feet, and then Finch led me off the trail and around a large boulder. We traversed the uneven ground for about fifteen feet before we spilled into an open area. It was beautiful, perfect for a private picnic.

"I take it this isn't part of the trail."

"It's not. She must have noticed it during her hike."

"I wonder how many people know about this spot."

"Not many. There is virtually no wear and tear on the ground."

How on earth did Agent House stumble upon this place? I knew at some point I would need to hear the story straight from her. I scanned for anything unusual as I walked the area. I stopped when I came upon the area where the victim had died. The leaves on the ground were still stained with her blood. I noticed a few boot prints. There was no mention of them in House's report, so I figured trampling law enforcement had left them.

I turned to Finch. "Did you see the body while it was still here?"

"I did."

"What were your first impressions?"

"That it was a terrible thing to have happened to that young lady. Agent, I'll be honest with you." He shoved both hands into the back pockets of his trousers. "Dead bodies aren't something we find around here. Even with the extensive hiking, the trails aren't difficult and there are no dangers of falling off a cliff. The most we'll encounter is a twisted ankle. I could splint the heck out of a limb better than I could solve a crime."

I was beginning to understand the finger pointing, at least from the perspective of the Park Service.

"Do you think it'd be easy to kill someone on one of these back trails?"

"On a few of the trails, yes. But most of them have a good amount of traffic."

"What about this one, Fern Creek?"

"It's one of the many trails that can lead a person into and out of the park. Right where we're standing is the edge of the park boundary. We have a couple of backdoors into the park. The Lost Trail is one of them. Keep following Fern Creek and you'll run smack into that trail. She could have found her way in via that route. But to answer your question, yes, someone could have easily done this without being seen. This is a popular trail, but some days, there are only a handful of people on it, even on a weekend."

"So someone might have passed Piper on the trail."

"Yes. I imagine if the news stations picked up the story, you might find someone. I think most people would remember a girl like that if they passed her by."

I had to agree with Finch. Six-foot tall model types

may not stand out on the sidewalks of New York, but they would on a hiking trail in Marin County. "Piper was a tourist on her first visit to Muir Woods. Seems a little fishy that she somehow found herself in this spot."

"You think someone forced her to this location?"

"It's possible, but they'd first have to make their way along the busy main trail. I don't see how you can force someone through that crowd."

Finch nodded.

Piper most likely came to the park with someone she had met in San Francisco. I knew she had left the hostel alone but it was apparent that she had hiked with someone. I didn't believe Piper was the victim of a random crime. She went to the park with someone else that day, and that person was opportunistic.

Chapter 9

A couple of days had passed since the Carlsons had read the riddle. Jerry was eager to get on with their next task, but for that to happen, he needed to figure out what the message meant. Vicki wasn't as good as Jerry when it came to deciphering the clues, and he suspected part of her lack of ability had to do with the fact that she didn't want to rush things and leave the city.

Jerry sat quietly in the hotel room while drinking coffee. He and his wife had spent the day shopping and were back for an afternoon nap. She was the only one occupying the bed. Jerry chose, instead, to take advantage of the quiet time and the fresh pot of brew he had ordered from room service to think through the riddle.

Good fortune comes in many forms. Find the right one for your next clue. Jerry repeated that thought while he sipped the hot and black. Every riddle they had received thus far had something to do with San Francisco, particularly the city's Chinatown neighborhood. No other instructions were included; figuring stuff out was part of the process. They knew each riddle would lead them to a specific location where they would receive the answer to unlock their next task.

Fortune… fortune…

His body jerked and his eyes widened. It's so obvious: fortune cookies. Every Chinese restaurant serves them after a meal, but which one?

Jerry moved over to the desk and searched for popular Chinese restaurants on his laptop. He scanned the results, hoping something from the name or location would jump out at him, but nothing did. *There has to be a better way of narrowing it down.*

He revised his search for restaurants only in the Chinatown area but it didn't help much. Most of the same restaurants appeared. He tried adding "delivery" to his search, but nothing about the results told him anything useful still. Frustrated, Jerry looked at his wife; his sleeping beauty lay calmly under the covers, unaware of his irritation at not having a sounding board to help.

Maybe I'm coming at this wrong, he continued with his thoughts. *Many forms… Flavors? There are different flavors. I've seen chocolate-covered ones.* Still, the problem was who and where. And that's when he realized it wasn't about all the places that served fortune cookies.

On a hunch, he typed "manufacturing fortune cookies in San Francisco" into the search field. Bingo! The Golden Gate Fortune Cookie Factory popped up, and it was in Chinatown. *That's it! It's gotta be.* Jerry mentally patted himself on the back for his cleverness before draining the last of the coffee from his cup. It was time to wake his lovely up.

◇◇◇

As soon as he had figured out their destination, Jerry had dragged Vicki out of bed and into Chinatown. This time, he also wore his disguise: a pair of glasses and a mustache. It was important to Jerry that he and Vicki conceal their identities when meeting with their contact. She said he was being paranoid, that it didn't matter, but he insisted. As they walked north on Grant Street, she monitored the map on her phone. "We need to make a left on Jackson, and then it's the next left after that."

They continued to the intersection, turned left and walked half a block uphill where they found themselves looking at an alley. "Is it on a street? I would think a place of business would have their front door facing the street."

Vicki frowned at the phone. "Well, it says it's the very next left. It doesn't say if it's a road or alley."

Jerry ignored the alleyway and told her to follow him as he continued up the hill to Stockton Avenue. He made a left and started looking for the Golden Gate Fortune Cookie Factory.

"We passed it," she blurted. "According to the map, it's back where we were, in that alley."

"Let me see that phone," he ordered. But to his

surprise, the map clearly showed they had passed it.

"I told you so."

"Yeah, well, sometimes these maps have the wrong information and—"

Vicki didn't wait for her husband to finish his sentence. She turned around and marched back down the street. By then, Jerry had caught up. In the alley they passed a florist and a small fruit market, even a print shop.

"See? There are businesses here." They kept on walking until they reached the other end on Washington Street.

"Well, I didn't see any giant factory," he said smugly. "Think about it; how could a factory fit in such a small area?"

Again, Vicki ignored her husband and retraced her steps. This time, he didn't follow. As far as he was concerned, she was wasting time. He pulled out his own phone with a plan to call the factory for directions, but before he could dial, he heard a big laugh coming from the alley.

He looked up and saw his wife waving her hands over her head. "It's right here. We walked right past it."

Can't be. Jerry headed to where his wife stood, and sure enough, above a single glass door where one wouldn't think to look, there hung a red and yellow sign that read "Golden Gate Fortune Cookie Factory." The glass door was dirty and covered with smudges, which helped camouflage what was behind it. The nondescript entrance looked more like the backdoor to someone's apartment than what Jerry had pictured in his head.

Vicki pushed open the door, and the smell of baked vanilla and caramel flooded her nostrils. "Mmmm, it smells delicious."

The space was tiny, no larger than a long narrow apartment. Bags of fortune cookies for sale overflowed from the shelving near the entrance. Down the middle of the factory were three women sitting behind tables with metal contraptions that resembled waffle irons. They were busy making fortune cookies.

Jerry leaned in toward his wife. "You mean to tell me these three women make all the fortune cookies?"

"I guess," she responded.

A rope prevented the Carlsons from venturing any farther inside. Nearby, an old man sat in a chair and smiled at them. Next to him, in shaky handwriting, was a sign that asked visitors to pay fifty cents to take a picture. Vicki immediately opened her purse, fished out two quarters and turned them over to the old man. She then stood next to the closest woman making cookies and smiled. Jerry snapped a picture on his phone and on Vicki's camera, for which the old man asked for another fee.

Jerry started to grumble.

"Just pay the man," Vicki ordered. "It's only fifty cents."

Jerry grabbed a bag of cookies, handed the man four dollars and fifty cents and then whispered, "Chasing Chinatown."

The old man nodded, stood up and walked to the back of the factory. A minute later he returned and handed Jerry a red fortune cookie. Jerry cracked it open and read the fortune before turning to his wife with a grin on his face. "We have our answer."

Chapter 10

The neighborhood I called home, North Beach, had the nickname "Little Italy" thanks to the large number of Italian immigrants who had settled there long ago. It's still home to numerous Italian restaurants and delis, my favorite being Fanelli's on Columbus Avenue near Washington Square. We lived a couple of blocks away from the square in an old Victorian on Pfeiffer Street. I liked the area. It was quiet, and the neighbors were nice and respectful. It felt like home to me.

I parked my Impala directly outside our house, like I always did. Before I made it to the front door, I could hear Lucy laughing inside. I looked at my watch: 8:00 p.m. *She should be getting ready for bed.*

I opened the door and spotted my little one sitting on the stairs in her PJs.

"Hi, Mommy," she said as she waved.

I brought my left wrist up and tapped at my watch. "Shouldn't someone already be in bed?"

"I was waiting for you to come home."

That's all she needed to say to have me ditch the tough Mommy attitude. I put my purse down and climbed the stairs with my arms out to give her a long hug. "Mommy's missed you. Have you been good?"

"Yes," she said with exaggerated nods.

"Did you finish all your dinner?"

More exaggerated nods.

"Have you brushed your teeth yet?"

That time she grinned and shook her head. "Nooooooooo."

I pointed to the top of the stairs. "Get moving." I patted her behind. "Brush your teeth. I'll come by later to tuck you into bed."

I watched her scramble up the stairs until she rounded the corner before I headed into the kitchen, where I knew I would find Po Po.

"Oh, you home. Good. I made noodles for dinner. I warm some up for you."

My mother-in-law practically lived in the kitchen. Having her bedroom next door only encouraged it. I knew it was nearing her bedtime, so I told her not to worry. She had already changed into her nightwear. Maybe. *I should really learn the difference between that blue dress and that blue nightgown.*

I usually try to get home by 5:30 p.m. On days I'm running late, which I try very hard not to do, I call and give her the heads up. Being late means I most likely missed out on walking the kids—well, Lucy anyway— home from school. On days I was able to meet them at school, Ryan took the opportunity to walk home with his friends. If work was hectic, I would text him, and he had the responsibility of walking his sister home before he could hang out with his friends. It would be that way until Lucy was eighteen.

Po Po ignored what I said and put a plate of noodles into the microwave. "While that's warming up," I said, "I'll tuck Lucy into bed and check in on Ryan."

"Don't take long. Microwave only need three minutes."

I hurried up the stairs. Lucy had just walked out of the bathroom, so I made like a monster and chased her into her room.

"How come you're home so late?" she asked as she climbed into bed and slipped under her covers.

"Mommy had to go to Muir Woods. Remember the park we went to with the really tall trees?"

"Oh, yeah. My neck hurt from looking at them."

"That's right; it did."

She yawned, and I took that opportunity to bring the covers up to her neck before giving her a kiss goodnight. Her eyes were slowly closing. *Yes!* I stood up and turned off the lights. "Sweet dreams."

I closed the door behind me and let go a couple of fist pumps. It had been a while since I'd had one of those right-to-bed moments. Usually she pummeled me with a series of "why" questions, or begged for a story, or the infectious giggles would attack her. But as she got older, the stalling happened less and less. Even the tantrums were fewer and farther between. Bedtime was becoming a natural occurrence and not a chore.

She went down quickly, so I was sure I had at least another minute or two left on the microwave timer. I stuck my head in Ryan's room. Empty. When he wasn't there, he could be found on the third floor. We had converted half of the top floor into a media/playroom, and he had taken to doing homework and playing up there so Lucy wouldn't bother him. He had her convinced that the floor was haunted, so she never ventured higher than the second floor. I'm sure some psychological damage was taking place, but hey, if it got Ryan to study, great. I would deal with the fallout later.

Ryan sat at the desk, his back to me, while he listened to music on his phone. When I placed my hand on his shoulder, he jumped, and I let out a laugh. "Got you!"

"Abby," he moaned, "I'm trying to study."

"And I'm trying to say hello." I gave him a hug and kiss. "History?" I asked.

"Reading comprehension," he corrected.

"How's it coming along?"

"Pretty good. It's one of my easier subjects. Math is the toughest."

Ha! Stereotype debunked. I pity the fool that tries to copy off my kid during a math test. He's following in my footsteps. I pinched myself as a reminder to look into a math tutor for him. I really didn't want him to struggle in any of his subjects.

I noticed a bruise on the back of his neck. "What happened here?" I asked, pulling his collar down a bit.

"Judo."

"Someone do a move the wrong way?"

"Sort of. We were practicing flips, and my partner didn't execute well enough. The back of my neck hit his knee."

"Ouch." I touched it gently. "Does it hurt?"

"No."

Ryan had come a long way from the little, whiny boy I remembered when we first met. I like to think I toughened the kid up and that his father was looking down at us with a smile. Judo, however, was the driving force behind his newfound confidence. He'd even started to take an interest in coming to the gym and hitting the heavy bag with me. I remember one day he got cocky and suggested we spar. It might have had something to do with him coming home after 5:00 p.m. on a school day and me doling out a week of no Internet, except for homework, as punishment. I told him, "Fine. Let's go."

We both entered the ring. Ryan had a silly grin on his face and started moving his feet back and forth like a boxer. He jerked his head from side to side. I suspected he thought I would take it easy on him. I didn't.

The entire session lasted a few seconds. He threw a jab and came up short. I followed up with a straight right and flattened his nose. I didn't draw blood, but I had made sure to put a little heat behind it, enough to sting. It was a friendly reminder to never underestimate his mother and taught him a lesson that girls are as tough as boys. That day also had me remembering how my father gave me my first black eye. It was his way of saying, "Come on. It's time you learn how to box."

I knew my father loved me, even if his ways of showing it were unconventional. He wanted two things for me: to be independent and to be able to protect myself. "If you can master those skills," he constantly repeated, "you'll be able to handle whatever life throws your way." I liked to think I was instilling the same virtues in Ryan.

As I left Ryan to his schoolwork and headed back downstairs, my phone started to ring. I removed it from my back pocket and answered, only to hear the haunting voice I hadn't heard in over a year.

"Ab-by."

The Monster!

The Monster was the nickname earned by one of the FBI's most wanted. I thought it fitting and refused to call him anything else. That's what he was, and it's what he deserved to be called. It had been over a year since I had last spoken to him, right before he slipped through our grasp. We never could confirm whether he left the country or even the state. It was like he vanished into thin air, never to be seen or heard from again. I had just stepped off the stairs onto the second level of our home when I responded.

"I would call you by your name, but you don't deserve that. They still call you Monster, or is it Prick nowadays?"

"Ah, you still have that mouth of yours."

"And you're still a scared man on the run." I moved quickly down the hall to the window that looked out over the front of our house. I gently parted the curtain and peeked, watching for any sort of movement in the shadows. Part of me thought he might have never left the city, but I knew that was unlikely. We had his picture blasted on every news station and newspaper in the state of California. Someone would have seen him. Hearing his voice again had me wondering how he had stayed underground for such a long period of time.

"Run? Who's running?"

"You mean to tell me you're still in the country?"

"Country? Why, Ab-by, I'm in your backyard."

My stomach dropped, and my heart lurched from my chest. I spun around and bolted down the hallway, then down the stairs two at a time. I still had my weapon holstered underneath my hoodie, and within seconds, I had it drawn. I sprinted by Po Po, telling her to stay in the kitchen. I didn't bother peeking out the back door, choosing instead to flip the light switch and burst onto the screened-in porch. It took seconds to clear the area before I moved into the yard itself. My heart thumped against my chest, and every sense I had remained on high alert. My breathing was elevated, but I remained focused. I hoped he had made the dumb mistake of showing up at my home. If you had asked me earlier how I would have reacted in this situation, I couldn't have told you. But that night, I discovered I was angry. *How dare that bastard come onto my property and threaten my family and me?*

I could hear the faint sound of laughter as I turned around searching the yard for him. It took a moment before I realized he was still on the phone I had shoved into the front pocket of my hoodie.

"Ab-by? Can you hear me?"

I brought the phone up to my ear.

"Guess what? I'm not there." More laughter. "You want to know what the best part is? The next time I call, you won't know whether I'm toying with you or not."

Chapter 11

That same night Jerry and Vicki were out on the town, taking in San Francisco's eclectic nightlife. They had caught a show at the Curran Theater and were enjoying a few cocktails at Bourbon and Branch, a speakeasy on Jones Street.

"What a charming bar," Jerry said as he looked around.

It certainly wasn't typical. For one, reservations were needed to receive a password to get in, as well as to receive the address. From the outside, a passerby saw only an unmarked door: no window, no sign, nothing. However, inside was quite the opposite. It was plush and ornate. The floors, booths, bar, and built-in bookcases were all fashioned out of polished wood. The wood finishes played up the era of Prohibition, but the lighting and crushed red velvet patterns lining one of the walls kept the vibe current and hip.

Unlike a bar packed with standing room only, this one had individual booths. According to the house rules, standing wasn't allowed around the bar—sitting only. And patrons took the term speakeasy literally. Everyone spoke in hushed tones, much like Jerry imagined they had back in those days.

Vicki beamed back at her husband. "Isn't the whole secret entrance so cool?"

"It is. I quite like it." Jerry looked at his watch before picking up his glass and swirling the amber liquor around.

"What's the matter, honey? You don't want to leave, do you?"

"No, not at all. But I'm wondering if we'll find what we're looking for here. It's almost midnight, and as much as I love this place, we have a task at hand." He was always the more pragmatic of the two.

"Well, I, for one, wouldn't mind having to extend our stay a bit longer if we had to," Vicki replied before taking a sip of her drink.

"I know you love it here, dear, but we can't stay forever."

Vicki relaxed her shoulders and held her glass with two hands. "I'm just so enjoying our time," she said with a pout before turning it into a smile and singing the city's famous song.

"Speaking of leaving your heart in San Francisco," Jerry said, triggering a burst of laughter from the two of them.

Vicki followed that up with, "Thump. Thump."

Anyone sitting next to them and hearing the conversation would think nothing of it except maybe that they were having a good time and cracking a few inside jokes between them. Pretty normal stuff, except the Carlsons weren't normal people.

They were in San Francisco, and they had a quota to fulfill—three down, two more to go. The way Vicki saw it, there wasn't any real rush; they were supposed to be on an adventure full of fun. So what if they played tourist a bit longer than they had planned? It hurt no one, and it gave their victims an extra day or two of life.

But now that they had their next directive, Jerry had become extremely focused. The answer they received earlier in the day from the fortune cookie factory was the word "heart." It allowed them to unlock their fourth objective, which called for them to leave someone's heart in San Francisco. He couldn't help but start planning. The kill was hardwired into him. Vicki as well, but she had an easier time controlling her appetite. Once Jerry fell into kill mode, there was no switching it off.

Vicki held up her rocks glass. "Here's to finding a heart, whether it be tonight, tomorrow or the next day."

Jerry nodded and *tinked* his glass against hers.

Vicki watched her husband. His concentrated stare in his glass, the bouncing of his left leg, the biting of his lower lip—she knew all the signs. She had done her best to prolong the inevitable, but it wasn't like she didn't look forward to what was coming up. She did. And thinking about it while watching her husband started to stoke her internal desires. She, too, would become cold and calculating. When she shifted into the same state of mind as her husband, she was equally as dangerous. Even Jerry wasn't safe. But he was unaware of that.

Chapter 12

The next morning, I gave Reilly the heads up about the phone call.

"Sheesh, Abby. Are you okay?" He sat up in his chair, and his eyes softened with concern, something I didn't always see from him.

"I'm fine," I answered. "To be honest, I was shaken at first, but only because the call came unexpectedly."

"Of course. That's a natural response. Remember, people like him are cowards. That's why they do their tormenting while hiding. He's a weak and pathetic man."

I couldn't have agreed more with Reilly. I wasn't afraid of the Monster but knowing that sicko was out there and I had to constantly watch my back was an irritation. I wanted nothing more than to put a slug in his head.

"Is that all he said?" Reilly asked, leaning back and drumming the armrest of his chair.

"Yeah. And then he kept laughing. I have no idea if he's still in the city or not. I didn't detect any background noise, and he called from a blocked number."

"I can look into getting a security detail outside your house—"

"That's not necessary."

"You want a new number?"

I took a moment to think about Reilly's offer. "No. I want to stay in touch with him. It'll keep me on my toes. Plus, if he feels like he can keep calling me, he might make a mistake, and that's how we'll get him."

Reilly lowered his glasses from his head to his nose. "All right. Keep me posted on the calls."

He looked down at his laptop and started to type but realized I was still sitting across from him. "Is there something else?"

"Uh, actually, you called me in here, but I brought up the phone call, and we never got around to why you called me in here."

Reilly threw both hands up in the air. "You're right. Sorry, been a little distracted lately."

"Everything okay?" I asked.

"Yeah, I'm fine. Thanks for asking. Listen, I received a call the other day from a Captain Richard Cavanaugh from SFPD, Central District. He said he has two detectives working a couple of homicides, and they're of the opinion that they might have a serial killer on their hands."

"Why is that?"

"He didn't go into the details too much, but he asked for a meeting with his two detectives and us. He wants our take on their reasoning. If it seems likely that they are right, he wants to know if we could help them out with a profile on their killer. As I told you yesterday, you're our best when it comes to stuff like this. Will you meet with them?"

"Sure. Not a problem."

"By the way, how's the investigation on that hiker coming along?"

"It's coming. I'll have more to convey later today after I do a little more digging."

Reilly nodded and went back to typing on his laptop, and I went back to my desk.

I was curious about the detectives' findings, since I had come to a similar conclusion with the Taylor case. I dialed the Oakland offices and asked for Agent House.

"Abby, good to hear from you. How are you and the family doing?"

"I'm doing well. The kids are busy with school, and well, you know my mother-in-law."

"That I do," House said, laughing. "I hear you got lucky and picked up my leftovers."

"Yeah, way to stir up the pot and pass it along," I joked.

"Seriously, though, I'm sorry you were handed this mess. Who'd've thought we'd find a frickin' body up there?"

"It's fine. Listen, I wanted to pick your brain a bit more. Mind if I stop by?"

"Sure. I'm in the office all day."

Time was a factor, so there was no sense in putting off

our meeting. I sent a couple of emails and stopped by the ladies' room before leaving. As I was about to enter the elevator, I heard someone call my name.

"Agent Kane."

I turned around and saw a man, a young recruit straight out of the Academy, hurrying my way.

"Agent Kane?" he called out once more. This time his voice wavered.

"Yes?"

"I'm glad I caught you. Special Agent Reilly wants to see you right away in his office."

"About what?"

"Uh, I'm not sure." He looked a little flustered. Poor thing, he only started last week. Heck, even I couldn't remember the guy's name. "I know he has a couple of SFPD detectives in his office."

That was fast. "All right. Thanks," I said and gave him a pat to his arm.

As I reached Reilly's office, I heard voices I didn't recognize. One was loud, boisterous and had an accent, and the other... Well, it wasn't anything—just forgettable.

As I turned into Reilly's office, I immediately stopped as if a force field had prevented my advancement. What I saw made me feel like I was teleported into an episode of *The Twilight Zone,* because standing in front of me, with that toothy grin of his, was Detective Kyle Kang.

Chapter 13

To an outsider, it must have looked like an old-time vaudeville act, with Kang pointing at me as he struggled to get at least one coherent word out of his mouth. "Wait, you *work* here?" He finally managed.

I folded my arms across my chest. "Apparently you still need my help."

"You're an agent?"

"I know. You were hoping for free tickets to the museum, right?"

His partner had put two and two together and burst into big belly laughs.

Reilly was in the dark. "I guess you guys know each other," he offered.

"Detective Kang and I have met on a few occasions, though I believe this is the first time he's discovering that I work for the FBI."

"Agent Kane is our best when it comes to cases involving heinous and sexual crimes," Reilly told Kang and his partner, "especially those involving a serial killer. She also has a tremendous understanding of how criminal organizations work, having run the Organized Crime and

Triad Bureau back in Hong Kong."

"Hong Kong?" Kyle repeated.

"That's right. Abby joined the Bureau about four years ago."

"Give or take a few months," I added.

"Look, Detectives, I'm doing your captain a favor here and allowing my agent to lend her expertise to your case," Reilly piped up. "You can take it or leave it. We have plenty to do around here."

Kang immediately pulled himself together. "No, we'll take it. I apologize if I came off as not wanting your help. I was caught off guard, that's all. My partner and I would be happy to hear Agent Kane's thoughts on our case."

"Well, with that said, why you don't you guys go play nicely?" Reilly suggested, motioning with his hands for us to get out of his office.

"Follow me," I said. "We can talk in the conference room."

As we walked down the hallway past L-shaped desks and glassed-in offices, I could only imagine what Kang thought—probably that I thought he was an idiot. I didn't know him well enough to make that judgment. We'd had a series of weird and unusual encounters. That's all.

"You guys want something to drink?" I offered as we passed the break room. "Coffee? Soda?"

"We're fine, thanks," Kang replied.

I led them both into the conference room and shut the

door behind us. It had large windows instead of walls. "I hope you don't mind." I walked around the room and closed the shades. "I can't stand it when people peer inside as they walk by." Neither said anything.

I took a seat opposite both of them and thought, before getting into the details of their case, I should make peace. We're all fighting the bad guys. "It's Detective Sokolov, right?"

The big Russian nodded.

"Look," I continued, "before we get started, I want to apologize if I led you to believe I was someone I wasn't."

"You could have pointed out you were an FBI agent the first day we met," Kang said.

I nodded my head. "I could have, but what took place that day wasn't a federal crime. There was no need to identify myself as a federal agent. I had a duty to help, which I did."

The two of them looked at each other, and then back at me.

"You're right," Kang said. "Now that we know what each other does, we can move on."

"Great. So fill me in on your case."

Kang did most of the talking as he told me about the two bodies, the details of each crime, and how the missing body parts connected the two.

"And other than the missing finger with the diamond ring, the other jewelry and money were left behind?" I asked.

"Yes. That's why we ruled out robbery. Same thing with the man with the missing teeth."

"Both victims were killed fast and quietly with a blade." Sokolov motioned across his neck with his finger. "Our guy knows how to kill."

"Exactly," Kang said, sitting forward in his chair. "That's why we think it's the same person. Both victims had the carotid artery in their neck severed. The killer then takes what he needs from the victims and leaves. They die quickly without the ability to call out for help."

One didn't need to be a brain surgeon to see that they were right. I agreed. "You got anything to go on? Witnesses? DNA? Any leads?"

Both detectives shook their heads.

"Where were the bodies found?"

"We found the lady in Fay Park on Russian Hill. According to the husband, she was out walking her dog late at night but never came back. She only lived two houses up the street. The husband figured she swung through the park, so he headed over there."

"Why did he think that?"

"She loved visiting that park, and apparently, she was prone to falling asleep if she sat for too long. Anyway, he finds her sitting on a bench with her throat cut and a finger missing. The dog lay by her feet unharmed."

"And the other victim?"

"Black male. His teeth were found first in a gold pan between Fisherman's Wharf and Pier 39. We found a body in the water with missing teeth. DNA match confirmed they were his."

"No witnesses from that crime scene either?"

"No," Kang said.

"From what you're telling me, I have no reason not to question your theory. Killing a person and then mutilating the body afterwards or during the process is typical of serial killer behavior. Clearly, there's some sort of meaning behind the missing body parts or in the way the victims were killed. Removing the victim's gold teeth and placing them in a gold pan suggests that the killer might be trying to send a message. Do you have a serial killer on your hands?" I tilted my head from side to side. "The evidence supports that theory, but more importantly, you really have nothing else to go on at the moment. What's missing here is motivation."

Kang turned both his palms up. "So what are you saying?"

"I'm saying that, if you can figure out the motivation, that'll tell you whether or not this person intends to keep on killing or if it was just a two-body hurrah. Typically, it isn't labeled a serial killer unless there are three bodies."

"So you're saying we should wait until there are three?"

"Actually, I don't agree with that argument. I think you

can have two bodies." I laced my fingers together and placed them on the table. "Look, there are plenty of gang members who have killed more than three people, and yet, they don't get the label. The reason is motivation. Their killings are either a result of a robbery, retribution, or simply being in the wrong neighborhood. The motivations for those types of deaths aren't to gain attention or to seek out sexual gratification."

"We think he's collecting body parts."

"Now *that* is motivation that's more in line with a serial killer."

Listening to Kang, I couldn't help but make comparisons to my own case and wonder if all three crimes could be connected. Whoever killed Piper Taylor had killed before—I knew that much—but I still needed to determine what motivated my killer. Kang thought his killer collected body parts, which was textbook serial killer. As far as I knew, Piper wasn't missing any limbs or organs. Would that immediately eliminate my victim from being associated with his? I also had to assume that Kang might be wrong.

"I'm investigating a homicide right now where evidence suggests my killer has killed before."

"What homicide?" Kang asked.

"An FBI agent discovered a body on Mount Tamalpais over the weekend. The victim had an axe sticking out of her chest."

"I heard about that one," Sokolov piped up. "Young

girl, like a model, right?"

"That's the one." I filled Kang and Sokolov in on the details of the crime and what I had learned from the medical examiner's office. After I finished, Kang leaned back in his chair and chewed on his fingernails before speaking. "You're thinking there might be a connection?"

"I hadn't ruled it out yet."

"The medical examiner's theory seems plausible. But you also said no body parts were missing."

"There's the rub. I don't know now if there is a connection, but three bodies in the same time frame that aren't gang related is too much, even for the Bay Area. These crimes aren't typical, and we can't ignore that."

"I agree," said Kang.

Sokolov nodded his answer as well.

"So now what?" Kang asked.

I'd had no idea the meeting would end that way, but I couldn't ignore my gut. "I think we should combine our efforts and work the three cases together."

Chapter 14

Because we were employed by different law enforcement agencies, it made sense for each of us to retain the lead on our individual cases and continue to share information as we acquired it until something in one of the three cases suggested we work differently. I had to admit, Kang did not come across as an idiot, nor did Sokolov. My impression was quite the opposite. They were nothing like the two detectives I'd gotten saddled with while working a case in Detroit.

I bade goodbye to Kang and Sokolov, unsure of what I had gotten myself into, and headed out of the building. The Oakland satellite office, where Agent Tracy House was stationed, was my next stop. I wanted to hear her take on the crime and catch up a bit. It had been a while since we had last spent time together. I called ahead to let her know I was on my way and she suggested we meet at the Starbucks around the corner—the air conditioning in the office was on the fritz.

House arrived before I did and acquired a table in the far back, away from most of the customers. She waved and smiled as I walked toward her and gave me a hug when I reached the table.

"I got you hot water." She slid a paper cup toward me.

"Thanks." House knew I had a specific taste for a special green tea that I always carried with me. I removed the lid from the cup and dropped a pinch into the water. I returned the cover to let it steep a bit before taking a sip. "I really appreciate you taking the time to talk to me about the case," I started. "I know your write-ups are detailed and—"

"Don't worry about it," she said, waving her hand. "I totally get it. I'm the same way. What do you want to know?"

"Walk me through everything as you saw it."

House recapped that Saturday morning for me, leaving out no details as I listened and sipped my tea. Only when she finished did I ask my first question.

"So you don't think the body was moved there?"

"I wondered that as well, but I did a perimeter search shortly after finding the body and couldn't locate any evidence of a body being dragged or even a trail of blood. All bodily fluids were confined to the spot where the body lay."

"And you didn't see the victim until you were in the clearing?"

"That's correct. In fact, I wandered into the clearing from the back side. I was on Fern Creek Trail, heading south toward Muir Woods, but veered off it by accident. That's how I stumbled into that area. Had I stayed on the trail, I wouldn't have found it. Some hiker would have smelt the decomposition days later, though. You think someone put the body there?"

"Not really. Ruling it out, I guess."

My pieces of the puzzle were starting to grow. Piper met her killer sometime after leaving the hostel. If she headed straight to the ferry building, that left a tiny window where she could have met up with someone. If I closed in on those few hours, eventually I would squeeze the killer into the open.

"I know the girl left the hostel alone, so she had to have come into contact with someone she trusted to hike with along the way."

House leaned forward in her chair. "So possible meeting points are the ports from where the ferry leaves and arrives, the ride across the Bay and the park."

"There's one more place. Earlier, I questioned a girl that works at the hostel. She said Piper mentioned a store that sold organic cotton candy."

"Organic?" A look of discontent appeared on House's face.

I didn't blame her. I, too, found it a bit ridiculous.

"Looks like you know what you need to do." House made a wringing motion with her two hands.

I pursed my lips before speaking. "I do wonder whether she knew her killer before that day or if she actually met the person on that trip."

"Most likely a man: an extremely charming one," House said. "Piper was pretty, probably received a lot of attention, and the right kind could have caused her to lower her guard."

"She also traveled alone. Solo travelers are usually open to the idea of doing something with other travelers."

House nodded in agreement. "Cost saving could have brought them together. How did they get to the park from the Sausalito? Bus? Taxi?"

"The girl from the hostel mentioned a bus, but I don't think this was about saving money. She met someone she took a liking to, and they decided to travel to Muir Woods together."

"I would suggest that perhaps the death was accidental, and the person is on the run out of fear. But I saw that axe." House paused. "Looked pretty darn intentional," she finally said.

"Sure did. I don't even think the killing was a spur of the moment thing. I think the killer spotted Piper and decided she would be the victim." I quickly filled House in on what I had learned at the medical examiner's office.

"So you have a guy who's killed before. He likes girls, tall pretty ones. If you want, I can run a check and see if we get a hit for other tall, pretty girls found dead, axe or not."

"That would be helpful."

"Makes sense to me," House said as she took a sip of her latte.

"The strange thing is, nobody has stepped forward with any information. I have no witnesses—which is unusual considering the park ranger who took me to the site said the trail was a popular one."

"It's the damn media. Unless the news is sensational or a hot topic, they pay it no attention. I bet most of the people there that day don't even know they were hiking around a dead body."

I agreed with House on that one. I needed to get the Taylor case some media love. Someone had to have seen something. "I've got an axe, and that's it. According to the forensic people, they found plenty of DNA from the girl but nothing to suggest another person, except we know she didn't just axe herself."

"Nope." House nodded as she sat back.

"There's something else," I said as I scratched the side of my cup with my fingernail. I filled House in on Kang's two homicides and his collector angle.

"What's the connection? Timing?"

"That, and the idea that Piper's killer has killed before."

"But you said the woman's finger was removed, and the man had his teeth pulled. Piper had no visual mutilation. Did the ME find something?"

"No. That's where it breaks down. Unless…"

"What?" House said, her words hanging.

I thought about what Kang said, about his guy being a

collector. There had to be more, something bigger than the taking of body parts. And that's when it came to me.

"Unless it's not about collecting but about staging. Gold teeth left in a pan. Staged. According to the report, they found the woman sitting on a bench. Could she have been propped up that way? A hiker killed in a beautiful clearing instead of hidden away in the brush. Maybe this is about presentation. A performance."

House took a deep breath as she pondered what I had said. I knew she would call bullshit if she thought it. That's what I liked about her. Business was business and our friendship was our friendship.

Her eyes shifted back on me after a few seconds of staring out the window. "That's a wild theory… Wild enough to be true."

I thanked House for her time. She had proved to be a great sounding board, and I had a new angle to pursue.

Chapter 15

Fay Park was located on the west side of Russian Hill on Leavenworth Street between Lombard and Chestnut Street. I had walked by it twice before realizing the immaculately groomed backyard with the white gazebo I kept passing really wasn't someone's backyard but the park. A closer inspection revealed a tiny sign near the small, gated entrance. *Mental note: Things I love about this city—they have tiny, quarter-acre parks sandwiched between homes.*

The park was gorgeous and had, not one, but two white gazebos separated by a rectangular plot of grass with inverted corners. Four symmetrical plots of blooming flowerbeds surrounded each gazebo. Two sets of stairs led down to the second level, where there were rose gardens. There were a few benches as well, but the one that caught my eye was located on the first level between the two stairs. It's where the body was found.

I sat on the bench and understood why the victim loved to sit there. The view was idyllic and peaceful. *I wonder how the killer found out about this park or how he even came upon her. Certainly he didn't happen by and say,*

"Hey, I think I'll kill that lady." If she had fallen asleep, it would have been the perfect opportunity. But the park was small and not well known. I found it hard to believe that the killer had happened upon her by coincidence. *Had he spotted her earlier and followed her home? How long did he watch her? Days? How did he know she walked her dog every night?* He knew her routines. He stalked her.

And what about the cutting of the finger? I stood up and looked around, hoping something might pop out. He had taken her finger with a diamond ring but none of her other jewelry. I pulled out my phone, pulled up the report Kang had emailed over and scanned it until I found what I was looking for. *Interesting.* For some reason, I assumed it had been her wedding ring finger that had gone missing. It wasn't.

Kang said the victim lived two houses up, so I searched the report and found the address. The street number was odd, so she lived on the left side of the street. I counted two houses and stopped in front of a beautifully renovated, two-story Victorian with a very ornate, colorful, wood-trimmed façade.

The home sat high, away from the sidewalk, with stairs that required three switchbacks on their way up to the front door, mimicking the famous crooked street nearby. It was beautiful, but I couldn't imagine making that climb every day. As I admired the residence, something sparkly in one of the lower hedges directly in front of me caught my eye. I moved in closer for a better look. *Holy moly!* I found myself staring at a large, diamond ring. It was on a finger.

Could it be? I moved a few branches and answered my own question. It had to be the victim's missing finger. *But why leave it here? Why would the killer risk coming back to the victim's home to plant the finger? It makes no sense.*

If the killer had indeed placed the finger here, it felt more in line with the gold teeth in the pan. Both victims had suffered body mutilation with the body part moved to another location, away from the body. Was the body part the killer's objective or was the kill? Was the removal of the body part a way to prolong the kill? He was trying to make a statement, but about what, I wasn't quite sure. It was a strange way to communicate, but riddles from killers aren't unheard of.

Still, that's not what I thought the staging of the body parts was trying to do. And why did I continue to think Kang's killer also did my hiker? Aside from the medical examiner's findings and my hunch, nothing more connected the two crimes. Unless…

I pulled out my phone and dialed.

"Kang, here."

"Kyle, you've got it turned around."

"Abby is this you?"

"Yes, it's me. Did you hear what I said? The motivation—it's wrong. Your guy isn't collecting."

"What is he doing?"

"He's thrill killing."

Chapter 16

I wasn't far from the Central Precinct, so I told Kang and Sokolov to meet me at the vic's home while I waited for CSI to show and process the scene. The detectives were speedy and arrived in ten minutes. As they approached, I pointed to the bush.

Kang leaned in and immediately reeled his head back, his expression soured. "I can smell it. How did you know to look here?"

"I didn't. I was looking at the victim's home when the sparkle from the ring caught my eye. I'm assuming your guy placed it here."

Kang stepped out of the way, and Sokolov moved in for a look. He wasn't fazed one bit by the slightly decomposed limb. "Good catch," the Russian said.

"That's it? Good catch?"

He shrugged as he looked at me. I had inadvertently riddled the man.

"It's the victim's middle finger. There's symbolism behind it."

"He's giving us the middle finger?" Kang asked.

"Close. Look at the house. It's a renovated Victorian,

picture perfect and probably photographed by every passerby. The way the killer placed the finger on the bush, it's as if it were giving the home the middle finger."

"Wait, I'm confused," Kang said, lumping himself in the same camp as his partner. "Earlier you talked about thrill killing, and now you're talking about a middle finger."

"Serial killers can be categorized by their motives. Hedonistic is one of the categories. Killers that fall in this category derive immense pleasure from killing."

"So our guy loves killing."

"Exactly, but not any type of killing. There's no sex, so he's not driven by lust, and he doesn't rob his victims, so it appears that money isn't a motivator. He's killing for thrills. He enjoys causing fear and even pain in his victims. He likes to see their eyes before, during, and after he kills them. It's most telling."

"Sounds like a real bastard."

"Very much so. It's all about the kill itself. Once it's over, they move on. So they can be very opportunistic or specific. It depends on their moods or their urges."

Kang rested his hands on his hips. "Okay. Say I buy into the thrill kill angle. Why go through the extra trouble of cutting off the finger and placing it outside her home?"

"I struggled with that exact same thought but it dawned on me. Victorian homes, the gold rush and redwood trees are all symbols of San Francisco."

"That's how you're tying the three cases together?"

Kang said a bit flippantly.

"It's how I am now."

Both men stood quietly, not saying a word. I was losing them. I couldn't fault them; they were looking at the facts and it sounded like I kept switching my thoughts on the killer's motivation. I had initially bought Kang's theory that the killer was a collector, but it was mostly because that's all they had, and it was a good start.

Finally, Kang cleared his throat. "With all due respect, Agent, are you sure you're not trying too hard to tie your case to ours?"

"Positive."

Kang shifted his weight. His expression told me he was finding it difficult to keep an open mind to the case. "Okay, then I think you need to help us out here. You're asking us to change our motivation based on your hunch that all three victims have the same killer. Honestly, I'm not seeing this thread."

"That's because you want a thread where A plus B equals C. The mind of a killer doesn't necessarily work that way. If someone collects things, they don't normally leave it someplace else. They take it with them. Cutting off a body part and leaving it elsewhere isn't collecting."

"It is still mutilation, and that's what connects our two cases and makes your hiker the third wheel. And, if I might add, you sound irritated that we're not taking your word as gospel."

Bite your tongue, Abby. Their fault isn't with you; it's their lack of knowledge. I let out a breath and responded with as much control as I could muster. "That sort of statement usually comes from people who think they know everything. I expected better from SFPD's finest. Remember, your department reached out to us for our expertise with serial killers."

At that point, I began to wag my finger at them like they were children. Probably a little overboard, but he had pissed me off. "This isn't a random shooting or a gang-banging incident, so investigating it like it is one is exactly why you're having a hard time grasping my methodology that ties these three cases together. So I'm—"

"This has gone far enough, we don't—"

"Do. Not. Interrupt. Me."

Sokolov stood stone-faced, while Kang's face showcased a range of emotions from shock to resentment. I should have been able to contain the situation and not let it get to that point. But I honestly didn't expect this sort of pushback from Kang. He didn't come across as the typical detective. He had smarts. They both did. Maybe that's why it irritated me. "Look, I'm sorry. We all want to catch this guy, and I know it seems like we, or I, might be grasping, but trust me, there's sound thinking behind what I'm suggesting."

The two detectives looked at each other, then back at me. "Go on, Abby," Sokolov said. "We're listening."

I'm not one to shy away from admitting I'm wrong. I've been wrong plenty, but I've been right more. And my gut told me I was right about this one. "Let's get back to the SF tie-in: gold rush, redwood trees and Victorian homes. This is the connection, not your body mutilation and not three murders in a specific time frame. San Francisco is what connects these three victims."

"So he could be making a statement about the city through things that represent San Francisco."

"Right. The Painted Ladies are a huge tourist attraction. Victorian architecture is as much of a part of this city as the hills are. It's what gives the city its charm."

"So our guy doesn't like Victorian homes, and this is his way of saying it," Kang continued.

"I think you're in the ballpark."

Sokolov snapped his fingers. "Panning for gold. The teeth in the gold pan are his way of paying homage to the San Francisco gold rush."

"Yes!" I said, pointing at him. "And the hiker. Well, the tallest living thing in the world is a redwood tree. The ones in Muir Woods are protected and can't be chopped down, but our guy found something else to chop down."

"A tall girl," Kang finished.

The three of us stood on the sidewalk quietly, letting the conversation sink in as the first vehicle of the CSI crew arrived. We'd had a breakthrough on the motivation, and the City by the Bay had a serial killer.

Chapter 17

After Kang had a few units from SFPD set up a perimeter and I had briefed CSI, we headed back to Central Precinct. Kang had commandeered the small interrogation room and turned it into our war room. He and I began making lists of San Francisco icons as well as popular attractions in the city and pinning them up on the corkboard next to a large map of the city which had the locations of the bodies identified by colored thumbtacks. I was busy adding to the list on the board when the door opened and Sokolov entered the room. He had a look of despair on his face, and his shoulders hung lower than usual.

He placed both hands on his hips. "Bad news, guys. The fighting between the Russian gangs in the Inner Richmond area has intensified. Boss wants me to head up a joint task force aimed at curtailing this ongoing war. I'm off the thrill kill case. Sorry, I must get started on it." Sokolov left, closing the door behind him.

"Well, that sucks," I said, not caring whether it was appropriate to say.

"Cavanagh did it on purpose," Kang said. "He considers you an extra body and doesn't think he needs three personnel on this case."

"But I don't work for him."

"He doesn't care. He wants to look good for the top brass. There's usually some type of political motivation behind every decision he makes. This Russian thing must be a hot button."

"We'll have to make do." I continued working on the list but stopped when I heard Kang chuckle to himself.

"What's so funny?"

"Nothing." His growing smile disagreed.

"Come on; give it up." He had tickled my curiosity enough that I stopped writing.

"Well, since it's the two of us and our last names are kind of similar…"

"I don't think they're similar."

"They totally are. How about we go by 'Kang and Kane: crime-fighting duo'?"

"Kang and Kane? Why not Kane and Kang?"

"Wait, how about the Asian Ks?" Kang painted an invisible marquee with his hands.

"Nuh-uh."

"Double K?"

"I don't think we need a nickname."

"Capital K and Lower K? Get it?" he said, moving his hand up and down.

"I wish I didn't."

He returned to his list, and I to mine.

"Kan-Kan?"

I nearly threw my pen at him. Inside, I giggled like a schoolgirl, but I wasn't about to let Kang know his stupid jokes made me laugh. Men think that, because they make me laugh, I must be into them. Next thing I know, they're hitting on me—all because I giggled. This relationship would remain completely professional. I wanted nothing more than to solve the case and return to the daily routine I had grown to like.

It didn't take long for us to make our lists. We had plenty of help from various tourist and travel websites, what with San Francisco being a top travel destination in the U.S. and all. After pinning up everything we wrote down, we took a step back and stared at the writing. It was overwhelming, to say the least.

"I'm thinking we need to pare this down somehow," Kang said.

"You think?"

To make sense of it all, we settled on the most popular and iconic themes, shooting for a mix of celebrity, sites, and city culture/history. I figured even the killer would need to keep his options limited and focus on only a few. In the end, our list looked like this:

Victorian homes	Chinatown
Redwood trees	Ghirardelli Square
Gold Rush	Cable cars
Golden Gate Bridge	Pier 39/Fisherman's Wharf
Golden Gate Park	The Big Earthquake
Alcatraz Island	Coit Tower
Lombard Street	Gay/lesbian capital

We included the three places the killer had already struck in hopes that our list would more closely resemble his. We stepped back and took another look at our board.

"Seems manageable," I said.

"I only have one question."

I turned to Kang. "What's that?"

"Now what?"

Chapter 18

The next day, Kang offered to take me to the location of the first crime scene where they had found the pan full of gold teeth. He'd said he would pick me up at my place since he lived nearby. I waited outside and watched him pull up in a dark blue Crown Vic. I saw that he had taken my advice—"Lose the suit for a day"— and dressed casually in jeans and a button-down.

"We're practically neighbors," he said, as I sat inside his car.

"Oh?"

"Yeah, I'm in Russian Hill—Hyde and Pacific. Took me five minutes to get here."

I nodded again and changed the subject. That morning, my mind was in case mode, and I wasn't about to let small talk snap me out of it. "This crime scene, it's near Fisherman's Wharf?"

"Pier 39 to be exact. Right off to the side is a small public space."

"Yup, I know the spot you're talking about."

A few minutes later, we were parked and walking toward our destination. I tried to focus on the case, but

Kang continued to derail my thought process with chitchat, until I finally asked him to give it a break. He didn't seem bothered by my remark: just smiled pleasantly as he shut up.

"It's right over here," he said, leading me past a ticket booth for boat tours on the Bay.

The public space was a paved area with multiple flowerbeds surrounded by seating. One of them was fairly big and had a centerpiece of roses.

"There." He pointed. "The area right in front of the rose bush."

We both climbed up the stone seating and onto the raised plot of grass.

"Who found the teeth?"

"A city worker hired to maintain the landscaping discovered it around ten in the morning. He thought it was a joke at first, until he realized the teeth were real."

"And it was just the pan and the teeth?"

"There was a little dirt and water to make it look like someone had just panned it."

"And the body?"

"Body was found floating near Pier 33 where the Alcatraz boat launches. It was almost completely hidden under the dock. Forensics confirmed that blood splatter on the dock was consistent with splatter that would exit the type of neck wound found on the victim. He was killed at that location and tossed into the water."

"But not before his teeth were pulled, right?"

"Yeah, time of death was estimated to be about one in the morning. We actually found the body first. Teeth were second." Kang turned to me. "Yesterday, you mentioned that our guy was a thrill killer. Why bother pulling the teeth? If I'm understanding this correctly, the rush is associated with the actual kill, right?"

"Normally, but not every killer fits neatly into that space. My guess is that our guy is confident enough with his kills, meaning he doesn't think he'll get caught and is comfortable enough to show off what he did. He also might have discovered that it prolongs the high he gets from killing."

"Well, if he wants to stroke his ego, why not utilize the body? It's a bigger visual."

"Good question. But if we're right about the symbolism—"

"Then he needs to connect the kill to San Francisco somehow. The gold teeth connect to the gold rush."

"Exactly. This killer has evolved beyond the actual kill, which tells me he's been at it for a while. He's smart, he knows what he's doing and he's perfecting his method. The positive in this is that they get cocky, which leads to sloppiness. I'm actually surprised he hasn't tried to start a rapport with the media. I'm sure he's wondering why they aren't reporting more on the discovery of the body. Do the media know about the teeth or the finger?"

"No, we withheld that information. We needed something to turn away all the freaks who come forth saying they did it."

I clucked my tongue repeatedly as I rocked on my heels. Around us, families were beginning to show up. Most were concerned with taking pictures of their kids in front of anything that looked remotely interesting; I doubt any of them would have even noticed the pan and the teeth.

"What are you thinking?" Kang shoved his hands into his front pockets.

"One thing is bothering me. Our guy is going through the trouble of creating these presentations, yet the public is essentially unaware of his efforts. Look around us; do you think any of these people would have noticed that gold pan? And the finger? Who would have seen that?"

"Hmm, interesting. If no one notices, what's the point? If he wants the public's attention, hiding a finger in a bush wasn't the brightest thing to do."

"Exactly. Maybe he doesn't care if the public sees it or not."

"Then why do it?" Kang asked.

"Maybe it's for an individual or a small group of people. He could be documenting the presentation and showing it to them."

"So what we're finding are the aftermaths of a personal show?"

"Could be…"

We both stood there quietly for a few moments while we chewed on our thoughts. It felt good to be out of the office, surrounded by clear skies and crisp air. The fresh air can work wonders on the thought process. I drew a deep breath and let it sit for a moment before releasing it. "You know, the girl at the hostel gave me a lead I haven't followed up on. Care to tag along?"

"Sure. What's the lead?"

"Cotton candy."

Chapter 19

Kang and I continued to discuss bits of the case on the drive over to Sausalito. It seemed like we were gaining ground, and I began to feel better about finding Piper's killer. Kang proved to be an excellent sounding board and had great ideas. I was surprised at how much I was enjoying working with him. Not that I thought it would be a disaster, but it can be difficult to pair up with someone new. Everyone has a different way of working. Kang, in many ways, was a lot like me. He was a problem solver, and he wasn't afraid to explore areas off the main path.

But then the conversation derailed, and we were off topic, once again. *Somebody give this man a bottle of Ritalin.*

"So you're from Hong Kong?" he asked.

"Born and raised," I answered as I stared out the window at the hordes of tourists walking across the Golden Gate Bridge.

"You don't miss it?"

"I miss some things."

"Mind if I ask what brought you to the States?"

Yes. I turned to Kang. He had his eyes on the road, but

I knew he was waiting for my answer. "Work and a change of lifestyle. Hong Kong was intense and became a bit too much. Have you been?"

He glanced at me. "To Hong Kong?" He shook his head. "Nah, only Beijing. I have some family there."

I nodded before turning back to the window, looking past the tourists, into the bay.

"How long were you a detective—"

"Inspector." I had cut him off.

"—with the Hong Kong police force. It was Organized Crime and Triad Bureau right?"

"A long time and yes." *What's with all the questions?* "Look, I'm sorry, but you keep steering the conversation away from the case," I said, shifting in my seat so that I faced him. "It's messing with my thought process."

"Sorry. It's…"

My eyebrow arched. "What? Spit it out now, or forever hold your peace."

"This might sound silly, maybe even stupid."

I hope not.

"But you remind me of someone I met a few years back."

Oh, God. Please don't hit on me. Please don't hit on me. Please don't hit on me.

"My partner thought I was reading too far into things, but once I found out you were an FBI agent and from Hong Kong, it's been on my mind ever since."

I hope that doesn't include the private time you have with yourself.

"A few years back, my partner and I met an inspector from Hong Kong who also worked for the Hong Kong Police Department."

"What are you talking about?"

"She was about your height, Asian and very knowledgeable in the field of serial killers," he carried on. "In fact, she actually helped us solve a case while she was here—one involving her missing niece. It's the reason she traveled to San Francisco in the first place. But here's the interesting part—and I'm sure you'll find this as puzzling as I did: this woman, the inspector, told us she was in charge of the Organized Crime and Triad Bureau. Imagine that. Same department you were in charge of. So my question is, how can two different women claim to be in charge of same department, at the same agency, around the same time?"

Good question.

Chapter 20

"I am not that person you're describing, if that's what you're alluding to."

Kang looked at me. "I knew there was something fishy happening. Out with it. I won't be able to focus until I know exactly what is going on here, Abby. Or should I call you Leslie Choi?" he asked with a raised eyebrow.

"Are you out of your mind?"

"What, did you get some work done to your face? You think a little plastic surgery, a name change, and a background story would be enough? Did you honestly think I wouldn't figure it out?"

"Let me explain."

"Oh yeah, I can't wait to hear this explanation. Gather around, kids. It's story time," Kang said with exaggerated excitement as he rolled his eyes.

If he doesn't shut up, I swear...

"Come on; let's have it. Hurry. I don't want you to have time to fashion another tall tale. Ha! A tall tale from a short woman."

"Are you going to let me speak, or just carry on with your babbling nonsense?"

Kang stared ahead for a moment before shooting a quick glance over at me. "Explain."

I giggled a little but caught myself from letting it rage into laughter. "Look, I'm not that woman. I realize we kind of look the same, but we are two different people."

"Wait, so there are two of you? You have a twin or something?"

"No," I said, shaking my head. "Leslie Choi worked for me and eventually assumed my duties when I resigned. We're actually friends."

"So there just happened to be two short, badass women in the same department?"

"Hey, maybe the Chinese people you know are all tall, but the majority of us are short, if you haven't noticed."

That comment broke the icy look on Kang's face, and he started to laugh, which triggered my funny bone, until we were both laughing our butts off. People passing by must have thought we were nuts, because Kang batted the steering wheel repeatedly while I threw my head back and forth. Eventually we calmed down.

"Leslie and I worked together for about six years," I said when I caught my breath. "I taught the woman everything she knows, and she'll back the claim up. Anyway, when she moved over to my department, we were like two peas in a pod. She was the perfect replacement for me when I left."

"But if I'm doing the math right, you should have still

been in Hong Kong when I met her."

"I was. After I resigned, it took us about eight months to prepare for the move."

"Did you know she was in SF?"

"Not at the time. I was so focused on our move that we actually lost touch for a bit. I found out later about her niece, after she had returned to Hong Kong. I think we just missed each other, with her going back and me heading over here."

"How often do you see or talk to each other?"

"Not as often as I wish. Out of sight, out of mind, I guess."

Kang shook his head as he looked forward.

"What a small world we live in."

"Yeah, tell me about it."

Chapter 21

We crossed the Golden Gate Bridge and exited the 101 Highway at Alexander Avenue. We were nearing the small port town of Sausalito.

"The shop is somewhere near the ferry terminal," I stated.

After Kang parked in an adjacent parking lot, we roamed around the shops, looking for one that sold cotton candy. It was a weekday morning, so the crowds were lighter than usual, more locals than tourists.

"There's a sweet shop over there." Kang pointed.

I followed his finger to a tiny pink and white shop with a sign that said "Naturally Sweet."

"That might be it. The woman at the hostel said the cotton candy was organic."

We entered the shop, and a sugary smell of sweets flooded my nostrils. The walls were lined with large, glass containers filled with an array of chocolates, hard candies and gummy everything. The place was a child's wonderland—mine, too. Behind the counter, near the corner, was the cotton candy machine. A teen girl wearing a blue apron was busy serving a family. From a door near the opposite side of the counter, a plump, middle-aged woman appeared wearing the same apron. She had short, brown hair and cheeks dotted with freckles.

Kang and I approached her. "Hi, are you the owner?"

"I am. How may I help you?"

I pulled out my ID. "My name is Abby Kane. I'm with the Federal Bureau of Investigation. This is Detective Kyle Kang with the San Francisco Police Department. Is there someplace we can talk privately?"

"Oh my. I'm not in trouble, am I?"

"No, you're not. We want to ask you a few questions."

She lifted up a hinged portion of the counter and came out to our side. "We can talk outside if that's okay."

"That's fine."

We exited the shop and walked to the side of the building, away from the foot traffic on the sidewalk.

"What would you like to know?" the shopkeeper asked with a forced smile.

"Your name would be a good start," I said.

The woman let out a nervous laugh as she fidgeted with her hands. "My name is Judy Huff."

"Relax, Judy. You're not in trouble."

She nodded and smiled, a little more genuinely this time. She seemed like a really nice lady, the type that mothered everyone around her, though I did get the feeling she had a fragile personality. God knows I've made more than one woman cry because of my tone, so I kept my questioning friendly.

I pulled out my cell phone and showed her a picture of Piper. "Did this girl come into your shop this past weekend? It would have been on Saturday."

She leaned forward for a closer look and started nodding. "Yes, I remember her. Tall girl, and very pretty, too. She bought some cotton candy."

"Do you know if she was alone?"

"Oh, she was with another woman," she answered, her chin bouncing up and down.

A woman? I wasn't expecting to hear that. "How old would you guess?"

"Let's see." Judy rubbed her chin and stole a look upwards. "She would have to have been in her late thirties, maybe even forty. Lively, though."

"How so?" Kang asked after clearing his throat.

"Well, she had a bunch of energy, seemed really excited, much more extroverted than the younger one."

I tilted my head. "Was the younger woman upset?"

"No, just a bit reserved, not as outspoken I would say. If you don't mind me asking, what's this about?"

"This young lady's name is Piper Taylor, and she was found dead on Mount Tamalpais."

"Oh, my God." Judy cupped her hand across her mouth as she slowly shook her head back and forth. Her eyes turned glassy, but she held it together. She used the back of her hand to dab her eyes dry. "Don't mind me. It upsets me to hear this. She was so young. Who would do such a thing? She seemed like such a sweet girl."

"Can you describe the older woman for us?"

"Lemme think, um… Well, she had brown, wavy hair that came down to right below her shoulders. She had light brown eyes and some color in her skin. She didn't wear a lot of makeup, only lipstick and a little mascara."

"Was she Caucasian?"

"Yes."

"How tall was she? Can you describe her body style?"

"I would say she was about five feet, seven inches. She looked to be in shape… Maybe there was a small pooch."

"Do you remember what she was wearing?"

Judy crinkled her eyebrows as she looked away for a moment. "I believe she had on khaki shorts. She had on a pink and white jacket with a tank top underneath." Judy leaned in and whispered, "She was spilling out of it if you know what I mean." She brought her hands up to her chest for emphasis.

"Anything else?"

"A light blue backpack—a small one."

"That's a pretty good description."

"Well, I spoke to her for a tiny bit. She wanted to know if it were possible to wave a cab down around here. They had plans to go to Muir Woods."

"Did you talk to them about anything else or hear them talk about anything?"

She shook her head. "It was just the cab. We were pretty busy that day."

"Do you know where they caught the cab?"

"Outside my shop, and it was a Yellow Cab."

"Are you sure of that?" Kang asked as he jotted it down on a small notepad.

"Absolutely. I gave them the number for the company."

"Is there anything else you can tell us about this woman?"

Judy leaned in once more as her eyes shifted between Kang and me. In a hushed tone, she asked, "Is this woman a suspect?"

"She's a person of interest," I whispered back.

"You know, I have this way of knowing if things are okay or not. Just do. I got that feeling about her. Also, it was strange that they were together."

"Why is that?"

"Well it seemed an odd pairing. She felt a little too old to be palling around with the younger girl, and I didn't get the feeling they were family."

"Anything else?"

"My store has a surveillance system."

Chapter 22

They say luck is nothing more than hard work crossing paths with opportunity. I guess we found the intersection that day. Fifteen minutes later, we had a digital screen grab of the mystery woman.

We thanked Judy and left our cards with her in case she remembered more. Kang emailed the picture to Sokolov and asked him to put an APB out on this woman while I had my office circulate the picture with the media, hoping for airtime. It was imperative we got the word out. Most of the people in that park or in Sausalito on that day were probably tourists and could be leaving the city at any moment.

Kang scuffed his shoes against the pavement as we walked back to his car. He looked to be as confused as I was about the recent revelation of our killer. "A woman, huh?" He finally said. "I thought for sure we were chasing a guy. You think that changes anything?"

"No. We stick with what we know, and we know Piper left the hostel alone, but when she arrived at the candy shop, she already had a friend. So they either met on the ferry ride over to Sausalito or at the ferry building."

Golden Gate Ferry is a city-run company that manages

the commuter ferries traveling back and forth across the Bay. The San Francisco/Sausalito route, with eleven crossings daily, was their most popular route. Neither of us could recall if the ports or the ferries had surveillance systems installed, but we intended to find out.

Because Yellow Cab was located south of San Francisco in Potrero Hills, we opted to pay a visit to the ferry company first. Their headquarters was located in Larkspur, about a fifteen-minute drive north from our location.

We identified ourselves to the woman at the reception desk and waited a few minutes before a white man in jeans and a polo shirt walked toward us. He seemed cheery for someone who was just told the FBI wanted to question him. He stuck out his hand with a sense of confidence and authority. "Hi, I'm Dan Harper. I understand you need information."

"That's correct. Is there somewhere we can talk?"

Harper led us down a short corridor and into his office. If he was bothered by our presence, he didn't let on. "Please, have a seat," he said, pointing to two chairs in front of his desk. "What can I do for you?"

I pulled out my phone and showed him the picture of our victim. "That's Piper Taylor. She was found dead on Mount Tamalpais over the weekend."

"That's terrible," he said, scrunching his face.

I showed him the second picture of the mystery

woman. "We believe this woman was with Piper shortly before her death. We're trying to ascertain if the two of them arrived in Sausalito together via your ferry."

Harper's head swayed from side to side as he let out a breath. "Wow, if you're wondering if a ticket seller might remember them, that's going to be a tough one, because there are so many locations you can buy a ticket, not to mention the Internet."

"We figured as much. We were more interested in knowing if any of your ferries have cameras or if the ports have them."

Harper shook his head. "The ferries don't, but the ports do. Unfortunately, we don't control those cameras. You would have to talk to the Port Authority for access."

We thanked Harper and exited the building. We were wasting our time following up small leads that may or may not turn up any useful information. I put a call in to Reilly and told him we needed help chasing down info.

"I have just the agent for you, Abby. Agent Austin Tucker joined us recently from Quantico and is eager to get his hands dirty."

Tucker turned out to be the nervous agent who'd stopped me at the elevators the other day. I took five minutes to brief him over the phone about the Port Authority lead and thanked him for helping out. When I finished my call, I joined Kang inside the car.

"Yellow Cab?" he suggested.

I nodded. "Let's hope we have better luck there."

Chapter 23

On our way over to Potrero Hill, we stopped off in the Mission for a quick lunch. We were craving decent Mexican food and had El Farolito in our sights. The place was a known haven for finger lickin' and belly fillin' food and always had a line out the door. Luckily, we missed the lunch crowd and only seven people were in front of us. I ordered a carne asada quesadilla and an horchata to wash it down. Kang settled on a carnitas super burrito and an aguas frescas. We were both starving and managed to mow through half our meals before coming up for air.

Still chewing a big bite, Kang made the first effort to speak. Fail.

He took a few more bites and another swallow before trying again. "You think if we find the driver and they remember Piper, anything will come of it?" he asked, wiping salsa from the sides of his mouth.

I shrugged to buy myself more time to chew. "I'm not sure," I said after swallowing. "I'm hoping that while they talked, he listened. Some of these cabbies pick up on every word their customers say."

"I've been thinking about our list."

"Yeah, and?"

"Chinatown is so synonymous with San Francisco. I feel like the killer might try to do something with it—maybe a tie-in with a dancing dragon or fireworks, or even Chinese food. Dim sum, perhaps."

"What's the body part associated with it?"

"You know, we may not need one. Your vic remained fully intact. He used her entire body as his performance piece."

"The Golden Gate Bridge is another large icon of San Francisco. Maybe *she* might throw someone over," I added.

"Are we officially switching from he to she?"

"I think so."

"There's no way for us to prevent *her* from throwing someone off the bridge. We would need round-the-clock surveillance."

I sipped my horchata and nodded my agreement. "Maybe we're still coming at it wrong, thinking too grand. Remember, everything she did was understated, almost hidden."

We were walking in circles when it came to figuring out where our killer might strike next. I was running out of ideas, and we were running out of time.

As I picked at my food, I started wondering what our next move would be if the picture of the mystery woman drew no tips from the public. The future looked dim. I tried to concentrate, but I could sense Kang's eyes boring into my skull. "What?" I finally asked.

He shrugged. "You have a healthy appetite."

"What's that supposed to mean?" I said, finishing the last of my meal and wiping my hands.

"I didn't mean that in a bad way. I've known a lot of women who were picky eaters or were full after a grape."

"Well, that's not me." I stood and grabbed my purse. "Come on; there's a cab driver we need to speak to."

A longer-than-expected drive later—Kang had gotten us lost, and I had put us back on track with the map on my phone—we arrived outside the Yellow Cab Company. We pulled into a parking lot and faced a sea of yellow. "Apparently, this is where all the cabs are when you need them," I joked as we climbed out of the car.

Kang chuckled.

We headed toward the large, white building, devoid of windows except one near the door. Attached to the building was a garage area where mechanics were busy working on cars. A short, stocky man in baggy jeans and a blue sweater walked our way.

"We don't do cab service here. You have to call."

"We're not here for a cab. We're here for one of your cabbies," I said.

Kang and I made our introductions to the man.

"Did one of my guys do something wrong? Which one was it?"

"Actually, we think one of your guys can help us with a

case. What's your name?" I asked.

"My name is Rod Warner," he said, pulling up his jeans. "I'm the shift manager on duty." He had Popeye forearms, except his tattoos were faded.

I produced Piper's picture and showed it to Warner. "Her name is Piper Taylor, and her body was found Sunday morning on Mount Tamalpais. A witness tells us that a Yellow Cab picked her up in Sausalito on Saturday and drove her and a friend to Muir Park."

"How can this witness be so sure it was one of our cabs? There are other cabbies out there with yellow cars."

"This witness gave our victim the number for your cab company."

"Oh." Warner rubbed the stubble on his chin. His fingernails and cuticles were stained with grime, yet clearly bitten down, which grossed me out more than a little.

"The call should be in the log book. Follow me."

Warner led us to a small office that looked more like a junk closet. There were stuffed filing cabinets that couldn't close completely and stacks of banker boxes filled with what I could only imagine was crap. "Have a seat," he said as he pointed to two mismatched plastic chairs. "I'll be back with the book."

Honestly, I wanted to douse the chair in hand sanitizer. The place disgusted me—especially his desk, which had a layer of everything old piled high on it. There had to be at least five empty coffee cups bunched together—one being used as an ashtray.

A few seconds later, Warner returned and sat in the cracked leather seat behind the desk. "All righty," he said as he flipped through a large, plastic binder. "Saturday… Saturday… Okay, here we go." He ran is stubby finger down the page. "Ah ha. Got it. Pick up at Sausalito pier in front of the Naturally Sweet store." He looked up at me. "That sound about right?"

I nodded. "You got a name?"

"Yeah. Vitaly Scherbo. Russian guy. Been with us for about six months. Looks like he hasn't been around since."

"Is that normal?"

"Some of these guys work a few days out of the week and that's it." Warner ripped some paper off an old McDonald's bag and wrote a phone number and address down. He offered it to me, but I motioned for Kang to grab it.

We thanked Warner for his time, and I called Vitaly as soon as we exited the building. An old woman answered.

"Phone's no good. Let's hope the address is real," I said as I pulled the car door open.

Chapter 24

It was a forty-minute drive across town, again. Vitaly's address was in the Inner Richmond neighborhood. His place of residence was on 18th Street between Geary and Anza—smack dab in the middle of San Francisco's Russian community.

Old row homes lined the street. The address led us to a light blue one that had a unit on top and one on the bottom—Vitaly's. Kang knocked on the door and took a step back. We waited a bit before he knocked once more, this time louder. I moved over to a curtained window to see if I could see inside, but the material was too thick and pushed tightly against the glass.

"Looks like he's not home," Kang said.

"Either that, or he doesn't want to talk to us."

I tried the latch on the wooden gate that separated Vitaly's building from the next. It was open.

"We don't have a warrant," Kang reminded me.

"We just want to talk." I pushed it open and entered the narrow space between the two homes. Behind the house was a small fenced yard with a few stubbles of grass making a go at life. A narrow slab of cement masqueraded as a patio and hosted a couple of beach chairs, and a bunch of empty Vodka bottles surrounded an overturned milk crate that played table to an overflowing ashtray.

"Looks like somebody had a party," Kang said from behind me.

Vitaly had the curtains drawn at every window, so I couldn't see inside from the yard, either. "This guy allergic to the sun?"

I stood off to the side of the glass door and knocked on it. A beat later, we heard the front door slam. We both spun on our heels and raced back to the front in time to see a man running away.

Kang and I gave chase and gained on him fairly quickly. I picked up the scent of stale alcohol being left in his wake. He was probably still drunk.

He cut across the street to the other side and was nearing busy Geary Avenue.

"Vitaly," I called out, "we only want to talk to you."

He didn't respond and continued running, now pushing people out of the way. He rounded the corner onto Geary. We followed and were both almost in reach when I heard Kang call out, "It's okay. I got him."

Before I knew it, I had blurted back, "You mean like last time?" With that, I lowered my head and put everything I had into a leap forward. I hit Vitaly in the back. Both he and I tumbled to the ground. Thankfully, he cushioned my fall.

I rolled onto my feet and turned in time to see Kang fall onto our guy. His knee went right into Vitaly's back, pinning him to the ground.

Within seconds, Kang had slapped a pair of handcuffs on him. He looked up at me when he finished, still breathing hard. "You had to be the one to catch him, huh?"

"It's more like I was the first one out of the starting blocks, so naturally, I was closer to him."

Kang shook his head and yanked Vitaly to his feet. I looked him in the face. He smelled like urine, but his breath was what sent my head reeling back. "Why'd you run?"

"Piss off!" he spat.

Kang spun him around, and we proceeded to walk him back to his house.

"Listen," I said, "you're not in trouble."

"Why the fuck you enter my property, huh?"

"We have some questions to ask you. That's it."

When we reached his building, we sat him down on the curb. "Vitaly, if we take the cuffs off, will you stay put?"

He let out a breath of air and nodded.

Kang uncuffed him, and I watched Vitaly rub his wrists.

"We don't care why you ran. Whatever the reason, we're not here for that. We understand you work for Yellow Cab."

He nodded.

"Last Saturday, do you remember picking up this girl

in Sausalito?" I showed him Piper's picture.

He shook his head.

"Take another look. It's important."

I watched him focus on the picture, and once again, he shook his head. "I don't remember this girl."

"Do you remember picking up anybody in Sausalito that day?"

"No. I don't pay attention to my fares. Fuck them. What do I care? Just pay me and get the fuck out."

Vitaly was a young man, maybe in his late twenties—probably a functioning alcoholic. Wouldn't surprise me if he had been drinking that morning. He lowered his head, giving me a bird's eye view of his thinning hair. It was hard to tell if he was lying or if he really couldn't remember.

"Hey, look, a girl is dead. Why don't you try a little harder?" Kang said, his voice heightened with irritation.

Vitaly continued to stare down between his legs with his mouth sealed tightly.

Why not help? What's the problem? "You remember her, don't you, Vitaly?" I questioned. "We know you had nothing to do with her death, so help us out. She was an only child. Did you know that?" I knew he didn't, but sometimes guilt can be a big motivator. Unfortunately, Vitaly continued to hide behind his Iron Curtain of emotions and resisted my attempt to tug on them.

I knelt down and handed him my card. "Call me if you remember anything, okay? It's important we find out what happened to her."

"We done?" he asked.

"Yes, we're done," I answered.

Vitaly stood up, and we watched him head back to his apartment. After he slammed his door shut, Kang turned to me. "You think maybe he's the—"

"The killer? I don't think so." I rested my hands on my hips and twisted my torso from side to side. All that driving around had made my body stiff.

"We know he picked up Piper. He might have been the last person to see her alive. Maybe we should bring him in for more questioning."

"On what charge?" I asked.

"No charge. We're questioning a potential witness, except we take a really long time to get him his coffee so that sitting in that room starts to gnaw on him. He'll talk soon enough."

I liked Kang's thinking, but it was risky. Vitaly could completely clam up in that sort of environment and never trust us. Once that happens to a witness, forget about them saying anything, short of it being beaten out of them. "No, we have to do this on his turf, where he won't feel threatened."

Kang studied me for a minute before nodding. "All right. I'll put a patrol car outside in case he feels like taking a walk."

Chapter 25

The plan was to circle back to Vitaly's apartment later that night, after he'd had a chance to sober up more but before he had a chance to start his next binge.

"You want to hang out at the precinct while we wait, or shall I drop you off at home and pick you up later?" Kang asked.

I opted for home. It was nearly four in the afternoon, and the kids would already be back from school. "Just give me a ten-minute heads-up before you come by."

I watched Kang drive off before turning and heading up the walkway to the house. Before I hit the porch stairs, the smell of something delicious awakened my stomach. If there was one thing Po Po was good at—definitely better than I ever would be—it was cooking. She had learned the same way most women from her day and age had learned: by watching and helping their mothers in the kitchen.

Po Po had an encyclopedia of Chinese dishes memorized in her head; not a single one existed on paper. Where she grew up, pens and paper were scarce commodities. They'd had no choice but to remember everything. Po Po also had a finely honed palate and could identify almost any ingredient in a Chinese dish—a remarkable ability. Our stomachs were lucky to have her.

"I'm home," I called out as I walked into the house.

As usual, my loyal daughter was the only one to greet me at the door. *Maybe I should get a dog to increase those numbers.* I gave Lucy a hug. Afterward, she grabbed my hand, and we walked toward the kitchen. The smell inside the house was divine and caused a watery flash flood to drench my tongue.

"How's everything?"

"Everything fine. Ryan upstairs doing homework, and Lucy help me make dinner."

Hmmm, maybe Lucy will be the one to carry the tradition on and memorize over a hundred recipes. "It smells wonderful."

"I make scallops and mushroom rice, oyster chicken, melon soup, and steamed pak choi."

My knees weakened upon hearing the menu. I'll admit it; I frickin' love Chinese food, and not because I'm half Chinese, but because it's frickin' awesome. When I was growing up, my father—the proud Irishman—had very little say in what we ate; that was my mother's domain. But every once in a while, he'd sneak into the kitchen and whip up his favorite, shepherd's pie.

I peeked over Po Po's shoulder for a look into the pot, but she backed me off with a long wooden spoon. "Not ready. Ten minutes."

I had learned early on not to argue with her about cooking times. Even if the dish looked finished, ten minutes often meant the difference between good and food porn.

I sulked and looked at my watch—it was ten to five. To pass the time, I headed upstairs to see how my other child fared. Lucy grabbed the back of my shirt and walked in step behind me, all while mumbling. I had no idea what she was saying or who she was talking to. Whenever I asked her who she was talking to, she smiled and asked me a question. I don't think she was even aware that she was talking. *My luck, Ryan's constant joking that she's probably talking to an evil spirit that will appear one night from a pool of black guck will surprise me and come true.*

Ryan was in his room, shockingly. I had gotten so used to him being upstairs in the media room. I imagined in a few years, he'd be asking if he could make that his bedroom, which would be strange considering my office was up there and I might cramp his style.

"Whatcha reading?" I asked, standing at his doorway with Lucy. He was on his bed, lying on his stomach. I had noticed he was reading more these days.

"It's the autobiography of Bruce Lee. Did you know he was born in Chinatown?"

"I did not." *I did. He's one of Hong Kong's biggest heroes.*

"And he had a dojo in Oakland."

That I did not know. "The book sounds interesting."

"Yeah, my friend Christian lent it to me. I met him in judo class. Maybe I can start taking kung fu classes, too."

My boy was becoming quite the martial arts enthusiast. He had already been involved in judo for over a year now and had even won a couple of small tournaments at his dojo.

"Is there a school nearby?"

"I dunno. I'll ask at the dojo and let you know, okay?"

"That sounds perfect. But right now it's time for dinner, so table that book and come downstairs."

Dinner that night lasted for forty-five minutes, longer than usual, but the conversation was good and so was the food. Afterward, Lucy rushed over to the couch and started playing games on her tablet. "Uh huh," I said. "Did you finish your homework?"

She remained quiet, pretending she didn't hear me.

"Lucy, don't make me ask you twice."

"Awwww, Mommy," she groaned.

"No games until it's finished. Understood?"

"But I'm tired."

"Next time, do your homework as soon as you get home, and that way, you won't have to worry about it later." I grabbed the tablet out of her hands. "You'll get this back when I see your homework finished."

I watched her stomp her tiny feet up the stairs before I turned to her brother. "And what about you?"

"All done. I'll be upstairs reading."

Awesome!

By the time Po Po and I finished clearing the table and doing all the dishes, it was nearing six thirty, which was more like eight for her. Her eyes looked tired, and I knew she'd had a long day. Still, at seventy-one years of age, she was pretty active—and she was up every morning at five thirty.

"Let me finish wiping the counters," I said before taking the cloth from her hand.

"I help," she insisted.

"Nope. Get out of here."

She nodded. "Okay, I take a bath now."

Since she had fixed an amazing dinner, cleaning up was the least I could do. *I'm so glad we have a dishwasher.* After I had finished in the kitchen, I retired to my office to give my case more thought.

As always, I made a pass over all my notes and the case files for the three victims as a reminder of what I already knew. Sometimes looking at the information with a fresh head helped me to see things differently. That wasn't the case that night. As much as it felt like we were making progress, my gut told me otherwise. So did the headache that lingered near the base of my skull.

I still had a little trouble buying the idea that my killer was a woman. Typically, serial killers were white males. It's not that women didn't kill—they do. They just don't fit neatly into what has long been regarded as the profile of a serial killer. Times were changing though. A case I had worked in Detroit a few years back was proof.

I pulled out my phone and pulled up the suspect's picture. It was grainy, and the angle was typical of most surveillance cameras, a top down visual. She didn't look like a killer, but the good ones never do. *Who are you? Why are you killing people?*

It was a little after eight, and I was still lost within my thoughts, when I received a call from Tucker, the newbie agent.

"Agent Kane, it's Agent Tucker. Sorry to bother you at home, but the early evening news didn't feature our mystery woman."

That didn't surprise me. None of the news stations had reported on the crime. Only a couple of small papers had made mention of Piper's death: the *Marin Independent Journal* and the *Sausalito MarinScope*. To most of the media, her death wasn't newsworthy enough. Translation: It wasn't sensational enough to move papers or spike ratings.

"That sucks."

"Yeah, well, I called a bunch of them back, and now they have all promised to feature it on the late news."

"Oh? What made them change their mind?"

"I hope you don't mind, but I gave the case a nickname, something they could sell."

"What name did you give them?"

"The Cotton Candy Killer."

Chapter 26

Vitaly Scherbo slouched on his couch. Sweat had soaked his shirt, and his bouncing legs showed no sign of losing their beat as he drifted in and out of his thoughts. A bottle of vodka he had removed from the freezer stood unopened on the small coffee table in front of him. The icy frost that had once covered the narrow bottle was nothing more than a tiny moat circling the base.

For three hours the bottle had stared at Vitaly, urging him to indulge one last time. It was always one last time. He didn't want to drink, but the pain he felt inside wouldn't disappear, and only the clear elixir from his homeland had the strength to dull it, if only for a few hours.

Vitaly had come from a well-to-do family; his father had made his fortune in aluminum after the fall of Communism. While his older brothers had been anxious to involve themselves in the family business, Vitaly had preferred psychology over the production of goods for commerce. He had dreamed of becoming a psychologist, a profession that hadn't been highly sought after in his hometown of Krasnoyarsk, Russia. Therefore, it hadn't been a common pathway at the universities where he had lived.

He had studied overseas to obtain a proper education in his field, receiving his undergraduate degree in London and his master's in New York, and was currently working on his doctorate in clinical psychology in San Francisco. For a year and a half, he had attended the University of San Francisco and excelled. Only recently had he taken on a job as a cabbie, not because he needed the money—his father paid for everything—but to do what he loved doing: studying people. He had planned on writing his thesis paper based on his observations and conversations with his fares.

By the sheer nature of who Vitaly was and what he was studying to become, anyone who entered his cab became subject matter. He was a very astute person to begin with, and not much got by him—a positive trait, Vitaly thought. Life had been perfect until that day across the bay when he had picked up those three people in Sausalito.

He'd followed his procedure, never straying, not even the tiniest bit. As soon as the passengers were in the car and their destination called out, Vitaly had done what he always did with each fare: he struck up a conversation. He studied their movements. He listened to their conversations. It had been no different with the trio in the back of his cab that day.

He had thought it strange to find a forty-something couple palling around with a woman in her early twenties. It would have been perfectly fine if she'd been their daughter, but she wasn't—he didn't need to be told that. She looked nothing like them, the ages weren't quite right, and their conversation only confirmed it.

Most people would have seen nothing wrong with the situation, and that was expected; most people hadn't made a career of studying people and learning the ins and outs of criminal psychology like Vitaly had for the last nine years.

It had been this area of expertise that made Vitaly first notice the man and the way he looked at Piper like a ravaged animal waiting to feast. And though he had tried hard to cover his intense stares with smile and laughter, the man swallowed often, licked his lips, and wiped sweat off his brow, even though the temperatures had been in the low seventies. It was as if he would pounce on her at any second. The more Vitaly watched, the more he'd thought something was wrong.

And then things got worse.

He had begun to take notice of the woman. He saw through her laughter, and hair flips, and her touchy-feely hands that always seemed to follow her way-too-agreeable nods; it had been clear that her role was that of an older sister, someone trustworthy. It's as if she were putting on an act, too. They were two wolves in disguise, talking up a baby sheep. The mannerisms of the woman were nothing like the man. Hers had been polished enough that the untrained eye wouldn't have blinked, but Vitaly had seen through her veiled deception.

As for the young girl, she hadn't found anything

unusual about her companions. It didn't appear as if the girl had been forced to go anywhere. She was agreeable and friendly with the older couple. They were friendly. They were normal. They'd had her convinced she was in a safe environment.

Vitaly tried to converse. He watched. He listened. He diagnosed. He feared. The young woman had been willing to chit-chat with him, but the other two only responded with malevolent stares. *She does not know. You must say something.*

At first, Vitaly hadn't believed what his mind had concluded. Surely, he must have gotten something wrong or jumped too hastily to his conclusions about the man and the woman. But what if he were right? The signs were there. Why couldn't it be true?

Based on his observations, the woman was likely a sociopath. She was charming, very likeable indeed. A lot of people are friendly, but coupled with continuous lying, it starts to build a case. For instance, Vitaly found it very unlikely that this woman had visited the Amazon. The woman hadn't stopped talking since she sat down inside the car, and she had told the most elaborate of stories fueled with adrenaline and involving high risk—a common characteristic.

Her low-cut tank top had barely been able to contain her full chest. The flimsy bra had been more for style than form. Was that enough to peg her as a sexual person, a clear trait of a sociopath? Vitaly wasn't sure. There were many more telling signs, but hadn't been able to make a full determination without further observation.

And the man—did he know?

If she was a sociopath and the man knew it, Vitaly got the impression that he didn't care. Why? Based on Vitaly's backseat diagnosis, the man was a psychopath; they tend not to be bothered by those kinds of things.

The man's forced smiles and occasional chuckles had checked the box for superficial charm. He had moved in his seat and twiddled his thumbs. Psychopaths were known to suffer a never-ending battle with boredom. The way he looked at the young woman, in a predatory way. She was a prize to him, something he could have used to feed his psychological need. She was not human; she just *was*. To Vitaly, those signs had suggested that the man felt no remorse or conscious for his actions. Of course, Vitaly couldn't prove any of it. It had all been just observation.

In the end, Vitaly had been left with two half-baked diagnoses that could go either way.

On their own, both the man and the woman could be dangerous. But if Vitaly's theory had been right, that the man had been a psychopath and the woman had been a sociopath and they had formed a relationship to fuel each other's needs, then that young woman was in grave danger.

On his way back to the city, Vitaly had replayed the drive over and over in his head. He wept as he thought of how he had done nothing, said nothing. He had let that poor, young girl exit the back of his cab and leave with those very disturbing people even though his gut had screamed for him to do something.

When he read the paper the next day, he had seen the mention of a dead hiker found on the mountain, and he knew who it was without even reading the rest of the article. He was responsible. His emotions only twisted further into a ball of self-hatred. He had known and had done nothing. He ignored all the signs.

I should have told them.

Vitaly knew it was wrong to withhold the information from the police, but he was scared—scared of what might happen to him, scared that maybe he might be implicated, or worse, that the couple would find out and come after him. After all, they knew what he looked like. His name had been clearly displayed on the cab license.

Streams of remorse trailed from his puffy eyes as the guilt inside burned through his chest. Vitaly reached toward the coffee table, past the bottle of vodka, for the true answer to his pain.

Vitaly's problem wasn't that he was an alcoholic. Deep down, he knew the real reason he had done nothing and had said nothing. He had known this reason for a long time— most of his life. Even though he had gone his own direction, left Russia and studied abroad for years, those were safe things. He'd had his father's money to protect him and his father's business to fall back on. The truth of the matter was that Vitaly was, and always has been, an honest-to-goodness coward.

And that's why Piper Taylor was dead.

Chapter 27

I was at my desk, with my back facing the door, when I sensed someone standing behind me. I thought it was Lucy, who I had put to bed over an hour ago. She had overcome her fear of the third floor and started sneaking up on me while I worked. "Lucy, is that you?"

"No," said a voice in a poor imitation of a little girl.

I spun around in my chair and found Kang leaning against the doorframe with a smile on his face. My initial reaction had me jumping back a bit in my chair. "Dammit, Kyle. What are you doing here?"

"I thought we were going to hit up that Russian kid again."

"I know that. What I mean is, what are you doing sneaking up on me inside my home?"

"Your Po Po let me in. She said you were up here and that she was on her way to bed."

Kang hadn't bothered to call and had shown up at my doorstep at nine. Of course Po Po had let him in, not because she knew him, but because she didn't. And it wasn't because he was a police officer, because he wasn't wearing a uniform. No, she let him in because he was

Chinese, and she thought I had a date. She had sent him up the stairs unannounced.

Agent House had asked me once if it bothered my mother-in-law when I went out on dates, being that I had married her son and was now a widow. I had told her Po Po wasn't bothered by it. At first, I'd thought she would be, but one day, she had told me that she was fine with me dating other men; she didn't expect me to honor my late husband's memory by remaining single. And plus, she thought me remarrying and having a man around the house would be good for the children. What she was against was me dating a man who *wasn't* Chinese, and that's why she had sent Kang straight up. I could have been naked in the bath, and she still would have sent him up.

I told Kang to wait downstairs while I freshened up.

"You look fine. You don't have to do that for me."

"I'm not doing it for you," I called out as I walked into my bedroom.

To which he responded while heading downstairs, "All I'm saying is that you look good."

Was that a real compliment or a flirty compliment? I laughed it off. Ten minutes later, I walked downstairs in jeans, a hoodie and my Oakland A's baseball cap. Kang had made himself at home in front of the television.

"You like baseball?" He stood up and turned the TV off.

"I like the A's."

"We should catch a game sometime. I have a cousin who works for a radio station in Oakland, and he's always giving away tickets."

I grabbed my purse. "That sounds great." *Free tickets to an A's game? I'm all over that.*

<><><>

Twenty minutes later, we arrived at Vitaly's apartment. We were about ten steps from his front door when a gunshot rang out from inside. The front door was locked, so we hurried through the gate and toward the backyard. The curtains were open, and I could see Vitaly slouched to the side on the couch, lit only by the blue hue from the television. The rest of the apartment was dark.

I reached for the handle on the sliding glass door and pulled. Surprisingly, it was open. Kang and I entered and discovered that Vitaly had sustained a gunshot to the head—self-inflicted. He still held the weapon in his right hand; it looked like a Sigma 9mm.

Kang had already pulled out his cell phone and dialed 911 for an ambulance. I knew they would call it a DOA when they got here, but it was procedure. *Why did you do this?* Vitaly had seemed fine earlier, a little hung over and a little freaked out by our showing up on his doorstep, but generally fine. *Was he hiding something?*

While we waited for the ambulance and the detectives

from the area precinct, we poked around the apartment and discovered he was first and foremost a student. "I guess this explains all the missed days," I said, looking at a bookshelf full of textbooks. Most of them were psychology and sociology books.

"I'm going to take a look in the bedroom," Kang said.

I nodded and continued poking around the living room area. There was an unopened bottle of vodka on the table in front of the couch where Vitaly sat. *Something had him troubled.* The table was a filthy mess: two filled ashtrays, a couple of empty coffee containers, crusted food spills, and used napkins. I was about to find Kang when my eye caught something scribbled on one of the napkins.

"Kang!" I shouted.

A beat later, he returned to the living room. "What is it?"

I pointed at the napkin.

Kang picked it up and read it out loud. "'I'm sorry, Piper.' He knew something."

"Whatever he knew, it was enough to make him blow his brains out."

Chapter 28

"Yes, that's the way. Yes! Yes! Yes!" Vicki vocalized in rhythm as she lay on her back. A muscular black man lay between her legs, rocking the bed on its frame each time he buried himself inside her. She gripped his meaty arms, her nails biting into his dark skin as she shook her head from side to side. "It feels so good. Don't stop," she said breathlessly.

Enough of the lamps in the hotel room were left on to create a relaxing mood while providing enough light for Jerry to film everything. He sat in a chair near the TV stand watching the thousand-dollar-an-hour black stud earn his pay. They had found his ad on an adult escort site that touted "a black anaconda between my legs." Jerry responded to the ad and arranged for a time, with the condition that, if he didn't live up to the advertised promise, he would be turned away.

The six-foot-two man went by the name Sampson, except he didn't gain his strength from his hair. Vicki had squealed when he had entered their hotel room earlier. "What a fine specimen."

She'd grabbed hold of his arm with one hand and

fondled his chest with her other. This wasn't the first time the Carlsons had brought another man into their bed. It was a treat for both of them, because Jerry enjoyed watching, and Vicki got variety. It also wasn't the first time Vicki had taken a black lover.

She had ordered him to drop his pants immediately. "No sense in wasting everybody's time."

Sampson had unbuckled and let his pants fall to the carpet. He wore no underwear and was true to his word.

Jerry had started filming Sampson and his wife from the moment they hit the bed, obtaining all of the requisite porn angles. After forty-five minutes and three wailing orgasms from Vicki, Jerry thought he had enough of that type of footage and attached the handheld camera to a travel tripod. It allowed him to operate the zoom function with one hand while he used the other to stroke his semi-erect cock. He watched for a while as Sampson continued his effortless thrusting.

Eventually, his eyes wandered from the action to the television near him. He had left it on earlier and forgotten all about it, really. The sound had been muted, so he turned it up a tad to listen to bits and pieces of the news report. It didn't seem to distract the two on the bed. Sampson had flipped Vicki over to her hands and knees, and she had started rocking against him.

Jerry turned his attention back to the television. A graphic appeared next to the reporter: The Cotton Candy

Killer. *Huh, this is interesting.* He leaned in closer but had trouble hearing everything the reporter said due to his wife. The graphic then changed to a picture of two women captured by a surveillance camera. Jerry blinked his eyes and took a closer look. *That can't be.* He looked away for a second, then back at the screen and focused once more. *That woman... That's my wife. And the other one—that's Piper.*

He wasn't mistaken. He could pick Vicki out of any line up, even a photo like this that showed three quarters of a face from the top down. It wasn't the best picture and thankfully she was wearing a wig, which made a big difference in her appearance, but still. *How recognizable would she be in public?*

Jerry thought back to that moment. He had chosen to remain outside for a smoke and thus had inadvertently escaped being photographed. *I could have easily been in that picture; of course, I would have spotted the cameras and warned her.* Jerry usually didn't wear a disguise when he and Vicki were on the hunt, but seeing his wife on TV made him reconsider his actions. Until now, he had thought they were getting better with their crimes. This was a sloppy mistake, disguise or not. Vicki knew to look for cameras and avoid them. *She's losing her focus.*

The graphic changed to a nighttime shot of the actual store in Sausalito where another reporter stood. *The police must have talked to the owner of that shop.* Jerry thought hard about what that person might have noticed about them.

And then he remembered: Vicki had mentioned she had gotten the number for a cab company from someone in the store. That also meant a conversation took place. Eye contact had been made—more mistakes from his wife.

He switched off the TV right as his wife stopped her moaning. She lay under Sampson, hidden almost entirely by his muscled mass. She gave him a pat on the back, and he rolled off her. They both lay still, catching their breath.

"Did he cum inside you?" Jerry asked pointedly.

"No. I thought I would wait for later."

Jerry walked over to the bed, leaned down and gave his wife a long, loving kiss. She smiled back at him as he pulled away, her hands still holding the sides of his face. "I love you, darling."

"I love you, too," he said, grabbing a hand towel next to him and dabbing it against her forehead.

"Help me up," she said, reaching up with both arms.

Jerry pulled on both of them as she slid her legs off the bed and moved herself into a seated position. "Boy, that was fun, but I need to take a breather." She kissed her husband once more before moving over to the lounge chair and kicking her feet up onto the ottoman. "I'll be right here."

Sampson was still on the bed, sitting back on his legs and still rigid as ever. Jerry lay down. He grabbed beneath his knees and pulled back on his legs, all while thinking about his dilemma. He should have been bubbling with excitement as he watched Sampson slather lube around his shaft and maneuver himself into position. But Jerry was too busy problem solving. His and Vicki's situation had suddenly changed and not for the better. Jerry looked over at his wife. She smiled at him, unaware that her picture had been broadcast across the airwaves and labeled as the Cotton Candy Killer. *What to do?* He drifted farther into his thoughts, oblivious to Sampson's forceful entry.

Chapter 29

It was Thursday, five days since Piper Taylor had been killed—more than two weeks for Kang's victims, whose cases had gone cold. My investigation was the only thing breathing life into his homicides, and I had slammed into another wall. Vitaly's unexpected suicide was a huge disappointment. Clearly he had known something about what had happened to Piper, and that information had died with him that day.

There was a glimmer of hope, though. Tucker had begun to field calls regarding Piper's death thanks to the media's broadcast of the Cotton Candy Killer. Some people reported having seen her at the Ferry Building near Market Street; others had seen her on the ferry itself or at the Sausalito port. None of them could place the woman—yet. It seemed as though Piper's beauty overshadowed anyone next to her. Our mystery woman might as well have been invisible. *Is that why she picked Piper?*

Case reports and notes from my investigation covered my desk. It all looked familiar, but I diligently went through the information again. In between sips of tea, I studied the reports from House and Kang. I looked over the ME's report and the reports from the park rangers and the FBI field office out of Cleveland. Nothing chipped away at the mental wall that had erected itself.

It was a tough day at the office. Question after question fished for answers in my head, but they all came up empty-handed. When I find myself in a situation like I did that day, I bury myself in the information. I continue that approach until somehow, someway, I punch through.

"Agent Kane."

I looked up and saw Tucker walking toward my desk, bright-eyed and eager.

"Sorry to bother you, but I wanted to update you with my progress on accessing the surveillance cameras at the docks."

I pushed back from the desk a bit. "What did you find out?"

"Getting access was easy. I've already pored over the footage that coincided with the timeframe you gave me."

"And?"

"I captured footage of Piper Taylor at the San Francisco ferry building, but she was alone. Well, she looked like she boarded the ferry by herself. The footage in Sausalito also showed her exiting the boat but again, by herself."

"Are you sure?"

Tucker's shoulders rose, and his voice softened. "I'm pretty sure, but I think it would be a good idea for us to both look at the footage."

I followed Tucker back to his desk where he played the video footage on his desktop.

"This is from the ferry building in the city." Tucker scrolled slowly until we saw Piper enter the frame.

"Keep going," I said.

The angle of the camera was from behind her, slightly off to the side. I could make out part of her face, but the clothes and the backpack were what confirmed it for me. I watched her move slowly toward the ticket taker.

"She doesn't talk to anyone," Tucker said.

"Hold on. Back the footage up until right before the ticket handler."

Tucker did as I said.

"Right there. The ticket handler—Piper doesn't turn over a ticket to him."

"Huh?"

"Rewind a bit farther and watch everyone in front of her." Sure enough, everyone in front of Piper handed over a ticket except her. The man behind her handed over a ticket but not the woman and two kids. "You see that? He paid for the woman and two kids. My guess is that person in front of Piper is our woman and she turned over both of their tickets. That's our Cotton Candy Killer, and they met before the trip."

We watched the footage of them exiting the boat in Sausalito. Piper and that same woman were together again, except this time, she had removed her large raincoat and hat. Our suspect's clothes and hair now matched the description from the owner at the sweet shop.

"You mentioned that she left the hostel alone," Tucker confirmed.

"According to the young woman at the front desk, she left alone, and as far as that girl knew, had planned on traveling to Muir Woods by herself. She said it was 'an easy trip.' There wasn't much time from when she left the hostel to the departure of the ferry, about an hour and a half."

"If she stayed in a hostel, she walked," Tucker said. "It's not that far, and as a tourist, it's another opportunity to see the city."

"So, a twenty-five minute walk."

"At the most, unless she stopped somewhere."

"Do me a favor. Pull up Google Maps and let's take a look at the obvious routes. Let's see if there's anything worth making a stop for outside of a coffee."

Tucker moved his fingers over his keyboard and a map of San Francisco appeared in his browser. He zoomed in so we could see both the hostel and the ferry building in frame.

"Well, the most direct route is to take Sacramento Street down to Drumm Street. From there, she could travel south to Market and cross over Embarcadero Drive to the Ferry Building or go north to Clay and cross over."

"She passes The Embarcadero Center on the way," I noted. "What girl doesn't like shopping?"

"I'll find out if the Center has cameras on the property and get access. We might get lucky."

I thanked Tucker for his help and returned to my desk, thinking how grateful I was to have a young agent who put everything he had into whatever I asked of him. Even though I knew Piper could have met this woman earlier in the week, my gut told me that wasn't the case. With time racing, I wondered whether this woman was a local resident or someone passing through town. If it was the latter, every day was a day she could wrap up production on her show and take off. Flushing her out of hiding was my best shot and the only way I would find her. I had to keep squeezing.

Chapter 30

Kang was sitting quietly at his desk and reviewing his notes when Sokolov took a seat at the desk opposite him. "What's the word, boss?"

Kang straightened his tie before leaning back and giving his partner his full attention. "We've made progress but not enough to where I think we have a handle on it and are closing in."

"The Cotton Candy Killer. I saw it on the news. Catchy."

"That was Abby's doing."

"Abby? You two are on a first-name basis?" Sokolov raised his eyebrows, furthering his curious response.

Kang waved off his partner's insinuation that something other than work was taking place between him and Abby. "It's not like that. We're friends. No need to keep it so formal."

"Friends…" Sokolov pushed up his lower lip as he nodded, his smile growing.

"Yes. Friends. You know, like you and me."

Sokolov coughed out a loud laugh.

"What?" Kang raised his shoulders, his palms held out.

"That's a weak rebuttal." Sokolov squeezed his eyelids tighter. "You like this woman, yes?"

"Don't you have some dried fish to eat?"

"I've known you a long time, my friend. You can't pull the wool over this Russian," Sokolov said as he jabbed his index finger into his own chest.

"You don't know what you're talking about."

The bald detective lowered his head and steadied his eyes. "I'm like KGB. I know everything."

Kang wasn't interested in any more Abby talk. "How's your task force coming along?"

Enthusiasm returned to Sokolov's voice. "I've put together a good group of men—five altogether. We were able to rent a small office in Inner Richmond for our base of operations."

A surprised look settled on Kang's face. "How did you manage that?"

"Important case. I didn't question when the captain suggested it."

"What's the plan of attack?"

"We focus on rebuilding a list of the players and start surveillance. We'll see where this takes us." Sokolov leaned back in his chair with both hands behind his head. "How close are you to finding this cotton lady?"

"Not very close," Kang said, still futzing with his tie.

"You still think she killed our two vics?"

"Good question. I'm more confident that she killed that

hiker. It'll either pan out, or it won't."

"Maybe you keep coming at it from another angle. The captain expects both cases to be solved."

This time, Kang saw none of the playfulness in Sokolov's eyes he had seen earlier. His partner, as always, was a solid sounding board. As much as he liked working with Abby, he had an obligation to make progress on his two cases.

Kang stood up. "I'm heading out for a walk. Need to clear my head."

"My time is limited," Sokolov said. "But if you need anything…"

"I'll let you know."

Kang exited the precinct and headed toward Chinatown. A walk through his favorite part of town never let him down, and it usually helped him work through his cases. But that day, he also wondered if it would also help him work through the feelings he had begun to have for Abby.

Chapter 31

I looked at my watch; it was quarter to four. I had agreed to have coffee with Dr. Green at the Starbucks on Bush Street. He had sent me a text asking if we could meet Thursday afternoon. I liked Green and knew he had developed a crush on me, but romantically, he wasn't my type. On the other hand, I didn't want to keep making excuses. *It's coffee. What's the big deal?* So I said yes. Plus, the top medical examiner in the city wasn't a bad guy to have on my side. I may need a favor or two from him down the line.

Green was already inside waiting for me and waved from a table in the far corner.

"Hi, Dr. Green. It's nice to see you again."

He stood up and pulled my chair out for me. "Oh please, this is a personal meeting. Let's use our first names, Abby."

Okie dokie. I smiled and took my seat.

"May I get you something?"

I removed my tin of loose-leaf tea from my purse. "Hot water. I kind of have an addiction," I said with a shrug. I sensed Green's attempts to make this feel like a date. It was, but not the kind of date he had pictured in his head.

"Well, I'll get us some pastries to share."

Before I could object, he had popped out of his seat and taken off.

I sat quietly, spinning my tin can around between my index finger and the table. I wondered what we would talk about. Would we resort to the expected and discuss the case or work in general? Or would he surprise me and hold a conversation that didn't have anything to do with a dead body?

Green returned with a chocolate brownie and one of those everything bars, along with my cup of hot water. He had already ordered himself a large coffee ahead of time. I fixed my tea and picked up a fork. There's no way I would let a chocolate brownie sit in front of me without a taste. No can do.

"I heard through the grapevine that you like to box," he started off.

Wow, that came out of nowhere. I can't remember mentioning it. "I do. My father taught me how when I was a young girl. I got away from the ring for some time, but since my move to San Francisco, I've fallen back into it."

"It's a great way to keep the body in condition."

"That's mostly why I picked it up again. I run as well, but boxing tends to give me a more balanced workout. And you? What do you like to do for exercise?"

"I wish I could say something impressive like muay

thai fighting, but sadly, I can't. I enjoy hiking. I love being out in nature. Not only is it beautiful, it's very peaceful."

"I'll agree with you there. I try to get the family over to Golden Gate Park as often as I can. I know the nature found there is nothing like hiking, but it does the trick."

"Oh, it certainly does. I love the park. In fact, I live nearby."

From that point on, the conversation steered itself all over the place. At one point, we exchanged embarrassing stories about our childhood. Green's were particularly entertaining. He had hippie parents who liked taking him on weekend camping trips to Bolinas with other families. He said there was a lot of nudity, pot and music. I laughed, hard.

"Oh my, I can't believe you had to endure that."

"At the time, I thought it was normal." He laughed. "I didn't know otherwise. My parents were, and still are, big-time nudists. That fun, magical place where we vacationed was a nudist colony." We giggled. "I liked swimming in the pool and roasting marshmallows over the campfire at night. What about you?" he asked.

"My mother thought I was a lesbian from age sixteen to age twenty-eight, the year I married my late husband." We both laughed as Green tried to get an apology out about my husband's passing. Thankfully, he didn't ask more about it.

I had a nice time with Green. It felt like we could talk about anything, and I was a bit surprised when I looked at my watch and saw that an hour had already passed. I told Green I'd had a very nice time talking to him, but I needed to get back to the office.

We were still chatting when we exited the coffee shop and I heard someone call my name. I spun around and saw Kang walking toward us.

"Kyle, what are you doing here?"

"I took a walk through Chinatown and decided to loop back on Kearny Street."

"You know Dr. Green, right?"

Kang looked down at my coffee date without his usual smile. "Green," he said with a quick nod.

Green looked up at my temporary partner without the smile I'd seen all afternoon and returned the same abrupt reply. "Kang."

Methinks they know each other. Fun had left the room, and awkward had taken over. I didn't know what to say, so I excused myself to go to the bathroom.

◇◇◇

"How do you know Abby?" Green asked when he and Kang were alone.

"We're working on a case together. I assume that's what you're doing?"

"Oh no, quite the opposite. We're on a date." Green beamed and pocketed his hands.

Kang jerked his head back. He wasn't expecting that.

"Cat got your tongue? Yeah, don't look so surprised. Abby and I hit it off. I know you're thinking I'm not her type, but I'll have you know, it's all fun and laughter when she's with me." Green had puffed his chest out a bit.

"How... how long have you—"

"Been seeing her? Well, let's see..." Green began a count on his hand. "This is the third time." *I'm not lying. Everything I've said is true.* "Things are really moving along for us. I'm pretty serious about her, just so you know. You're not interested in her, are you?"

"We're partners on a case. That's all."

Kang looked away. He hadn't gotten the impression that Abby was involved with someone. To think he had spent the last half hour thinking about her, even working up the guts to ask her out. Kang actually thought she might even be out of his league, but seeing her with Green... well, not only was it a shock; it actually made him jealous. It didn't help that it was Green.

Kang and the medical examiner had a history. Their relationship had been fine until he worked the Top Chef Killer case a few years ago. It was during that time that Green had met Inspector Leslie Choi and had become smitten with her. Kang didn't think her feelings had been mutual. Anyway, Green developed a jealous streak over all the time that Kang and Choi spent together and how well the two got along. From that point on, Kang and Green's relationship had deteriorated. This was yet another case of Abby/Leslie déjà-vu.

"Yeah, she probably wouldn't be into a guy like you anyway. Plus, I already have dibs on her." Green bounced his eyebrows at Kang.

You smarmy little shit. Kang took a deep breath, forcing his face to relax. *Calm down, Kyle. You're not dating her. Don't get upset because someone else had the balls to ask her out while you pretended not to like her.* He straightened up to his full height to make Green feel tiny. "Tell *Abby* I'll catch up with her later."

Chapter 32

Jerry had been looking forward to the night tour of Alcatraz he had booked a few days before their arrival in San Francisco. But now, with the situation with his wife, it dampened the excitement. If the Cotton Candy Killer news piece blew up, they would have to flee the city before completing their five objectives—a no-go in his mind. The entire situation angered him.

They had a list of precautions they'd agreed to follow. In fact, it had been all Vicki's idea. She was the one who had implemented layers of planning to lessen their chances of being caught. Over the last couple of years, she'd spent measurable amounts of time refining the way they would complete their kills. For this trip especially, she'd thought of everything from fake aliases and passports to dummy prepaid credit cards and bank accounts that were replenished through their bank accounts offshore. They had disguises packed in their suitcases, even a plan for what to do should they find themselves on the run and separated.

Jerry had been against it all from the very beginning. He preferred to slice and dice on a whim and couldn't care less about a trail that led back to him. But over time, she had slowly helped him change his methods. Now, he had become obsessed with following the rules to a T.

He still hadn't mentioned to his wife that her picture had made the late news. They had stayed in the hotel all day, contentedly lying in each other's arms between screwing and ordering room service. A threesome always seemed to bring them closer.

Jerry turned to the night table and peeked at his watch. It was encroaching on half past four. They would need to get ready soon.

"Why are you watching the clock?" Vicki asked playfully. "Don't you like being stuck in bed with me?"

"We have tickets for Alcatraz, remember? I don't want to miss the ferry."

"Oh, that's right," she said absently. Vicki had no interest in visiting the prison. She thought it strange that Jerry wanted to visit a place that could become a reality in their line of business.

Jerry looked at his wife. "You still don't want to go, do you?"

She pouted her lips and lowered her chin. "No."

"Tell you what; stay here and relax. Order more room service. I'll go by myself. It's not a big deal."

"Are you sure?"

"Positive." *The less interaction you have with the news-watching public, the better.*

Jerry kissed his wife reassuringly. He slipped out of

bed and stepped into the shower but not before asking her to join him. Keeping her in the hotel seemed easy enough, but how would he stop her from watching television or surfing the Internet? She might discover what he had been hiding from her. And then what?

Jerry wrestled with the problem while he lathered and scrubbed his wife's back. He thought of telling her, but decided the right thing was to keep quiet. They did not have a plan for something like this. He knew she would never have bothered to give it any thought, because she was confident they would never end up in a situation like this. She would be devastated to know she was the one who screwed things up.

Jerry wished it had been his mistake. Of course he'd have to take a beating for it, but it would save his wife the embarrassment. Should she find out, Jerry feared she might lose her confidence. He couldn't have that. As a team, they both needed to be strong. A panicked wife creating more problems was the last thing he needed.

As they toweled each other off, he casually mentioned that she should nap so she would be fresh and ready to continue the fun when he returned.

"Jerry," she said with a smile, "you've been so attentive all afternoon."

Upon hearing that, Jerry dropped to his knees and snuggled his face between her legs. Vicki laughed and tried to push him away, but he held tight and kept his face buried and his tongue moving. It didn't take long before Vicki succumbed to pleasure once again.

Jerry continued his husbandly duties on the bed while looking at his watch every few minutes. He intended to leave at the last possible moment, with his wife tired and completely uninterested in moving. When the time came, he kissed her and bolted out the door. Even with all that could go wrong, he still wanted to tour Alcatraz.

Chapter 33

Vicki hadn't moved, still content to lie in the same revealing position that her husband had left her in. But boredom eventually set in. She rolled over twice to the other side of the king-size bed and fetched the remote off the nightstand. She pushed the power button, and the flat screen powered to life with previews of movies available on the hotel's on-demand system. She flipped through a few of the channels but didn't recognize any shows. She clicked the remote once more, turning the television off.

What to do? It didn't take her very long to figure that out. She dressed, put on her face and left the comforts of the room. The Carlsons had been staying at the Parc 55 Wyndham on Cyril Magnin Street near the edge of the Tenderloin. She had wanted to book one of the many charming boutique hotels in the lower Nob Hill area, but Jerry had reminded her of her rule that they be as inconspicuous as possible. The large Parc 55 hotel made it easy for them to blend into the sea of faces that other guests, and the hotel staff, saw on a daily basis.

Union Square, the epic center of San Francisco shopping, was only a few blocks over, and that was the compromise. Vicki had thoughts of buying new lingerie, something to surprise Jerry. The concierge directed her to the Victoria's Secret inside Westfield Center, only a two-minute walk in the opposite direction of the square.

Once there, she spent thirty minutes searching for the perfect outfit. She continually switched back and forth between the classic bra, panty and garter belt ensemble versus the cute, see-through négligée. She came close to buying one of each but, in the end, opted for what she thought her husband would like best: stripper wife.

Vicki didn't bother to browse the rest of the shopping center; instead, she hurried over to Union Square. She had wanted to shop at Macy's ever since they landed in San Francisco. Almost two hours had passed when she received a text from her husband that he had returned and wanted to know why she wasn't in the room. Vicki had completely lost track of time. *It seems like he just left.* She texted him back that she had finished shopping and would be home soon. Vicki hurried down the four flights of escalators to the ground floor. She had intended to be lying on the bed in her new outfit when Jerry returned. *So much for the big surprise.*

She exited Macy's at the north doors, facing Union Square. Before she could turn left, in the direction of her hotel, the most beautiful voice caught her ear. Her head turned from side to side as she searched for the owner of that soulful voice. Her ears led her across the street and up the stairs into the square.

There, a young man sat on a chair, strumming a guitar while he sang into a microphone. It wasn't a song Vicki had ever heard before, but she loved it. None of the passersby seemed to notice the man as they crisscrossed the wide open space, hurrying from one store to another with large shopping bags in tow.

His high tenor with its angelic notes easily cut through the city noise. He wore a pork pie hat that allowed his golden locks to peek out. The rest of his outfit consisted of a brown sport coat and jeans with scuffed leather boots.

His eyes were closed and had been since she first had seen him, while his left foot bounced to keep time. Vicki moved to within five feet of the singer, listening and watching until he finished his song. She clapped, and he thanked her with a warm smile as she removed a five-dollar bill from her purse and placed it in the open guitar case on the ground in front of him. He nodded and smiled once more before strumming the beginnings of another song. Eventually, other people gathered, and Vicki lost her private concert.

She turned to leave but not before smiling at him one last time. When she was out of his sightline, she removed her phone from her purse and texted Jerry, "You'll never guess what I found."

"What?" he replied.

"The heart we've been looking for."

Chapter 34

Jerry moved as fast as he could. His heavy backpack slapped against his back with every stride taken. He was thrilled about Vicki's text message and didn't want to ruin it by arriving too late. When he got there, a bubbling of perspiration covered his face and the chest area of his brown shirt showed signs of spotting.

"I power walked here," he said, bent over and gasping for air.

Vicki rubbed his shoulder. "Gee, honey, you didn't have to do that."

He looked up at her. "You're wearing your wig."

"Yeah, I know. I kind of like it. Maybe I should grow my hair out."

"I don't think you'll need it this time."

"Well, he's already seen me in it so…"

Jerry stood up but still rested both hands on his hips. He twisted his neck, searching for the singer. "Where is he?"

"There," Vicki said. She gripped his shoulders and faced him in the right direction. The two watched the singer from a distance, enjoying his melodic tones.

"He's pretty good."

Vicki smiled and snuggled her husband's arm. They watched for a few more minutes before Jerry spoke again. "We can't take care of business around here. It's too public of a place."

"What do you suggest?"

"When he's done, we'll follow him and see where that leads us. I brought our equipment."

A crowd had begun to form around the young man, allowing the Carlsons to move closer and still remain faceless. When he finished singing, Vicki and Jerry cleared out with the rest of the impromptu audience and took separate seats at a coffee shop about a hundred feet away. There, they waited patiently. An hour later the singer packed up his equipment and headed off.

The Carlsons split up, as they always did in those situations, and followed at a good distance behind their target. The singer walked up Powell Street until he reached the bus stop on Sutter. Jerry texted his wife that he would move in closer to the young man since he wouldn't be recognized.

Vicki continued in the opposite direction on Sutter for fifty yards before crossing the street and doubling back to hide around the corner from them.

A short wait and the number two bus arrived. The singer entered through the front doors with Jerry right behind. Vicki entered through the rear doors with her head down and a hat on and took a seat next to an elderly lady. The singer walked right by her without even a cursory glance and sat at the rear of the bus. Jerry sat two seats forward from him.

There the three remained until the bus reached Larkin Street, where the singer exited with Jerry close behind and Vicki trailing. The man stopped at a building right before the next street and headed inside. Jerry caught the gate before it slammed shut and thanked the singer even though he hadn't held it open. Together, they rode the elevator—the singer to the fifth floor, Jerry to the fourth. When Jerry exited, he quietly made his way up the stairwell to the fifth floor. There he saw four doors. *Not bad. I can deal with those odds.*

Vicki waited for Jerry's text in an alleyway next to the building, under the shadow of scaffolding. They were both in the zone at that point. There would be no confusion or hesitation. When they were this close to what they loved doing most, nothing could deter them—not even the presence of the police car that drove by.

Two minutes passed, and Vicki received a text from Jerry to meet him at the entrance in thirty seconds. The two moved quickly up the stairs, neither speaking a word. Jerry had already determined which apartment the singer lived in. If he hadn't, he never would have texted. When they reached the fifth floor, Jerry held up a hand with one finger, then his other hand with five fingers, signaling apartment number sixteen.

He helped her remove her sweater and the spaghetti strap top underneath before unclasping the black bra that kept her full 34Cs from jiggling. She slipped her top back on. The flimsy material stretched thin, displaying the location of her large areolas while the chilly air kept her nipples pointed. She fixed her hair, freshened her lipstick and dabbed her neck and wrists with a perfume sampler. Jerry then kissed his wife and handed her the blade, which she slipped into the back pocket of her jeans.

From the stairs, he watched his wife walk confidently down the carpeted hall until she reached the musician's door, the last one on the left. She rang the doorbell and put on a smile. A few seconds later, she waved at the peephole. *Come on; open the door*, Jerry thought. A second later, the seal of the door cracked.

He watched his wife bat her eyelashes as she squeezed her arms together. She said something to the singer and began to playfully walk her fingers down his chest as she backed him into his apartment. That was Jerry's cue. He moved out of his hiding spot and down the narrow hallway, ready to play his part.

When he arrived, Vicki had already stuck her blade directly into the singer's voice box, disabling it. Jerry closed the door behind him and revealed his favorite carving knife. The man stumbled backward at the sight of Jerry. His eyes stretched wide. His mouth dropped open. His left hand still had a grasp around his neck, but it could not contain the bloody leak. The singer shook his head no. His watery eyes pleaded for mercy. Jerry nodded yes. His darkened eyes promised no such thing.

Chapter 35

It was six a.m. and chilly. The fog had rolled in thick that Friday and settled across the entrance to the Bay and most of the city. When I arrived at Union Square, visibility was better. It was unusual to see it slither so far south. I spotted a couple of black and whites parked near the northwest corner of the square and made the walk.

The taped-off area looked smaller than usual and piqued my interest right away. I flashed my credentials to the uniform on perimeter duty, and he let me through with a nod. It wasn't hard to spot Kang amongst the crowd of law enforcement and forensic personnel.

"Abby. Thanks for coming so quickly. I had the team hold off on processing the scene so you could get a look at it in its original state."

I looked around for a body but didn't see a sheet. I finally had to ask.

"There isn't one. There's only a heart." Kang motioned for me to follow. "Every year, these large heart-shaped sculptures are painted by different artists and installed around the city. The CowParade exhibit inspired San Francisco to do the same but with painted hearts to play off the song 'I Left My Heart in San Francisco.'"

I thought Kang was pulling my leg until I saw the bloody organ sitting on top of the installation. It was housed inside a small, acrylic box as if it were on display. It was.

"They glued the box to the installation. We'll probably damage it when we pry the box off." Kang shook his head in disappointment.

I leaned in for a closer look. It still looked fresh. "Any idea how long it's been here?"

"Green's office hasn't had a chance to give an official ruling, but I'm guessing no more than a few hours. The area is heavily trafficked except for a narrow window in the early morning."

I looked at Kang, and we both knew what the other thought. "I can't believe we missed this one," I said. The song was iconic San Francisco. And the killer took it literally. "I wonder where the owner is."

"Who knows?" Kang blurted.

I watched him flip his jacket collar up and pull it tight around his neck. "I have my men interviewing the people around here and knocking on the doors of the shops in the area, though I'm not hopeful. Most of these stores don't open until ten in the morning. Even so, a couple of drops of super glue, a firm press to the installation—the killer could have done that without even stopping."

Kang looked around before turning back to me. The lines in his forehead had deepened. "You still think the killer is your mystery woman?"

"She's the best lead I have."

"What about my cases?"

"She's also the best lead on your cases, because you have none. Why the awesome mood this morning?"

Kang didn't answer me and avoided my eyes by constantly looking around. This was a different side of him, one I hadn't seen before. *Where's the playful Kang I know?* I had thought we worked well together and were on our way to becoming friends. *Maybe he's a grouch in the early morning*, I thought, though he should know he wasn't the only one who had to drag his butt out of bed early.

I did another walk around the crime scene; there wasn't much to take in. I circled the work of art and did a larger, ten-foot perimeter. Nothing caught my eye. I also agreed with Kang about the area businesses not being open when the heart was placed on the installation; maybe the Starbucks a block up the street, but that's about it.

I gave Kang a pat on the back. "Come on; let's go."

"Where?"

"For coffee and answers."

Chapter 36

The night before, the Carlsons had checked out of the Parc 55 and into a charming bungalow on Russian Hill. Vicki couldn't understand why they had to move from the suite she had grown comfortable with. But when she saw night views of the San Francisco Bay from the private wraparound balcony of the house they had just rented, she forgot all about the Parc 55. The only explanation Jerry gave Vicki for the move was that a change of scenery would be nice and much more private. She figured she had obliged him with the faceless hotel, and he was trying to do the same with a place packed with personality. Their new abode had all the character of an old home, which she craved, yet it was completely modernized to suit their needs.

Of course, the real reason for the move was that Jerry's nerves had worsened over the last few days. The kill the night before, while executed flawlessly, had made it worse. Anxiety was a rare emotion for him. Vicki was usually the nervous one who wanted precautions and every move planned. But lately, Jerry had found the roles reversing. He couldn't quite understand why. He'd never cared about the details in the past. The kill was what mattered the most, not the how, who or where.

From the moment the two met on a night years earlier in a dive bar, Vicki had brought structure into his life. It had been hard in the beginning, but she stuck with him, and he had learned, or at least accepted, that this was a better way to continue what he loved doing most.

Both had been single back then, but spending time in that bar hadn't had anything to do with meeting someone of the opposite sex and had everything to do with filling their macabre desires. Jerry didn't care who he killed. He had been simply waiting for someone to exit through the back door. After hours without an opportunity, Jerry's patience had run its course. He had decided to head out back and walk the alley behind the bar in hopes of coming across someone—anyone.

A young man in a mullet and a sweat stained T-shirt with the sleeves cut off had presented the loudest mouth in the bar that night, and he'd been spreading his putrid body odor, all while his chest remained artificially inflated thanks to the beer muscles he acquired over the night. Vicki had trained her eye on the man. She had watched him carefully after he stood in front of her, babbling and trying to drag her onto the dance floor. She had nearly vomited in her mouth while he tugged on her arm.

Vicki had decided to take matters into her own hands. She had walked over to the loudmouth and whispered in his ear before heading out the back door as well. A few seconds later, the man had followed.

Jerry had heard the door open and the *click-clack* of heels on the pavement. *Finally*, he had thought as he'd ducked into the shadows. In one pocket he had possessed wire. In the other, a knife. He fondled both, unsure of which to use. He needed to see the person before deciding whether to deliver a close and personal kill or an angry torrent of slashing. He hadn't been able to hear the heels any longer, and he worried that he might have missed his chance. He took a risk and leaned out of his hiding spot. He saw no one. But before his anger could rise, the back door flew open, and out walked the man he had noticed earlier. *Perfect.*

Jerry removed the knife and readied himself. He could hear the scraping of boots against the asphalt as each step came closer to him. But suddenly, Jerry heard the heels again. They were fast and coming his way. *Two? Could it be my lucky night?*

Jerry relished the opportunity and made his move. He stepped out from his position in the dark, hand raised, knife poised to strike, only to find a strange woman standing behind the man. She had placed one hand across his mouth, holding him tightly against her. Her other hand had brandished a knife that had been driven deep into her mark, slicing through muscle and sinew. The man gurgled and grasped at his neck. Jerry still stood in the same pose, from which he had exited his hiding spot. The only change had been the mask of confusion that had spread across his face as he watched some other killer poach his victim.

"What the hell?" he blurted. "He was mine."

"Yours?" the woman responded. "I lured him out here."

It had been love at first sight. Jerry had helped Vicki stash the body, but not before giving it a few stabs. He had waited while she changed into fresh clothes. She then produced baby wipes for them both to clean their hands and arms. After, the two headed back into the bar for a drink. Jerry and Vicki had been inseparable ever since.

Chapter 37

We walked uphill from Union Square to the Starbucks at the corner of Sutter and Powell. The sign on the door said they opened at five in the morning. *Surely they had to arrive sometime before store hours.*

Inside the coffee shop, we faced a buzz of early morning commuters all wanting their caffeine fix before they faced the monotony of their office jobs. I walked up to one of the employees, a teen girl who was busy wiping a table. Lately, wherever I saw teenagers doing something, I wondered if one day my two kids would do that. It entertained me.

"Excuse me," I said, producing my identification. "Is there a manager I can talk to?"

"Uh, yeah." The girl swallowed before running off.

Kang and I stood quietly before he suggested getting a coffee. "I'll take a cup of hot water."

He slipped into line while I waited. Everyone had their faces buried in their smartphones, and the few who didn't were yacking away on them. It made me feel a little self-conscious that I didn't have something to do on my own phone.

A few seconds later, a woman in her early thirties approached me. She had her hair pulled back into a ponytail, and a pen was tucked behind an ear. "How may I help you, Officer?" she asked. Her tone was even and her face looked tired.

"It's Agent. My name is Abby Kane. I'm with the FBI, and we're investigating a crime that took place in Union Square early this morning."

She scrunched her eyebrows and followed that up with a breath of disappointment. "What does that have to do with my store?"

Uh oh, looks like I drew the short straw and ended up with the bitch. "What time do you and your staff usually arrive in the morning?"

"Jenny—that's the girl you talked to earlier—and another girl got here at four-thirty this morning, same time I did."

Kang returned and handed me my cup. I nodded my thanks. "I'd like to continue talking to you while my partner here talks to Jenny and the other one, if that's okay."

The store manager took a deep breath, and her face remained flat. "It's not, but I can spare a few." She then turned to fetch the girls.

"Boy, I'm glad you're taking that one," Kang said, raising his eyebrows.

"She and her minions arrived here at four-thirty this morning. They might have noticed something on the way in."

Kang nodded and took a sip of his coffee. We split off from each other when the manager returned.

"How do you arrive to work?"

"I catch the number three bus and get off at Union Square, then I walk the one block to the store." She couldn't have sounded more disinterested if she tried.

"Were there other people around when you exited the bus?"

"You mean in the square?"

No, dipshit, on the moon. "Yes, in the square."

She tilted her head to the side, and her eyes went blank for a moment before answering. "I was the only one who got off the bus. There were maybe a couple of people around, across the street. I guess they were walking to work. But it's not my job to conduct a census every morning when I arrive."

"Is there a problem, miss?"

"Yeah, if you haven't noticed, it's rush hour here, and every second I'm here talking to you is a second longer someone has to wait for their coffee. Next time, I'll come to your job when you're slammed and tell you to stop so I can discuss the intricacies of brewing coffee with you."

She was barking up the wrong tree, and I wasn't in the mood for any backtalk. "All that hot air escaping your mouth—not helping your situation. So either answer my questions, or I'll handcuff you right now and drag your sorry ass down to my office and question you there."

She folded her arms across her chest and relaxed her shoulders.

"Anything about these people pop out as different or unusual?" I continued.

"No." She shrugged. "I had my iPod on and wasn't paying attention."

That's how people get mugged. I shifted my weight to my left foot. "Did you notice the large heart at the corner?"

"Sure, it's only been there since the beginning of the year."

My eyes latched onto hers, and I lowered my voice. "Do not test me. Last warning."

She eyed me for a moment before giving me a slight nod. I suspect she tried to think through whether I could legally handcuff her and haul her in. Another remark and she would have found out. "Did you see anything on it, or a person near it or walking away from it?"

"No."

I took out my phone and produced the picture of our mystery woman. "Did you see this woman this morning?"

Her eyes slowly shifted to the phone. "No, she doesn't look familiar."

I hope Kang is having better luck than I am. I pocketed my phone. "Were you the first to arrive this morning?"

"I'm the manager. I have the keys."

I'm the manager. I have the keys. I want to make

everyone else in the world hate their lives as much as I hate mine. It took an extraordinary amount of effort not to sigh audibly and throat punch her. "Thank you for your time. Let me know if you remember something else." I left my card with her and walked toward Kang as he wrapped up his interview with the second of the two girls.

"You moved through both girls fast."

"The first one was a waste. I think she was stoned." I watched his Adam's apple bob as he gulped down the rest of his coffee.

"And the second?"

"Nothing," he said, wiping his mouth with the back of his hand.

I never got around to making my tea and Kang had already left the coffee shop. When I caught up with him, I grabbed him by the arm and slowed him down. "What's wrong? You've been in a funk all morning. If you didn't realize it, I'm the one that interviewed Medusa."

He shrugged and looked everywhere except at me. "Eh, what's it to you?"

"What's it to me? We're partners. I need to know that your head is in the game. But that's not all; I really do want to know what's bothering you."

"It's nothing." His distant look continued for a moment longer before he looked my way. "I'm sorry if I've been obnoxious this morning. I'm bothered that we're running into dead ends and now there's another body on top of the two I already have."

"Could have been four," I said with a smile.

Kang finally cracked and laughed as his shoulders relaxed "Yeah, you're right."

"Well, I'm glad the Kang I know is back. I missed him."

"Did you really?"

I punched him in the arm. "Of course I did. I need someone to tease."

The case was a headache for us both. The last thing I wanted was for us to contribute to that.

As we turned to walk back to Union Square, I spied a homeless person across the street. He was lying in the doorway of a business that had not yet opened. He might have seen something if he'd been there all night. I motioned for Kang to follow me, and we crossed the street.

It wasn't until we were closer that I realized I mistook his squinting for sleeping. He watched us until we stood in front of him. To break the ice, I reached into my purse, took out the remaining half of my Ghirardelli chocolate bar and handed to him. He hesitated at first, looking at the chocolate, then back at me. I leaned in closer, still holding the bar out in front of me. "Go on; take it."

He cautiously reached up, took the candy from my hands, quickly removed the paper and bit into it, though his eyes never left us. His wrinkles cut deep into his leathery skin and barely moved as he chewed. When he reached up and brushed a chunk of matted hair out of his face, it fell right back.

"What do you want?" he finally spoke, propping himself up a bit.

"Have you been here all night?" I asked.

"What's it to you? I'm not breaking any laws."

"No one said you were. We only want to talk."

"You a cop?" he asked. His eyes shifted to Kang and then back to me.

I showed him my identification. "I'm an FBI agent. My name is Abby Kane. What's yours?"

"People call me Simon Says."

A chuckle escaped Kang's mouth. "What? Like the game?"

Simon shot Kang a look. "Hey, Long Duck Dong, you on a school field trip?"

"I'm a detective with the San Francisco Police Department," Kang shot back.

"I'm a detective with the San Francisco Police Department," Simon mocked in a teasing voice.

"Don't mess with me, pal."

"Don't mess with me, pal," Simon continued, but this time, he added a lisp and pushed timidly away with his hand. I nearly burst out in laughter, but kept it together. *Time to separate the children.* I waved my hand between them, breaking the staring contest. "Both of you cool it right now!"

Simon took another bite of the chocolate. He still had Kang in his sights.

"Simon!" I said loudly. "Pay attention to me, okay?"

He shifted his eyes off of Kang and onto me.

"You see that large heart down there?" I asked, pointing toward Union Square. "Did you see anyone messing with it last night or early this morning?"

Simon looked down the street, and his eyes went vacant. I thought I had lost him, but then his beady gaze found me again.

"Someone vandalized it," I continued. "We're looking for a woman." I held out my phone so he could see the picture of our mystery woman. "Did you see her, Simon?"

He squinted again, slowing his chews as he concentrated on the picture. "I saw her."

"Where, Simon? By the heart?"

He shook his head. "I saw her the other day. Over there," he said, pointing across the street to a diner.

"You saw her go inside?"

"No, she stood near the building, peeking around the corner. Then she got on the number two bus."

"You remember the time?"

"It was near sunset. I don't know exactly when."

"You did a good job, Simon. Thank you for your help."

He held out his hand and rubbed his thumb and index finger together and, for the first time, cracked a smile. Surprisingly, he had all his teeth.

"I see everything that goes on around here. I got me a photogenic memory. That's why they call me Simon Says."

I took a twenty out of my wallet and handed it to him. "Well, Simon Says, do me a favor; don't spend that on booze."

"How about breakfast? My treat," he said with a wink as he waved the bill back at me.

I smiled. "I'm on duty. I'll have to take a rain check."

As we walked away, Kang mentioned that the buses were equipped with cameras. "If we can locate the bus she boarded, we'll know what stop she exited at."

"Good call. I'll get Agent Tucker started on that."

"So, uh, does every man you meet ask you out?" Kang asked, with a chuckle.

"Of course not," I said, putting my cell phone up to my ear. "You haven't."

Chapter 38

When I got to the office, I received a text from Tucker. He had identified the buses on the route that afternoon and was working on securing footage from the surveillance systems. We were making progress. *Keep squeezing, Abby.*

Back at my desk, I closed my eyes. I could feel the beginnings of a headache percolating and I wanted to head it off before it gained traction. I dug into my desk drawer, and removed a bottle of aspirin and shook two into my hand. I must have been dehydrated, because in the break room, I gulped down water like a dog after a Sunday run in the park. *I need to get more sleep*, I told myself, but really, I knew sleep wasn't the culprit. It was the case.

I returned to my desk determined. I picked up the photo of my mystery woman and stared at her. *It may be slow and hard, but we're getting closer to finding you.* My gut had that tingling feeling—the one I get right before I turn the corner on an investigation. I knew if we kept on closing down the angles, we'd find our way. The question was, would we find her before she struck again?

I had a feeling she wasn't done yet, that she believed she had more work to do. A body in Fay Park, one near Pier

39, another in Muir Woods and now a fourth in Union Square. All these locations were popular attractions in the city. Did she have a grudge with San Francisco? Was she wronged in the past and this was her payback? *What's driving you?*

The other thought that had snuck its way in to my head was the abrupt change in Kang's demeanor. I had sensed earlier in the morning that he had doubts about the investigation and how it was being handled. I won't apologize for making my case my priority, but I did believe Piper's killer was responsible for Kang's previous victims and the owner of the heart.

Kang had seemed like a straight-up guy from the beginning. Sure, I gave him a hard time, but I could see that he was one of the good ones, someone who believed in police work and did the right thing. I also had the impression that he liked me, and we worked well together. I appreciated having a partner instead of flying solo.

But still, why the attitude? It had come out of nowhere. It's not like he was an a-hole from the beginning. I genuinely felt I could count on Kang to work with me and not against me—unlike so many men I had encountered in the past. I had to hope he would continue to trust me.

I sent Tucker a text, asking for an update. While I waited for a reply, I headed to the break room again, this time for some hot water. I passed a slew of empty desks—a lot of agents were still out in the field. Some days, the office is a madhouse, and others, it's a ghost town. *I wonder what everyone is working on.*

I removed a pinch of tea from my canister and dropped it into a mug filled with hot water. I watched the water turn color as the leaves settled on the bottom. I placed a napkin over the top of the cup to keep the heat in so it could steep and took a seat at one of the tables. A few seconds later, my phone beeped. The text from Tucker read, "Still looking."

I thought more about our mystery woman between sips. It seemed so strange for a woman to be this violent. Removing a heart? That was serious stuff, not something I'd expect from a female killer. A man? Yes. To get at the heart, one has to actually pry the chest apart. I'm not saying a woman couldn't be as vicious or possess the physicality needed to do the job. I've seen them chop people into pieces like their male counterparts, but they always had a partner in those crimes. Did my mystery woman have a partner?

Just then, Reilly entered the break room. He didn't see me, as I was tucked away in the corner. I watched him head straight for the soda machine and feed a dollar bill into the slot. A beat later, a Pepsi rolled out the bottom. It wasn't until he turned around, bottle pressed against his lips, that he noticed me. "Abby. I didn't see you there."

"I'm small."

He took another sip as he walked over to my table and sat.

"You know that will rot your teeth."

"Yeah, that's what I hear," he said before taking yet another powerful gulp. "How's the Cotton Candy case coming along?" he asked as he swallowed the burn in his throat.

"Slow and hard."

He nodded. "The partnership with those detectives working out okay?"

"Sokolov was put on another case. It's just Kang and I. We're working well together and making progress."

"Good to hear. Let me know when you get a break in the case."

He pushed back from the table and stood. I watched him tilt his head back and guzzle as he exited the room.

I finished the rest of my tea and stood up to return to my desk when my phone notified me of an email from Green. He said the heart belonged to a young male, fairly healthy, no obvious signs of disease or substance abuse. From the deterioration of the tissue, he approximated that the heart had been out of the body for about ten, maybe eleven hours by the time it was reported to the police at six thirty in the morning. I copied and pasted that part of the email and sent it to Tucker and Kang, leaving the other half of Green's message for my eyes only.

He wrote that he enjoyed our coffee date. I had to admit, I'd had a pretty good time. He asked if we could meet again, maybe for lunch or even dinner. At first, I wasn't sure if I wanted to make it lunch, let alone dinner, but then I realized I had spent the same amount of time with him at a coffee shop and it had been fine.

Deep down inside, I knew Green had a crush on me. I didn't want to lead him on, but I did enjoy our conversation and wouldn't mind talking with him again. I found him interesting, and I honestly didn't feel like I had given him any indication that our relationship could be anything more than friends. But I knew how men operated: return a smile and suddenly they think I want to give them head. *Is that what it's come to? I have to watch who I smile at, or else I'm on the hook for head. Sheesh.*

Chapter 39

I was still at my desk when Tucker showed up a few hours later. He had an intense look plastered over his face, but his approach showed signs of weakness in the knees. I appreciated his seriousness, even if I made him nervous.

"What's the news?" I asked.

He reached into the inner pocket of his jacket and removed his cell phone. A moment later, a video clip played on the screen.

"We found her. Not only that, but I believe we found our victim as well."

I grabbed his cell phone and studied the footage. There was no doubt in my mind that the person entering the bus through the rear doors was our mystery woman.

"Go back into my camera roll. There's another video."

I swiped the screen and pulled up the second video. It showed a young man with a guitar exiting the bus. I looked up at Tucker. "The medical examiner said the heart belonged to a young male."

"Both individuals exited the bus at Larkin and Sutter," he added. "It's a residential area in the lower Nob Hill neighborhood. My guess is either she followed him, to his place or she lives in the area."

I agreed with Tucker. "Great work, Agent. Email Detective Kang and me those videos, and get ready to head out with me." Earlier, Reilly had mentioned that if I had the chance to take Tucker out into the field, I should do it. He needed to get his feet wet. I questioned whether it was too early, but Reilly said he didn't want to coddle the kid.

"Okay," Tucker said with a large smile.

After he left, I called Kang and updated him on Tucker's find. "The sooner we can organize a knock-and-talk, the better chance we might have at finding someone who saw something."

He agreed, and we made a plan to meet at the location in forty-five minutes.

"Bring a couple of extra bodies," I told him. "I have a feeling about this one."

◇◇◇

The Carlsons had just completed another marathon sex session to celebrate the completion of the heart Attraction. Because they were in a new place, they had done the deed in all the rooms and finished in the bedroom, where they both lay breathless and sweaty. Jerry had quickly faded into a deep sleep—not unusual—but Vicki remained alert and energized. She hopped out of bed right as Jerry began to snore.

In the kitchen, she opened the fridge and poured herself a glass of orange juice before taking a seat on the balcony, still nude. The crisp air gave her goose bumps, but it felt so refreshing that she didn't mind. She stared at the sparkly reflections that covered the bay and fell into an aimless gaze until an uptick in the breeze awakened her.

She took another sip of the juice and was reminded of the charm that had fallen off her bracelet. She had noticed it missing when she gave Jerry head earlier. She had eight altogether. The missing Eiffel Tower charm was the one she adored the most though, because that's where Jerry had proposed to her. But mostly, they were reminders of where they had killed together.

She knew she'd still had the jeweled piece when they were watching the musician in Union Square, even when she stood in the alleyway waiting, because she had been playing with it. After they dispatched him, they came straight back to the hotel, packed and moved to the cottage, where shortly after, they had begun their sex-a-thon. *Did I lose it at the apartment?*

She thought about telling Jerry but decided against it. He would only tell her she should be more careful. Plus, at the time, he had begun to do her doggie style, and she temporarily forgot about it. Even though it had only cost a few Euros, to her, it was priceless, and she had to have it back.

Vicki thought briefly about returning to the apartment

and the dangers that would entail. The other likely place she thought she might have lost it was in the alley outside the musician's building. While waiting, she had placed both of her hands behind her butt and leaned against them instead of the building's exterior. It could have caught on something and, in the process, have been pulled off the bracelet. But being in the vicinity was a bad idea. Jerry would never let her go back there if he knew that's what she was thinking. She realized then it was a plus she hadn't mentioned it.

Vicki made her way to the master bedroom. She could hear Jerry snoring before she even entered the room. He lay on his stomach with a pillow stuffed under his chest and head, his bare ass looking back at her. She poked her husband in his arm. "Jerry." She did that twice more, but still, he didn't stir. She figured she could cab it over to the location and take a peek in the area where she had stood, and if she didn't find it, she would come back to the cottage right away. Jerry would never have to know.

Vicki dressed in jeans and a black sweater so as to blend with all the other people who wore black in the city. She'd had no plans of wearing the wig, since she had worn it that night, but seeing how it looked with her outfit changed her mind. She grabbed her oversized sunglasses to differentiate her look and then called for a cab.

◇◇◇

Tucker and I met Kang and his crew of officers at the corner of Larkin and Sutter. We weren't sure what we were looking for. Her apartment? His apartment? A body? Who knew, but we had to start somewhere.

Given that we had no idea how far they might have walked, there was a great deal of ground to cover. Our plan was to start with the buildings near the stop. Kang's men split up and tackled Sutter. Kang, Tucker, another officer and I took on Larkin, they on one side of the street, Tucker and I on the other.

The Sutter team was already handling the building on the corner, so Tucker and I walked north to the next one, past a small side street. We got lucky with a resident exiting and were able to slip inside the lobby area.

We counted sixteen mailboxes in the five-story building. The first floor was a lobby, no apartments.

"Four per floor. Should be easy," Tucker said.

"Take the second and third. I'll handle the fourth and fifth. Remember, if you stumble upon anything suspicious, you call me before you do anything? Got it?"

He nodded. "And if I find the body?"

"Don't touch it. Don't puke."

Tucker hoofed it up the stairs while I waited for the elevator. *Did he live here? Did she ride up with him? Did she strike up conversation to relax him, to have him lower his guard? Was she flirting, making it easier?*

The elevator doors opened onto a dimly lit hallway.

The light directly outside the elevator had burned out, and the rest looked like they were all low wattage. *Talk about cheap management.* I breathed in deeply. The air was slightly chilly with a touch of mustiness. My nose didn't catch a whiff of death, but my other senses tingled as if it should have.

Chapter 40

Vicki had the cab driver drop her off one block north from the location of the bus stop. She had decided she was better off approaching the building from the opposite direction *and* on her terms. No surprises. She thought about paying the driver to wait but decided against it. *No need for a witness should something go wrong.* She tossed the cabbie a twenty and exited the vehicle.

For a minute or so, Vicki stood at the corner and watched the building. Street traffic was sparse, and there didn't seem to be any people walking the block. *Might as well get on with it.* Vicki adjusted her purse on her shoulder before crossing the street. Her right hand dipped inside the bag and fondled her blade, ready for any confrontation she might encounter.

She walked confidently at a pace she thought would mimic a person who lived in the neighborhood. A few steps past the building, she stepped into the alley. *Where are you, little one?* She scanned the area methodically, not wanting to overlook the small charm. It could have slipped into a crack or been covered by a piece of rubbish. Rather than kick the debris around, she picked up each item, eliminating any doubt as to whether she had checked under each one. It didn't take long for her hopes to diminish as the area she searched widened. Vicki let out a deep breath, resolving to what she knew she had to do: return to the apartment.

◇◇◇

I hadn't had any luck with the first three apartments—two were empty, and the occupant in the third had a very poor command of the English language. So there I stood, facing the last apartment at the end of the hall, expecting to have a similar experience. I was pleasantly surprised when the door opened and revealed a cheerful, old lady who was exactly my height.

"Hello. May I help you?" she asked with a pleasant smile. She had light blue eyes that popped against her snow-white bob, which was neatly tucked behind each ear. She wore a pink blouse with a pearl necklace draped over it and a checkered skirt that fell slightly past her knees. I could tell she was of the generation that believed in dressing for the day, even when she had no plans to leave her apartment.

I smiled back at her. "Hello. My name is Abby Kane. I'm with the FBI. I'd like to ask you a few questions."

Concern drew her lips together. "Yes, of course. Please, come inside."

She stepped back, opening the door wider. Before I could ask my first question, she told me to take a seat on the couch, said she would be back with some tea and then scurried off to the kitchen.

I hadn't expected to have a long conversation; all I wanted was an opportunity to show her a few pictures. With her enthusiasm for entertaining an FBI agent, I got the impression she didn't receive many visitors. Besides, it wouldn't kill me to make the time, and she had said the magic word: tea.

I sat there quietly, taking in her décor. That woman loved horses. They were everywhere in the form of paintings, sculptures and stuffed animals. Even the throw blanket she had on her couch featured a scene of horses running through an open field.

"Let me guess; you like horses?" I said as he reappeared with a tray.

She laughed as she put it down on the coffee table. "I rode for many years as a young woman. I had my own horse, Betsy. She was a Dutch Warmblood who had the most beautiful, black coat you have ever seen. It shined under the sun like a freshly polished shoe." She walked over to a built-in bookshelf and removed a picture frame and a small box. "This is me at the Summer Olympics in Helsinki. I won a silver medal, thanks to Betsy."

I did a double take at the frail woman who now stood before me. "That's you?"

"Yes," she said with a chuckle. "Most people find it hard to believe that I'm an Olympian."

She then opened the small box she held in her other hand. I drew in a sharp breath. "That's beautiful. I've never seen an Olympic medal firsthand. Incredible."

Her proud smile lit up the room.

I wanted nothing more than to pepper her with more questions about her life, but duty called. "Thank you for sharing." I removed my phone and pulled up the picture of my mystery woman. "Have you seen this woman?"

She squinted and leaned forward before shaking her head. "She doesn't look familiar, though I might have seen her and can't remember." She poured me a cup of tea. I noticed the familiar hue, and I got excited. I had expected black tea, maybe Earl Grey. I reached for the cup and before it reached my lips, I inhaled and couldn't believe my nose. *This can't be.* I took a sip. *It is!* "This isn't *Tieguanyin*, is it?"

"Why, yes, it is. I happen to have a certain fondness for it."

"Oh my God. So do I. It's the only tea I drink. In fact, I carry a tin around with me." I dug around in my purse and pulled it out so she could see it. "People think I'm nuts to carry tea around."

She waved off my assessment. "I used to do the same thing. It's not a tea that people commonly keep on hand."

"Tell me about it. I tell everybody I drink green tea, because if I mention that its oolong tea, they always ask what the difference is, and I got tired of explaining."

"A lot of people drink green tea, but oolong—now that's a tea worth carrying around."

I was completely and utterly in love with this woman. We talked about our addiction for a few more minutes before I steered the conversation back to the case. I pulled up the video footage that Tucker had sent me. "I have some video of her. Does this help?"

She watched the video twice before shaking her head once more. "I'm sorry, but I just don't recall seeing this woman around. She doesn't look familiar at all. I'm very sorry."

So was I. As much as I wanted to stick around and continue chatting with her, I had a killer to stop.

Chapter 41

Jerry muttered under his breath as he stared out the window of the moving cab. He was furious, a fact that his beet-red face made very apparent. He chewed on a thumbnail that barely existed; it was the only way he could keep himself from exploding. He thought more than once about killing the cab driver to ease his nerves but had the resolve to hold back, something he couldn't have done years ago, before Vicki's calming influence.

Over the years, she had taught him self-restraint—said it would lead to a more prosperous life of killing. She was right, but he hated it. He hated denying himself the pleasure of killing on a whim. But what complicated matters for Jerry was his slew of anxieties, most of them compulsive.

Once Jerry bought into something, he had to see it through. It's the only reason he could kill so pragmatically. Never in a million years had he thought he would take orders on how to kill a person and then deliver. That would have been too much trouble.

Jerry preferred organic kills, those that happened naturally with no disruption. He had once explained to Vicki that he likened this new method of killing to having sex with a condom. "When I'm in the moment and everything feels right and the next move should be to slip inside but I have to stop, get the condom, rip it open, slip it on… It ruins the natural rhythm of things."

Jerry's impatience with his wife's insubordination had come to a head. She had pushed every one of his buttons with this last outing. *How stupid does she think I am?* He knew where she had run off to. He had noticed that her charm had gone missing. *That stupid thing. It's not even real gold.*

Jerry wrestled with the idea of how to keep his wife under control. She was jeopardizing their gameplay. How could he expect to continue with her exhibiting that sort of behavior? *I told her not to go there. I had forbidden it.* At least, he thought he had. He was sure he did. It didn't matter. The question he now proposed to himself was whether he should kill her. It would eliminate the problem, and he felt confident enough that he could go on without her. But there was a hiccup: he loved her.

◇◇◇

Vicki didn't need to wait very long for someone to exit the building and allow her to slip inside. She pulled on the heavy, glass door of the rickety elevator and entered. The small space reeked of mechanical oil used to keep the gears of the old lift lubed and functioning. She hit the fifth floor button and proceeded to take the slow ride up. There was no bell or lighted number to announce her arrival, only the grating of metal when she slid open the manual doors.

Down the carpeted hall she walked, mindful of not dragging her feet or letting the heels of her cross-trainers drum the floor. *No need to notify any of the residents that someone is outside.* With each step closer, Vicki became increasingly aware of a tightening in her stomach. It wasn't something she had experienced very often. She didn't flinch when gutting a man, nor did it bother her to stare into someone's eyes as their lifeblood spurted from a wound on their neck. Excitement would be the word to best explain those feelings. This was different. She had never before returned to a location while the body was still there. It wasn't something that interested her, nor had she ever had any reason to.

She also noticed that her throat had dried when she swallowed, causing her to cough twice into her closed mouth. *Strange,* she thought. When she reached the musician's door, only then did it dawn on her that the door was probably locked. Jerry had been the last one out; surely he had locked it. All this sneaking around and risk could be for naught. Vicki shook off those thoughts and reached for the doorknob, wondering and hoping. With a quick twist of her wrist, the door clicked open. Her husband had fucked up.

She entered the apartment and locked the door behind

her. On the floor, surrounded by an oval of soiled carpeting, lay the musician. His eyes were still open, but dry, and staring absently at the wall. Most of the blood coating his skin and clothing had dried to a crust, except around the gash in his neck; there, it looked to still have a gel-like consistency. The strong smell of iron lingered in the apartment but was nonexistent in the hallway. It surprised her that it wasn't worse, all things considered.

She moved closer to his body, careful not to step on the carpet that had absorbed fluids. *Plush carpeting serves a purpose.* His face was devoid of color, and his mouth lay partly open, allowing her to see his dark, bloated tongue. She noticed a slight belly had formed from the gases slowly building inside of him—a big fart waiting to explode.

Vicki carefully searched the area around his body and slowly branched out in a circle. She found nothing and started to wonder if the charm might be under him. *That would be a bummer.* She didn't want to get her hands dirty. *Maybe he has a broom or something I can roll him over with. What a drag.*

<><><>

The fourth floor was a bust, but the company and the tea had made up for it. After thanking Virginia Ayton for her time—I had noticed her name on the picture she had shown me—I handed her my card and told her to call me if she should remember anything. Secretly, I hoped she would. I so wanted to learn more about her interesting life. *Would it be weird to ask her to meet for coffee after questioning her?*

I headed for the stairs with that thought lingering and wondered if Tucker had beat me to the fifth floor. I counted sixteen steps with badly worn carpeting before reaching the top of the stairwell. There were no surprises, just another dreary hallway staring back at me. There was a difference, though: I could detect a hint of carpet freshener. *Someone cares on this floor.*

Before I knocked on the first door, my phone beeped. It was a text from Kang asking for an update. I replied that Tucker and I were still in the first building and that I hadn't had any luck. I told him I wasn't sure about Agent Tucker. He responded with similar results on his end. So far, things weren't looking so good. And it didn't get any better, as I encountered a moment of silence after knocking on the first door.

Door by door, I made my way down the ghost hall. No one seemed to be home, and not a peep could be heard. I knocked on the second-to-last door and thought I heard a noise. I had: my stomach telling me to feed it. I let out a soft breath. My earlier hopes of moving forward in the case were slowly fading. That's the thing with police work; the highs were high, and the lows were low. A lot of exploring was needed to produce any sort of meaningful result.

I kicked my heel into the carpet and twisted it as I

waited for someone, anyone, to answer my knocking. I waited a few more seconds before turning to the last door on the floor. *Come on, number sixteen; make my day.*

Chapter 42

Vicki was on her hands and knees, craning her neck for a better look under the couch, when she heard the knock at the door. She jumped up at the sound. Her first inclination was that she had mistaken some other noise for a knock, but then she heard it again. Someone was definitely on the other side of that door. *Just be quiet. They'll leave eventually.* But the knocking continued. *Persistent fuckers, aren't we?*

Vicki looked at the body sprawled out in front of her. Inviting them in for coffee was out of the question. *Did he have a girlfriend? Did she have a key? If he'd had one and she did have the key, she wouldn't be knocking, dummy.*

Again, three succinct knocks rang out.

Vicki quietly walked up to the door and leaned in toward the peephole. *A quick look couldn't hurt.* Standing outside she saw a short, Asian woman dressed in a dark blue pantsuit. *Who the hell is that? A Realtor?*

"Open up," the woman said. "I know you're home. I can see your shadow moving under the door."

Vicki looked down. *Damn!* She quickly counted her options.

Ignore her.

Answer the door and politely tell her I'm busy.
Kill her.

"My name is Abby Kane," the woman said with a raised voice. "I'm with the FBI, and I want to ask you a few questions. It'll only take a few moments of your time."

Shit! Vicki had to reconsider her options. Quick!

She moved into the bedroom, yanked the brown comforter off the bed and covered the body. She then stripped off her pants, shirts and shoes and wrapped one towel around her head and another around her body. A splash of water to the face and she returned to the door.

Surely that agent wouldn't come into the home of a half-naked woman. Vicki put on a smile and cracked the door open enough to peek out.

◇◇◇

"I'm sorry to disturb you," I said. The woman staring at me from behind the door looked as if she had just stepped out of the shower.

"Bad timing." The woman forced a laugh. She was being polite.

"I'll get to the point." I held up my phone and showed the woman the picture of my suspect. Her head jerked back instantly, and her forehead crinkled.

"Do you recognize this woman?" I asked as I moved the phone closer to her face. "Looks like you might have."

She pulled her head back farther. "No, not at all. I can barely make out her features." Her eyes fluttered back and forth between the picture and myself. "It's a terrible photo."

Why thank you, Master of the Obvious. "She's a suspect in a case."

She shrugged. "Is that it? I'm sort of in the middle of a bath, and I'm running late for an appointment."

"No." I pulled up the video. "See if this helps."

She barely watched before she started shaking her head.

"You live in the building long?" I asked.

"Not long. Maybe six months."

"It empties out during the day. This is the second apartment I have encountered where someone was home."

"Oh, well, I work from home. I'm a writer," she replied. Her nose turned up a tad. I guess she wanted to show me that her nostrils were clean.

"That's nice," I said, biting my bottom lip but never taking my eye off her.

"Well, Ms…"

"White. Evelyn White."

"…Ms. White, thank you for your time." I produced one of my business cards and handed it to her. "In case you remember anything."

"Sorry I couldn't be of more help."

As I turned to walk away, what she said stopped me dead in my tracks.

"Good luck finding them."

Chapter 43

Jerry ordered the cab driver to pull into the alley next to the building. "Here's fifty bucks. Wait here for me," he said while handing the cabbie the money. "I have another hundred for you when I get back, okay?"

The cabbie nodded. "I'll be right here, boss."

Jerry eyed the brown-skinned man for a second before nodding and exiting the vehicle. He hurried to the front of the building, hoping the security gate had been left open. No such luck.

Fucking A. Dammit, why did she have to disobey me? He distinctly remembered telling her to forget about that charm and that returning to that apartment was a risk. Yes, it had all come back to him. The conversation had taken place over dinner and drinks. At least, that's how he remembered it. Or did he? Jerry ignored the voice that said otherwise, the one that swore the conversation had never happened. Jerry hated that voice. So cocky. So condescending. "You always have to be right," Jerry whispered under his breath. "Not this time."

His left hand remained in his front pants pocket, fondling the ivory-handled razor that Vicki had gifted him a few Christmases ago. She'd said he needed to add some pizzazz to his kills, and a man's shaving blade was the perfect way to do it.

Jerry looked around. There was no one on the block, so he resorted to his last option and starting calling apartments, hoping someone would buzz him in. A few seconds later, someone did. Jerry pulled open the metal gate and entered the building.

◇◇◇

I spun around and shoved my foot into the crack of the door right as she tried to close it.

"Excuse me!" she exclaimed. "Your foot is—"

"You said 'them'." I wedged my foot farther in and placed my left forearm against the door.

"What are you talking about?"

"You referred to 'them' as though I were asking about two people, but I had only shown you pictures of one person. Why?"

Her eyebrows narrowed and her head shook vehemently. "I don't know, probably because you said so."

She's lying, Abby. "I didn't say anything about two people." I leaned into the door, feeling even more resistance. "Ms. White, you mind letting me in?"

"I will not." She then kicked and stomped on my foot, trying to force it out. "You have no right to—"

That's when I interrupted her by throwing my shoulder forward. *Smack!* The door struck her forehead, and the woman released her grip, allowing me to slip inside.

Right there before me, lying on the living room floor, was a body. Well, I saw a foot sticking out from under a blanket. I assumed the rest of the lump was a body. I turned to face White and realized she had recovered from the doorbutt faster than expected. She caught me on the chin with a right. It sent my face off to the side and my blood pressure skyrocketing.

She had set up for another strike, but I was faster and ducked. I countered with an uppercut to her jaw and snapped her head back. I then followed that with a combination punch and backed her up. She was noticeably dazed from my efforts, but I wasn't taking any chances. My chin still stung from her cheap shot. I gripped the towel wrapped around her and yanked her forward, stepping to the side and sending her to the floor. She surprised me by rolling into a tumble and back to a standing position, minus both towels. And a wig.

"It's you!" I gasped as she suddenly became very recognizable.

"You think you got me," she seethed, clad only in her underwear. "I'm going to kick your short ass back to China."

"Great. After that, you can buy lingerie that fits the body you have, not the body you want."

That set her off. She let out a scream and moved toward me. My first instinct was to step to the side, but I was still pissed that she had punched my face. I stood my ground and allowed her to barrel toward me for a tackle. She was taller than me but, for some reason, had lowered her attack and aimed for my midsection with her arms stretched out and her face down. *Perfect.* I timed a knee strike and could hear the crunch of her nose against my kneecap before she crumpled to the ground.

I jumped onto her back, driving my knee into it and pinning her to the ground. While I proceeded to handcuff her, she kept screaming that I had broken her noise. *No shit!* Her face was a red Niagara Falls. After cuffing her, I leaned down and said, "The next time you want to act like a tough bitch and pick a fight, realize you might be doing so with an even tougher bitch."

Chapter 44

Jerry exited the elevator and turned to the right, ready to make his way down the hall. He could already hear the commotion coming from the apartment and see that the door was open. *Fuck me!*

As he took a step forward, heavy bounding footsteps made their way up the stairwell. Within seconds, a young man in a suit came into view. Jerry, the quick thinker, immediately played the worried resident and pointed at the commotion at the end of the hall.

"Stay here," said the young man as he removed his weapon and faced the hallway.

Jerry deduced that suits meant government, and that was a bad thing, considering there was a dead body at the end of that hallway. Before the young man could manage two steps forward, Jerry pounced on him from behind, taking him by complete surprise. He wrapped one arm across the suit's chest to hold him still as he cut deep across the throat with the shaver, not once but with a rapid, sawing effect, until he had nearly severed the head. He let go, and the man fell to the floor, his limbs still twitching. Saliva spewed from Jerry's clenched teeth with each breath. Kill mode had taken over. There would be no stopping him now—short of killing him.

He moved quickly and quietly toward the apartment. What he found wasn't unexpected but very opportunistic. There, with her back to him, was a tiny woman in a suit. *Perfect.* Looking to perform the same move twice, Jerry quietly advanced.

◇◇◇

Hearing the noise in the apartment directly above hers, Virginia Ayton immediately knew something was wrong. She hurried over to her phone, preparing to dial 911, when she saw a uniformed officer outside on the sidewalk talking to another man. She hung up the phone and opened her window. "Officer! Officer!"

Kang was talking to Officer Greg Loui when they both heard a woman's voice shouting. They both looked around, searching for the source.

"Up here."

Kang looked up to the building and saw an elderly woman waving at them from a window. He immediately headed toward the building entrance. "Is something wrong?" he shouted up to her.

"Yes, something terrible is happening in the apartment above me."

Virginia buzzed both men into the building, and into

the elevator they went as another resident exited. Kang accidently hit the fourth and fifth floor buttons simultaneously. *Shit!* Couple that with the inch-by-inch movement of the old elevator, and Kang uttered a few more choice words that echoed in the metal chamber. They were trapped at least until the next floor, which Kang pressed the button for immediately. Seconds felt like hours as Kang repeatedly slammed an open palm against the elevator cage, rattling it each time. He continued to curse himself for that button mistake but even more so for not taking the stairs.

◇◇◇

A squeak from the floor alerted me, and I turned in time to see a strange man with a blank look on his face moving toward me. Both of his arms were covered in blood. I rose to my feet fast enough to counter his swinging right with my left forearm. That's when I noticed the razor in his hand. *There are two of them?*

I delivered a punch to his right eye, hoping a knuckle would catch his eyeball. No such luck. I tried to move out of his reach, but a lucky grasp from his flailing left arm clamped down on my jacket and held me within striking distance of his blade. I immediately lifted my right leg, ready to retaliate with a foot strike to his gut. But in that moment, I remembered my father's advice. "Abby, there's an artery in the foot. If you can hit that blood vessel at its most vulnerable point, where the top of foot meets the leg, you will cause extreme pain. If you're lucky enough, you'll sever it, rendering the foot useless."

I didn't know if what my father had said was true, but the heel of my shoe raced toward that area like a blade on a guillotine. I hoped to hell he had been right.

"Arrrgggghhh!" The man cried out as his eyes clamped shut.

Bingo! I batted his hand off me and followed that with a knee to his groin, causing him to double over. I moved back as I reached inside my jacket for my weapon with my right hand. That's when I felt the sharp pain on my left thigh. I looked down and saw blood beginning to soak through the cloth. My pant leg had been sliced, and his arm was swinging back toward me for another attempt. I hopped back just in time, causing him to miss, but he had momentum on his side, and he closed in on me quicker than I could have imagined. *What happened to rendering the foot useless?*

The situation was dangerous. He was taller and outweighed me. I knew I would lose if he took me to the ground. I needed distance and continued to back up. I needed to remain on my feet. But luck wasn't on my side.

My left foot was kicked out from under me.

Even though she was handcuffed, my suspect had free use of her legs. My mind raced, looking for my next move as I fell to the floor. I still had my hand on the butt of my weapon, but it slipped off when I hit the ground.

A smile grew on the man's face as he fell on top of me in a straddle position. His right knee prevented me from drawing my weapon, but I at least had a grip on my Glock. Little did I know, things would get worse. My other suspect rolled over and slammed a leg down across my neck, choking me in her attempt to help keep me immobile.

I looked into the eyes of the man on top of me. His pupils were obscenely dilated and saliva dripped from his clenched teeth like a rabid dog. There was no talking my way out of this.

My options were limited. I had to act fast or add my name to the list of victims. I twisted my right hand for a better grip on my weapon's handle. My index finger was still outside the trigger guard. I thought if I could fire a round, it might confuse the man on top of me, maybe even hit him and give me a splinter of an advantage but I couldn't be sure of the angle of the barrel. The last thing I needed was to shoot myself in the hip.

"Move your leg," he growled at the woman.

"Just kill her already," she yelled back as she complied.

"What the fuck happened to you?" he asked.

"What does it look like, you stupid fuck? She broke my nose."

At that point, I watched the man lean toward the woman, stick the blade into her neck and pull down, opening her throat. She gasped, and her body shook. She twisted and turned in a panic as she drained before her own eyes.

Without missing a beat, he focused back on me as if he hadn't done what he had just done. I could still hear the woman's gurgling panic off to the side as it began to calm. She was dying. He then placed the blade against the side of my neck. It felt warm. *Her blood?*

In life, there are no do-overs. Over the years, I've learned that people have a better shot at success if they trust their instincts. It's the wavering that causes the problems. Earlier, my instinct had presented an option to me. The question was, would I follow my own advice, or would I waver?

◇◇◇

The elevator slowed even more, if that were possible, as it neared the second floor. The cage bounced twice after stopping, and before Kang could react, the officer hit the fifth floor button again.

Kang knocked the officer's hand away, and quickly gripped the handle of the heavy metal door and yanked back, stopping the elevator from moving again. "Are you kidding me?" he asked, looking the officer in the eye. "Did you not notice how slow we were moving?"

Unaware of his stupidity, the patrol officer shrugged. "Sorry. I thought—I mean, what are we racing toward anyhow?"

Kang felt like punching the guy, fellow officer or not. "I don't have time to explain this shit to you if you can't grasp the situation." Kang shoved pass the officer, knocking him back with his shoulder as he slipped through the narrow opening of the elevator.

Kang used his long legs to his advantage and bounded up the steps two at a time until he reached the top floor. He didn't bother waiting for the officer, who was still hurrying one step at a time.

At the top of the stairs, Kang saw Tucker. He was a mess and looked gone. *What the hell is going on?* Officer Loui caught up to him just then. "Call backup and get an ambulance over here. Now!"

Kang stood up and removed his weapon. His long gait propelled him down the hall to the apartment with the open door. He could hear a commotion. He raised his weapon, ready for anything. With his gun out in front, he leaned cautiously into the opening.

Bam!

Chapter 45

The bullet had ripped though Jerry's upper, left thigh, causing him to rear back in pain and give me my slim advantage. I yanked my gun out of its holster, aimed up, and fired again. His bottom jaw exploded from the impact of the bullet. I fired again, catching him in the neck. He fell forward, his full weight resting on me. I started whacking him as hard as I could as I tried to wiggle out from underneath him. That's when I saw Kang standing in the doorway.

"Don't just stand there. Get this guy off me!"

Kang looked as if he had seen a ghost. I couldn't understand his reaction. Clearly, I wasn't dead. He stumbled forward, holstered his weapon and pulled the man off me. He held his hand out, and I grabbed it, allowing him to pull me to my feet.

"Are you okay?" he asked with that weird grimace still displayed on his face.

"I am now. What's wrong with you? Why are you looking at me all funny?"

He grabbed me by my arms and turned me around so I faced the hanging mirror on the wall. Staring back at me was an Asian Carrie. I'm not talking about a few splatters on the face; it literally looked like someone had dunked my entire head into bucket filled with blood and sprinkled bits of flesh about my cheeks and forehead.

I knew I had crap on my face—I could feel it—but I wasn't expecting to see that. I nearly vomited in my mouth before rushing into the bathroom to wash. I stuck my head under the shower faucet and used shampoo and soap liberally. It completely and utterly grossed me out.

While in there, I tied a shirt I had found around my thigh to curb the bleeding. With my adrenaline rush depleting, I began to feel a throbbing in my leg. The cut was deep enough that I knew I would need stitches and walking for the next few days would be uncomfortable.

My jacket hadn't survived. It was badly soiled. I slipped it off knowing the forensic team would want it, but I wasn't about to hang out with my face painted with human matter.

The two other officers who were searching the other street arrived then as well.

"Shit," one of them blurted as they entered the apartment. I couldn't blame them. The living room was a minefield of bodies with fresh blood everywhere. It wasn't a pretty sight.

Kang had already removed the blanket to reveal a body with a large hole in its chest. "The owner of the heart."

"He looks so young," I said. The body was stiff, still in

its rigor state. The cool air of the Bay area had helped to slow decomposition. It would have been a few more days before the smell would have signaled the neighbors on the floor.

Kang walked around to where I stood and gave my shoulder a gentle squeeze. "You okay?"

I nodded. "A little bruised, and some stitches to my thigh are in order, but I'll be fine. Probably need a new suit though," I joked weakly.

Kang gave me a small courtesy smile. "There were two of them?" he said, still serious.

"It makes much more sense. The whole heart removal bugged me. That action was more in line with a male killer."

Kang nodded in agreement and pocketed his hands.

"You check for ID yet?" I asked.

"Yeah. They had nothing on them. But the wig probably explains why no one could place her after that day on Mount Tamalpais. She probably only used it on kills or I guess for returning to crime scenes. We got lucky here."

I walked over to where she lay and glanced at her from the same angle in the picture. The resemblance was unmistakable to me, even with her short, black hair. I let out a long, lingering breath before punching Kang in the arm. "We got 'em."

"*You* got 'em."

A lot of elements in the case had been stacked against

us, but there we were, staring at our two dead sickos. I never thought it would play out this way, violent like this. I always hope to walk the bad guys into the jail cell, because death is easier than a life behind bars.

I looked around and realized Tucker wasn't there. "Have you seen Agent Tucker?"

"Abby," Kang said, his hand gently squeezing my arm.

"What? Where is he?" I asked, though the look in Kang's eyes had me answering my own question.

He shook his head. "He's gone. His body is outside, at the end of the hall."

My knees buckled a bit, but with Kang's help, I was able to catch myself before I fell.

"Take a seat, Abby." Kang ushered me to a chair.

"No." I shook my arm free from his grasp. "I need to see him."

"Abby, it's not pretty."

He stepped in front of me and tried to stop me, but I pushed him out of my way and exited the apartment. From there, I saw Tucker's body at the far end of the hall. He lay face down, his body crumpled as if he were cold. I fell back against the wall. My legs lost their urge to stand, and my body inched its way down the wall into a sitting position.

Why? It was the only question I had.

My eyes never left Tucker, not for a second. I couldn't have looked away even if I had wanted to. I didn't. I felt Kang's presence next to me and his hand on my shoulder. A beat later my vision blurred.

Chapter 46

The trip to the hospital cost me two hours from my day and earned me a week off, mandated by Reilly. I argued with him over the phone, but he wouldn't have any of it.

"Abby, the FBI isn't going anywhere. We'll still be here after a week."

"But the case! There are still a bunch of loose ends, and Agent Tucker—"

"Let me deal with him. I don't want you anywhere near the office. Have you thought about counseling? Do you want to talk to someone?"

"No, I'm okay," I said in a lowered voice.

"No one faults you for what happened. I don't fault you. Do you understand that?"

I heard Reilly, but I wasn't listening. He continued on about how he was behind me one hundred percent and that procedure was followed and what occurred was an unfortunate accident.

"Remember, Abby; you almost lost your life, too, so don't beat yourself up about it. I'm glad you made it. Go home and be with your family." Reilly hung up, and that was the last we spoke of Tucker.

Later, the hospital discharged me with a pair of crutches. The doctor told me to avoid vigorous activities, or I would risk tearing my wound open. Not a problem. I had already accepted my mandatory time off and looked forward to a little R&R with the family.

I never told them what exactly had happened. I never do. I gave them the downplayed version of events, the one that favored me. No need to make them any more upset than they would be once they saw I was injured—though I think Ryan was beginning to catch on to my tall tales. I was in my home office, a challenge getting there with crutches, when he stopped by to talk about my injury.

"I already told you," I said, careful to keep the tone of my voice even.

"Come on, Abby; you didn't think I would believe the story about you climbing a fence."

Uh, yeah, actually, I did. Okay, telling them that a fence caused the big gash on my thigh might not have been the best answer, but at the time, I thought mentioning anything close to being attacked with a razor would be too much.

Anyway, I had thought I had everything under control until Ryan called me out on my B.S. Don't get me wrong; I love that he had become comfortable with speaking his mind but questioning me, even though I lied—not a fan of it.

"I have a job that can be dangerous at times—"

"Duh!"

"You want the real story?" I asked, raising my left eyebrow.

Ryan nodded.

I leaned back in my chair and rested my hands in my lap. "While apprehending a suspect, he attacked me with a sharp knife."

"Why didn't you shoot him, Abby? You have a weapon, too, right?"

"I do, and I did."

"Did you kill him?"

That's a first—talking to my kid about killing someone. How does one prepare for that? At that moment, I would have preferred the why-does-my-penis-get-hard question. But life doesn't work that way.

Ryan was becoming wiser to what it was I did for a living. I figured I might as well be truthful. The truth is always good, right?

"Why do you ask that?"

He shrugged and looked down at the carpet.

"Well, to answer your question, the suspect received a fatal gunshot wound from me. So yes, he died." I didn't bother to add any more than necessary, figuring less was more.

"Oh…"

Ryan eventually looked up at me. "It was self-defense, right?"

"Yes, Ryan. That man intended to hurt me more than he already had. I had to protect myself."

A smile formed on Ryan's face. "You're awesome."

Secretly, it made me feel good to know my kid thought I was awesome, but I was a little worried that it was because I had killed someone. "You understand it's not okay to go around shooting people, right? Even an FBI agent like me is not above the law."

"Yeah, I know that. It's just cool having a tough mom."

My heart jumped. *He called me his mom.* I almost cried. Luckily, I held it together. I think if I hadn't, he might have rolled his eyes and taken the compliment back.

He seemed satisfied with my explanation, because he headed back downstairs to his room. I closed the door to my office right as my eye let go a tear. *My son had finally called me Mom.*

Chapter 47

Only three days had passed since the incident in the apartment, and I was already antsy at home. The kids were in school during the day, and Po Po and I had talked each other out. My only contact with work came through a small memorial service we had at the office for Agent Tucker. Reilly didn't balk when I said I would show for that. Tucker's family lived in Tallahassee, Florida, and that's where the body would later be flown for funeral arrangements, but only after Green had completed an autopsy. Standard procedure.

Kang did his best to keep me clued in on things on his end with text messages and phone calls. I knew I could count on him for updates. Even though *we* were both certain we had our killers, the Prosecutor's Office sought more proof. We had yet to identify the John and Jane Doe killers, and that proved problematic. Even their prints came up empty. We found no record of them. We still didn't know if they were from out of town or locals. There were a lot of questions and not a lot of answers. Those pesky but required details kept blocking what should have been a slam-dunk ending.

When Kang finally stopped by to check on me in person, similar to his last visit, Po Po sent him upstairs to my office unannounced. *It's a good thing I don't work in the nude.*

"We caught a break."

I spun around in my chair in time to see Kang enter my office. Before I could react, he took a seat next to me and started talking. "A day after our investigation at the apartment, one of the uniforms on perimeter patrol mentioned to me that he'd spotted a cab driver parked in the alleyway next to the building."

"I like it when people do their jobs, don't you?"

"Yeah, I already gave him an earful. Anyway, he never got a name or plate, but he said it was a Yellow Cab. So I visited our friend at the cab company—"

"The one with the grungy nails and an office that resembled the city dump?"

"That's the one. He did some digging and came up with two names for me. I questioned them both."

"And?" I asked, my body tensing a bit.

"One of them was the driver in the alley that day."

I smiled at Kang. "Good work, Detective."

"Thanks. By the way, how's the leg?" he asked, pointing.

"Meh. It's slowly healing. What's to say? Tell me more about this cab driver."

"Immigrant from Pakistan." Kang removed a small

notebook from his jacket. "His name is Yousuf Ijaz. He confirmed that our guy was his fare and that he had promised him $100 to wait in the alley. The pick-up address was a home on Russian Hill."

"Near you?"

"Nah, this was a nice house on the east side with views of North Beach and the bay. Above my pay grade." Kang chuckled. "I got a search warrant and hit the place ASAP. We found plane ticket stubs, originating from Toronto, suggesting they're Canadians."

"Married?"

"Seems like it. We also found multiple passports and fake facial hair. Looks like the guy sported a disguise as well. They're pros, and know how to cover their trail. Right now, we're working with authorities in Toronto to ID them. Our findings don't stop there, though."

I gave Kang my best Oliver Twist impression. "More, please."

"We found a laptop with pictures and videos that document their crimes."

I threw myself back into my chair. "No way!"

"Yeah, pretty stupid, huh?"

"How incriminating is it?"

Kang leaned forward. "Devastating. One of the videos shows the woman striking your vic with a hand axe." His hands emphasized his words. "Pretty gruesome stuff, and it nails the case shut. We're pretty sure their real names are

Jerry and Vicki Carlson. Once we confirm it, we can file the case away."

"What you do mean 'file it away'? What about the staging at the crime scene? Or our theory that it was done for someone else or a group of people?"

"We solved the murder. We found our victim's killers."

"Did we? I think we found two of the people involved. There's more to it. I can feel it."

"Why couldn't the photos and videos be souvenirs, something to inflate their egos? Maybe they got off watching themselves in action. There are plenty of documented cases where a serial killer keeps photos or clothing or something from the crime scene."

"I hear you, but this is different. If it were for their pleasure, why go through all that extra trouble of coming up with presentation that tied into an SF icon? It makes no sense. Something or someone else prompted them to act this way."

Kang leaned back. His ego and mood deflated and swooshed out of his lips.

"Look, I know if we keep digging, it prevents you from closing the case on your end, which keeps your a-hole boss on your back. It also prevents me from closing my case. But we both know there's more to this story."

I knew that was the last thing Kang wanted to hear. To be inches away from putting this case to bed and then realize there might be more to it had to be irritating. The other part of the equation: if I was wrong, Kang got skewered. Not an easy decision. Cavanaugh didn't care about the truth. He cared about stats. Kang said the department had a ninety-percent solve rate for their cases and staying there was what mattered. Cavanaugh made me appreciate Reilly.

"So what do you want to do?" he asked with a shrug.

"What else was on the laptop?"

"The photos and videos were the only incriminating thing we found. The rest were just personal files and programs."

"That's what we need to be paying attention to. It may give us a clue as to who else might be involved."

"Well, we combed all their email and social media accounts, and nothing came up."

"My guess is you were looking for the wrong thing."

"What do you mean?" he asked, his brow crinkled.

"You were looking for evidence that ties them to our victims. We need evidence that ties them to their audience."

Chapter 48

"No way. I can't do that. If Cavanaugh finds out I'm intentionally derailing his closure rate, I'll be relegated to foot patrol faster than you can spew a quick remark."

Did he slam me or compliment me? "Look, I know I'm asking a lot, but if we're right, not only will we put away another degenerate, but this will put you in a better light with your captain. That has to earn you some extra donuts in the morning, right?"

Kang rubbed his chin and chewed his bottom lip. I had never seen a cop mull over a decision to chase a bad guy. Well, maybe I had, but this was Kang. This guy was straighter than a baton when it came to policing.

"Do you really need the laptop?"

"How else am I to find the information? Where is it now?"

Kang shifted in his seat and looked away. "It's bagged and sitting in the evidence room under lock and key."

"Will it be a problem to get it?"

"This evidence seals the case. If anything happens to it, or it gets damaged, or the contents get erased… we're screwed."

"Hulk be careful. Hulk no break laptop. Hulk promise," I grunted.

Kang shook his head. "I don't know, Abby. Can't you come down to the precinct? I can probably get you access for a few hours."

I looked at my injured leg and then back at him, triggering his eyes to roll upward.

"Come on, Kangster," I pleaded. "Kangman," I continued. "Kangis Khan. See? I can do the name thing too… Kangaroo." I batted my eyelashes, threw in a pout and waited for him to cave. It took two seconds. *You still got it, Abby.*

While I had enjoyed watching Kang succumb, I had a better solution than just snagging the computer. I really didn't need the laptop. If I could copy the entire contents of the hard drive, I'd technically have the laptop without needing the actual laptop. And to be honest, I really didn't need his permission for him to agree. As an FBI agent, I had the authority to confiscate the contents of that laptop for the purpose of my investigation if needed. I was being mindful of his situation with his supervisor—which was so unlike me. I sent an email to Reilly to keep him in the loop in case the SFPD found out and cried about my methods. He sent his usual reply. "Do what you need to do to get the job done."

Later that evening, Kang returned with the laptop, and I copied the entire contents over to an external hard drive. He was eager to get it back into the evidence room and was out the door as soon as I had finished. I didn't bother to wait for him to return before I checked out the contents.

"Anything yet?" Kang asked when he returned a half hour later with two plates of food. He noticed the look of confusion on my face. "Oh, your Po Po gave this to me on the way up."

He handed me my plate and proceeded to shovel beef and broccoli into his mouth. "She's a good cook," he managed between bites. "This is the real deal."

"Tell me about it. I overeat at every meal."

"So what's the latest?"

I swallowed before answering. "Nothing yet. I went through his email, his documents folder and the trash."

"So did we. We also looked through his photo organizer and video folders."

"What about his Internet history?"

"We looked at it, but nothing popped out."

I opened the browser. A quick scan showed a lot of SF searches for information on sights and attractions. It didn't take long before I found dirt. "Looks like they've visited the personals on a few adult directories. Escort services."

"Yeah, we saw that. He's got an active life back home."

"The searches appear to be for escorts here, not Toronto."

Kang stopped chewing. "Why would he want an escort

in SF?"

"Maybe he and the woman were platonic." I shrugged.

"No sex, just kills?"

"Yeah, it doesn't make sense to me either." I pulled up a few of the pages they had visited. "Well this is interesting. The searches are all for male escorts."

"So the woman wanted action."

"I wouldn't judge too quickly. We don't know that it wasn't the guy."

Kang's head bobbed from left to right as he continued to eat.

I tapped a finger on my desk. "You know, they could have been trolling for another victim."

"A male escort? What's the connection to SF?"

I raised an eyebrow at Kang. "You ever get out of Chinatown?"

He still had a puzzled look on his face while he scooped food into his mouth.

"San Francisco is a hotbed for porn production specializing in the alternative scene," I said. "Maybe they were planning something in the Castro. They've visited at least twenty different ads on this site alone. Let's see if they reached out to any men of the night."

I opened the mail program and checked the emails they had sent.

Kang must have noticed the smile on my face. "Did you find something?"

"They contacted a bunch of them. Let's see who responded." I checked the inbox on the days they were on the hunt for an escort. "I've found some replies."

"Well?"

"Hang on." I scanned a few emails. "Seems as though their interests with the escorts had to do with their size, and I'm not talking height. I see some back and forth with an escort who calls himself Sampson... Here we go. They had a meeting set up with him at the Parc 55 Wyndham."

"We don't have a victim named Sampson, so maybe he was a potential."

"I doubt that's his real name, but none of our victims fit Sampson's profile. He's a six-foot-three, muscular black man." I shrugged. "He's worth seeking out. Let's set up a meeting."

"You really think this escort was involved?" Kang asked.

I leaned back in my chair and patted my belly like a bongo drum. "I'm not sure. It could have been a legitimate hire for an adventurous threesome."

"Or there's more to it."

"Exactly. But we won't know until we talk to him."

Chapter 49

I set up a new Gmail account and typed out an email to Sampson, explaining that we were a Chinese couple seeking his services for a threesome. "Anything else you think we should mention?" I asked Kang.

"That sounds like a typical query. It should work."

I hit the send button, and the email swooshed its way to our escort. It was nearing nine at night. I told Kang I would text him when I had a response. As I walked him to the front door, he mentioned, "I know the manager of the Hyatt in Chinatown. I can arrange for a room if this thing gets that far." I nodded my agreement and said goodnight.

Ryan was the only one up; Po Po and Lucy had gone to bed earlier, at eight. Once I had tucked him into bed, I had the house to myself with no distractions.

I popped back into my office and continued with my search through the Carlsons' computer files. I wasn't hopeful with the escort angle. My gut told me he showed up, did his job and left. There had to be something we were missing. They knew how to cover their tracks and they had multiple identities, so they clearly had experience. Yet they had taken pictures and made videos of their crimes. Why go through all the trouble of disguising themselves and leaving no evidence or witnesses at the crime scenes, then erase all of that by keeping evidence of their deeds on their computer? Someone that good wouldn't do that unless there was a valid reason, like proving they had killed a person. Was that it? Did they document their crimes to prove they had done them? Was this about showmanship or proof? A contract killer might be required to provide proof. But I didn't believe these were contract kills.

I looked in the all the obvious places more times than I could count, thinking maybe I had missed something. To be sure, I looked in every folder. Sometimes people hide the good stuff in places that are right out in the open but where you would never think to look, like in an Applications folder—better yet, the Utilities folder.

I clicked on the Applications folder and saw a list of the usual programs that came loaded on a Mac. The only additions were Adobe Photoshop and Microsoft Word. I scrolled until I found the Utilities folder. Again, normal stuff needed to keep the laptop functioning. I didn't find any strange, out-of-place folders. *What am I missing?*

I began to think they kept a laptop primarily to store videos and photos and to surf the Internet. Outside of the escort emails, the rest of their email activity was tourist related: hotel and flight bookings, purchasing tickets to attractions and, of course, things to do in San Francisco. The same went for their online activity. Each corroborated the other.

The staged crime scenes, the pictures and videos—this was all for someone else. Another person viewed our couple in action, but how? Could they have hand-delivered the evidence of their deeds on a flash drive? If that were the case, then tracing their steps back to that person would be difficult, if not impossible.

I went back to their Internet history. The couple had visited the Kayak website a lot, and Kayak memorizes your last search. Maybe their next step could tell me more.

No such luck. The "to" and "from" fields were filled in with Toronto and San Francisco. What about a return flight? I dug back into the emails and found the airline confirmation email. They had purchased one-way tickets. Did they not intend on returning? Were they planning on staying in San Francisco? Were they last-minute travelers who bought their plane tickets days before travel? I went back to the airline confirmation email. The date they booked and the date of travel were separated by two days. I wondered if their travel plans were dependent on another trigger, like permission or instructions. Or were they simply not sure of their next move? *What am I missing? What else could tell me more about these two individuals that I don't already know?*

There were no Word files saved in their Documents folder. I even booted Word to see if there were recent files opened. None. I did the same for Photoshop, Excel and more. And then my eye caught their Games folder. *Hmmm, a serial killer that plays Angry Birds. Who would have thought?*

I opened the game. There appeared to be consistent gameplay since they had completed five levels. I opened a few other games, unsure if it would lead me to anything, but it was something to do. As I moved from game to game, all I gathered was that they liked to play the popular ones, all of them PG rated. I didn't see any shoot 'em up or fighting games. You would think a serial killer would rather play those than Mahjong or Solitaire. Go figure. I was a click away from closing the Applications folder and calling it a night when I spotted an app with a dragon icon. There was no file name, just a blank space next to the icon, which explained why I had missed it on the first pass.

I clicked on the app, and the screen went black. An animated, fire-breathing dragon materialized. It put on a brief show before morphing into the game's logo: Chasing Chinatown. I leaned back in my chair as both sides of my mouth climbed higher. *I got you guys.*

Chapter 50

It was near midnight when I received a text from Kang that he was standing outside my home. When I opened the front door, I was amused by his down dressing. He had on sweatpants, a hoodie and a baseball cap.

"What?" He asked, his body language defensive. "You said get over here as fast as I could. I was already in bed."

I motioned for him to hurry inside. "We hit the jackpot," I said as I skip-hopped past him and up the stairs. "Come on; I'll show you what I found."

I moved up the stairs and into my office as quickly as my leg would allow. Slightly out of breath, I pointed to the laptop. "Take a look."

Kang took a seat at my desk and stared at the screen. On it was a simple outline map of the world with the major cites of various countries represented by glowing red dots. A blue trajectory line connected Toronto and San Francisco.

"Is this some sort of a game?"

"Yes. It's a game that our killer couple has been playing."

"Wait, you got me out of bed to look at a game?"

I stood with my weight resting on one leg and my hand

on my hip. "It's more than a game. I've been poking around this program for the last hour or so, not to mention I had to crack a password to even get access. Let me explain. It's kind of like a travel log. It keeps track of their expenses and the miles they've logged and the most interesting—"

Kang held up his and interrupted me. "Hold on, Abby. I'm still not seeing the importance."

"Well, if you would zip it and let me finish, you would."

"Fine." He turned back toward the laptop, giving me the floor.

"As I was saying, the most interesting part of this all is that it keeps track of their kills."

Kang straightened up.

"That got your attention, didn't it?"

"Keep going."

"Not only does it manage their kills, but it *orders* them."

Kang looked back at me. "You mean this game, or whatever it is, asked for one dead guy minus his heart?"

"Not exactly, but close." I reached around Kang, took control of the mouse and moved the cursor over the listing of headings titled Attractions. "Each of these Attractions correlates to a kill." I clicked on Attraction Four, and the other headings and the map faded back. A large animated scroll appeared and unraveled, revealing a phrase.

"Good fortune comes in many forms. Find the right one

for your answer," Kang read out loud.

"Each Attraction has a riddle like that. Below the riddle is a place to type in your answer."

"And below that is a task," Kang continued. "Leave someone's heart in San Francisco. That's referencing the Tony Bennett song, 'I Left My Heart in San Francisco.'"

"That's right, and our last victim had their heart removed and left here."

Kang removed his cap and ran his hands through his hair as he leaned back in the chair. "Unbelievable."

"I think answering the riddle correctly reveals the task, because the first three Attractions all have the same thing, except the riddle and the tasks are different." I quickly took Kang through them.

"Why the puzzle aspect? If they're killing for someone else, why make it difficult?"

"It's a fun challenge—a game—so to speak. Most serial killers pride themselves on their analytical thinking, their ability to outsmart law enforcement and even their victims. I'd say this is right up their alley. Consider it an appetizer before the meal."

Kang leaned back. "Maybe the game aspect is twofold. It masks what is really taking place."

"That's a valid point."

"The only thing we don't know is what answer they gave for each riddle to reveal their tasks."

"Well, I crosschecked this fortune phrase with the

history of their web searches. While I didn't see any direct searches for this phrase, there were a lot of searches for Chinese restaurants."

"Fortune cookie," Kang blurted. "Chinese restaurants have fortune cookies and this riddle is about fortune."

"That was my initial thought, too, until I saw the search for fortune cookie manufacturers."

Kang snapped his finger. "The Fortune Cookie Company. It's located right in the middle of Chinatown. So that's the answer."

"It could be, but my hunch is it was something at that location."

"So they visit, recite the riddle and receive their answer. They then come back, plug it in and the task is revealed."

"Perhaps. It fits with the gameplay concept." I leaned against the wall and crossed one leg over the other.

"So we have a game that challenges the intellect, the skill, and the creativity of a serial killer. Talk about three ways to feed the ego."

"Yeah."

Kang rubbed his palms back and forth over his thighs. "You did good, Abby. You've certainly unearthed more about this case than I had thought there to be. But do you really think the creator of this app is masterminding the kills? Maybe it's only a game that someone thought up, and these two lowlifes decided to use it to add a little excitement."

"Possibly. I can't say that isn't the case."

"But you think someone is behind it."

"I do, and it's because of the staging involved with the crimes and the documentation. While a lot of serial killers have a signature, something about their kill that brands them, I don't believe the staging was a signature for the Carlsons."

"Too much work?"

"Yeah. The amount of thought put into the staging, not to mention covering their tracks—I still believe the Carlsons relished the kill. The staging aspect feels more like work they might have enjoyed or even a way to prolong the high of the kill for them."

"Could this simply be them seeking credit for their kills?"

I tossed Kang's question around in my head for a bit, even though I had initially discounted it. "It's not credit they're seeking. This is about proof. Credit would require reaching a large audience. That's not what they're after. The staging was small and hidden."

"Either way, I still can't shake the fact that we're talking about a simple app."

"This isn't coming from nowhere. This little game played a role in their kills."

Kang looked up at me, his eyebrows arched into half circles. "We have no hard evidence that someone is issuing a command to kill through it. There are no direct orders."

"It's a great way to hide the fact that an order was given. It's like the way the mob communicates over the phone; all of their conversations are indirect. Whoever is behind this is equally organized and set this up to avoid implicating themselves should something go wrong."

Kang's eyelids were heavy and his brow had relaxed. It was a lot to take in. I knew that, which is why it didn't bother me that he still questioned me. He wouldn't be doing his job if he didn't.

For a few moments, neither of us said anything. My gut agreed with everything I had told Kang. Whether he agreed as well was yet to be seen. He had his head down as he stared at the area rug on the floor. His arms were folded across his chest with his hands tucked between his torso and his biceps.

I recrossed my legs. It must have wakened him from his self-imposed coma because he looked up at me then. Maybe he sensed me staring at him. There wasn't an obvious sign to confirm my suspicions.

From the beginning, our relationship had been professional. Kang never crossed the line with me. I had said a lot of things that probably did but still, he always treated me with respect and as an equal. Could he loosen up a bit more? Sure, but I didn't mind things the way they were.

As I shook off my thoughts, I saw that Kang was still

staring. I didn't feel as though he were gawking, nor did I feel uncomfortable. Maybe it was his gentle eyes. Twice, I almost opened my mouth to break the silence but resisted. We were having a moment. I wasn't sure what it meant, but I also wasn't so quick to stop it. Slowly, I watched a smile form on his face. It started on one side and grew to encompass his entire mouth. I couldn't help but grin back; his was too contagious to ignore.

Eventually, the silence got the best of me, and I laughed. "You're staring at me."

"I'm thinking about the case."

"No, you're not."

"All right, I'm not."

"What then?" My left eyebrow rose, as I tilted my head to the side playfully.

"I'm realizing how good you are."

"As a person?"

"Yes, that, but I really meant as a cop."

"Even though I'm an FBI agent, I'll take that as a compliment."

"You know what I mean."

I looked at my watch; it was nearly two in the morning, and that triggered a yawn, which then turned into stretching my arms high above my head. I peeked at Kang as I reached for the ceiling. My shirt must have ridden up higher than it felt like. Before Kang arrived, I had changed into a T-shirt and a pair of sweat shorts—my normal comfort wear around the house. In my mind, it was the furthest thing from sexy.

Kang thought otherwise.

His eyes were intensely staring at my exposed midsection, and before I could stop myself, my mouth cranked into gear. "Are you checking me out?"

He quickly looked off to the side before settling his eyes back on me. "What?" he managed to say with only a slight crack in his voice.

"You were staring—wait—leering at me."

"I was not. It might have looked like I was, but I was thinking about the case, lost in my thoughts." He waved a dismissive hand at me and looked away. "You've got a big ego."

So I had busted his balls a bit for taking a peek. I was glad he had done it. It made him seem normal—goofy. And cute.

◇◇◇

Twice in one night, I found myself calling Kang while he was asleep.

"Abby?"

"Sorry. I know it's late, but I know what we need to do."

"It's four in the morning. Don't you sleep?"

I had been sleeping, but a trip to the toilet had ignited the cogs in my head and they started spinning. As I had laid in bed with pieces of the case flowing in and out of my conscious, clarity on our next move appeared.

"Are you listening to me? I said I know what we need to do."

"Is this about the case? Give it up. There's no hard evidence that someone was talking to the Carlsons through this game. We would be chasing a ghost."

"There's still one riddle left that hasn't been solved."

"So we guess the answer correctly, and the task is revealed. Where does that take us?"

"I'm not sure. But there's only one way to find out."

"And what's that?"

"Play the game the way the Carlsons would have played it. For real."

Chapter 51

Kang agreed to hear me out the following morning. I had known from the start I would be walking into a minefield of negativity, but I needed to get Kang on board. Add that I had ruined any chance he'd had at a good night's sleep and, well…

I sat at a sidewalk table in front of the La Boulange Bakery on Columbus Avenue. It was beautiful out, no fog but still jacket weather. I already had my tea steeping in a large mug when I spotted his tall frame poking up amongst the sidewalk traffic. I waved until he spotted me. The big grin on his face eased the tension in my chest. Maybe I had expected a fight where there wasn't one.

"Thanks for meeting me." I slid his usual, a medium black coffee, across the table as he took a seat.

"It's not a problem." He grabbed the cup and brought it up to his lips but kept his eyes on me while he swallowed. He then moved the cup far enough from his lips to speak. "And thanks for the coffee." He then took another sip before setting it down and rubbing his hands together quickly. "Brisk, isn't it?"

"A little. Look—"

Kang held up a hand. "Abby, I'm in."

My eyes widened.

"You can close your mouth. This is a good thing."

It took a moment for me to gather my thoughts and form a response. "Great." That's all I could manage.

Kang leaned back and rested his foot across his thigh. I knew then we were good and back on track. "I'm curious." I hesitated for a second, though I don't think he noticed. "What made you change your mind? You seemed so… I dunno, negative, last night."

He dropped his foot to the sidewalk and shook his pant leg straight. "To be honest, I trust your judgment. I don't think I would have closed this case if I hadn't been working with you."

"Puh-lease." I reached over and gave him a playful shove. "We both worked this case."

"Thanks. I appreciate you including me, but I know a smart cookie when I see one."

My wide grin allowed me to easily sip my tea, which I stretched out longer than usual. I didn't have an answer, and I could feel the heat in my cheeks increasing.

"About this game," Kang said. "How do you see it unfolding?"

"When the Carlsons killed that musician, they unlocked Attraction Five, probably by delivering pictures or video of the end result. I know the riddle wasn't solved, because the task has yet to be revealed. I propose we become Jerry and

Vicki Carlson and play the game the way it's intended."

"Last night, you talked about a person behind this game. How do we know he doesn't know what the couple looks like?"

"We don't, but if we can nab this answer to the riddle without alerting the hounds, we're good. I figure worst case scenario, the guy cuts off all contact and goes underground, and we'd be back to where we currently are."

"And if we succeed?"

"We keep playing and see where it takes us."

I watched Kang press his lips tightly together before swishing them from side to side. "We could be walking into an ambush."

"We'll take precautions."

"When do we start?"

I opened my shoulder bag. "Now. I've loaded the game onto my laptop."

I booted up the program. The map of the world and the Attraction headings appeared. I clicked on Attraction Five, and we watched the animated scroll unravel to reveal the riddle.

Hundreds of dragons churn the waters. Find them and find your clue.

"That's the riddle?" he asked.

"Yeah. I have no idea where to start."

Kang said it out loud a few times. I didn't even have a suggestion to make. I was completely stumped by what it could mean.

Kang shifted his eyes upward, to me. "This is a lot harder than I expected it to be."

I took a deep breath. "Let's take a step back. We know the way the kills are made tie into the city, so the riddle probably does as well. What's the link between dragons and San Francisco?"

"Chinatown." Kang sat up. The light had gone on in his head. "They're all over the place."

"There are dancing dragons during Chinese New Year," I added.

"It's May, though, but…" Kang raised his index finger. His mouth hung slightly open. "That's not the only festival that has dragons associated with it." He held that pose for a beat longer, his mind continuing to churn and keeping me guessing. "That's it!" He slapped his thigh repeatedly.

"What? Tell me."

"Today is the first day of the fifth month of the Lunisolar Chinese calendar."

"Huh?"

"This is the month of the Duanwu Festival—the Dragon Boat Festival, where dragon-themed boats race against others."

"Hundreds of dragons churn the waters," I said.

"That's exactly what the race looks like."

I punched Kang in the arm. "Your nerdy knowledge of all things Chinese is paying off."

"My what?"

"Nothing. The festival? Where? When?"

Kang whipped out his phone. "I don't know why it didn't come to me sooner. I've been to it many times. It takes place on Treasure Island, and there are literally hundreds of these boats gliding across the bay that day. It's a real sight to see. There must be a website." He tapped at his phone a few times and waited. "Got it. The race is this upcoming Saturday."

"Looks like the Carlsons have plans."

Chapter 52

After our revelation at the bakery, Kang confided in me regarding his growing concerns with Cavanaugh. As far as the politicking captain knew, the case was solved and filed away. "If he finds out we're digging further into it, he could order me to stop. Heck, I wouldn't be surprised if he slapped me with an insubordination charge. I'm not his favorite detective, you know."

I had an easy solution. I pulled rank and officially made the entire case an FBI investigation requiring SFPD's help, specifically Kang's. Reilly was on board. He saw the potential in this case, not to mention that it was already cross-border.

Toronto's RCMPs got back to us with a few unsolved murders that had a staging aspect to them. We were confident that the Carlsons were connected. That alone was enough to make it a federal investigation. Plus, Reilly knew it could be a big coup for the department. Cavanaugh wasn't the only one who looked to collect an "atta-boy" wherever he could. And because our case had been elevated, we had access to the resources needed to help us.

Even though we assumed the real Carlsons had never

met the mastermind behind the game, he might have seen a picture of their faces. The department arranged for a professional makeup person to come in and help us match the facial features of our couple and the disguises they used.

Kang looked more Asian than I did, but the artist had a way to help alleviate that through rubber prosthetics around his eyes. They also attached a bulbous nose on his face to match Jerry Carlson's and replicated the mustache found at the cottage. We both were outfitted with wigs. I wore contacts to change my green eyes to brown and got a new beauty mark on my cheek, which I quite liked. The entire disguise was fairly turnkey so we could apply it ourselves in the future.

In the days leading up to the big dragon event, a tactical team scouted the area and picked out a location where our safety team could position themselves and monitor the situation. Since Kang and I would most likely be on the move, another team of agents, dressed as spectators, mobile food vendors and security would follow us around. It was a large operation for a hunch, but as Kang had mentioned earlier, we had no idea what we were walking into.

The day of the races, Kang and I arrived at the island at eleven in the morning. We were wired so we could maintain radio contact with the team, who had arrived earlier to get into position. Reilly and his team were overseeing the operation from a tent disguised as a life insurance exhibit, something that would receive very little foot traffic, if any.

"Carlsons, Command Center is operational, and your perimeter team is in place. We're waiting on your go," Reilly said over the radio.

"We just parked and are heading to the entrance. Let us know when you have eyes on us," I responded.

The first agent to pick us up was Agent House. "This is ground security at the entrance. I have the Carlsons in my view. Proceeding to follow."

It didn't take long for the entire team to lock us in their sights and for us to spot them. I had handpicked every agent. It was comforting that I knew every one of them.

"Carlsons, do your thing. We're watching," Reilly chirped in.

"Hundreds of dragons churn the waters," Kang said.

We really didn't know what steps to take. All we knew was that the Carlsons had a riddle tied to fortune cookies and they Googled manufacturers. From that, we extrapolated that they had visited the Fortune Cookie Company in Chinatown and received their answer. Not much to go on, but how hard could it be? Solving the riddle wasn't the end goal. The kill was. It had to be a challenge that could be easily completed.

We headed down to where the boats were docked, thinking they might hold our answer. The boats were long and narrow like the skiffs used in rowing events, but they had a deeper and larger hull like a canoe. A dragon's head carved from wood was mounted on the stern of each boat. They were painted in a variety of bright blues, oranges, yellows, and reds. The dragon detail continued along the side of the narrow vessel, making the entire boat look like a beast moving through water.

"They look really cool," I said. "But I don't get the feeling that what we're looking for is here. It's too literal to the riddle."

"I think you're right. It's something else."

We turned around and headed back to the top of the festival grounds where the majority of the exhibits were and where there was a great view of the racecourse.

"What else do you know about this festival? Why do they race dragon-themed boats?" I asked.

"Well, there are a couple of theories. The most popular is the story of a scholar who, in a form of protest to government corruption, committed suicide by throwing himself into the Miluo River on the fifth day of the fifth lunar month. The villages were so impressed by his sacrifice, they used leaves to wrap rice into little triangles and threw them into the river. You and I know this as the rice dumpling snack called Zong Zi."

"That's how Zong Zi was invented?"

"According to the story, yes. Anyway, they did this to prevent the fish from eating the body."

I stopped walking and turned to Kang. "Feeding the fish rice so they don't eat a body? Are you messing with me?"

"No, I'm serious. Mind you, this supposedly took place in 278 BC. That's the way minds worked back then. Anyway, in their efforts to keep the fish snacking on rice, they paddled boats out onto the river to spread more rice around and that's how the dragon boat racing came about."

"Who's the scholar responsible for this commercialized myth?"

"I think his name was Qu Yan."

"Does he look like that guy over there?" I held my arm up and pointed to a Chinese man dressed in traditional ancient garb with a fake wispy mustache that hung from the corners of his mouth. Groups of people were having their pictures taken with him.

"Yeah," Kang mumbled.

"I guess he's the Dragon Festival's answer to Disneyland's Mickey Mouse." I grabbed Kang by his arm and dragged him toward the character. "Honey, look. It's Qu Yan!" I squealed. "I want a picture."

"He's not that popular. Bring it down a notch." The words squeezed out of the corner of his mouth.

We waited as the woman in front of us had her boyfriend take her picture over and over because she wasn't satisfied with his iPhone photography. After the fifth picture, my patience had started to grow thin. "What's the point?" I said through gritted teeth. "She'll probably slap multiple filters on it, and it'll look nothing like the original."

"Happy thoughts, dear. Happy thoughts."

Kang's response initiated a few chuckles from our listeners. I had forgotten briefly that we were mic'd. Finally, Miss Inconsiderate okayed a photo, and they left. I stood next to the man and hooked my arm around his. While Kang took out his phone to snap a picture, I leaned in and said, "Hundreds of dragons churn the waters."

Nothing. Not even a slight acknowledgment that I had said something. I tried once more, only louder and with a throat clear to grab his attention. Still, he only stared at Kang, who was suddenly bent at the knees with one leg stretched all the way back while he tried to maintain balance.

"What are you doing?" I asked.

"Trying to get the right angle."

"The right angle is you standing straight up and taking the picture, dear."

I had the opposite problem from the girl who had stood here before me. Smile cramp had started to set in, and Kang appeared no closer to taking the picture. He was of the mindset that he had something much more substantial in his hand than a phone camera.

I tugged on Qu Yan's arm, gaining his attention, and repeated the riddle once more. He only smiled back at me with a gentle nod. I then mentioned, "Team Carlson." Same response. What the hell was I doing wrong? Maybe Qu Yan wasn't our point of contact, but surely someone was. I doubted we were looking for an object. Qu Yan was the reason for this festival. If not him, then whom? Finally, grasping at anything, I said, "Chasing Chinatown."

At that point, Kang had finally snapped a picture, and Qu Yan had wriggled his arm free from my grip. At first, I thought he was in a rush to go elsewhere. I didn't blame him; I wouldn't want to spend another second with a wannabe pro phone photographer and his clingy wife. I still hadn't decided if I wanted to let this guy go. I could hear Reilly in my earpiece asking for an update. I couldn't say anything and was mindful not to accidently give the signal for everyone to move in—putting my hair behind my left ear.

Not having any other reason to keep clinging to Qu Yan, I relinquished and set him free, expecting him to hurry away, but he didn't. I watched him reach into one of the many folds in his robe and remove something. I couldn't quite see what it was, but he grabbed my hand, and in it, he placed a small Zong Zi.

"There's been an exchange," Reilly said over the radio. "Team, wait for the signal. Carlsons, are we grabbing this guy?"

I waited for Qu Yan to move out of earshot. "He gave me Zong Zi. It's a rice dumpling associated with the festival."

"Are we grabbing him?" Reilly stated once more.

"No. He's only the messenger. We need to keep

playing the game."

"All right, team. Let's wrap it up."

I showed Kang the dumpling before addressing the team. "Team leader, we will rally back at your position."

<><><>

The man dressed as Qu Yan watched the couple hurry away, like two kids who had just received a present from Santa Claus. He watched them disappear into the crowd before turning around and heading in the other direction. He avoided eye contact with any potential picture takers and made his way past a few exhibition tents to an area where only exhibitors were allowed. He didn't stop until he stood under a large olive tree, one of the few that still thrived since its planting during the 1935 Golden Gate Expo. There, he removed a cell phone from his robe and made a call.

A low scratchy voice answered the call. "Yes."

"Team Carlson check in for fifth Attraction. I give them answer."

"Thank you, Wei. This is good news."

"No. Not good news."

"Why do you say that?"

"Wrong couple."

Chapter 53

Jing Woo pressed the end button on his cell phone and set it down on the wobbly teak table in front of him. Even with a crack running the length of the tabletop, it was sturdy enough to hold the pot of tea that he always kept near him. He sat Indian style on an array of colorful silk cushions while leaning back against a larger, fluffier one that had been propped against the wall—not an office you would expect for the head of the local Triad gang.

Everyone had heard of Jing, but very few had ever met him. Most of his conversations took place over the phone or through other individuals, and he had an army of men who did his bidding. Jing liked it that way. It's what made him powerful, what made Chinatown impenetrable by outsiders.

Jing slipped the ivory cigarette holder between his lips and inhaled deeply, causing the cigarette to crackle and burn brightly. Swirls of gray circled his head, noticeable from the tiny bit of light that shone through a small, frosted window above his head. Large candles spread out around the room contributed to the ominous look by casting an array of harsh shadowing and flickering light. Furnishing was sparse outside of a few small tables and bookshelves populated with books and Chinese pottery. Like the table, they, too, were fashioned out of teak and decorated with either ivory or mother-of-pearl inlays.

Very few people were allowed inside Jing's retreat. In fact, only his most trusted advisor had carte blanche to enter. That man's name was Quai Chan, but he was commonly referred to as the Black Mantis.

Jing picked up a small bell and rang it. The entrance door to the room opened quietly, and a man slipped inside. Jing adjusted himself on the pillows as the shadowy figure approached until the red glow lit his face. "You requested my attention."

"Yes, Quai. Please, sit. I received an interesting call regarding Team Carlson. What do you know of them?"

"They have played the game well."

"They have, yes. Very creatively, too. Today, however, they did not collect the password for their final objective."

"Why is that? Could they not figure out the riddle?"

"No, no. That wasn't the problem." Jing took another long toke and allowed his exhale to linger.

"What then?" There was alarm in Quai's response.

"Another couple showed up in their place."

"Impossible," Quai blurted.

"Is it?" Jing brought his teacup to his lips.

Quai knew that was the end of the conversation. It was his job to discover the problem and fix it. He stood and bowed respectfully to his boss before exiting the room. His next course of action was to find the couple from the dragon race in a discreet way. Jing Woo and his crew were well protected within the borders of Chinatown, though on the outside, it was a different story. It was important they work from the shadows, especially when problems arose. That was how their kind thrived in their popular neighborhood.

Quai was an expert at his trade—intimidation. That's why he was called the Black Mantis: his ability to strike an opponent from out of nowhere without any witnesses gave fear to those who knew him and a short life to those who didn't. In addition to his savvy street smarts, Quai's ruthless ability earned him the title of Jing's most deadly assassin. His greatest asset was his height and weight. He stood no more than five-feet, five-inches and barely toppled the scale at one hundred thirty pounds; he was the most unassuming opponent a person would ever face.

Chapter 54

Back at the Bureau's office on Golden Gate Avenue, Reilly, Kang and I gathered around the laptop. I pulled up our fifth attraction and typed the word Zong Zi as my answer. The screen went dark, and a moving graphic of the word "Congratulations" appeared. Tiny fireworks shot out of the top of the letters. We all looked at each other, wondering if this were some sort of joke. The graphic design was reminiscent of what existed on the Internet back in the mid-nineties. Add to that the strangeness of celebrating another step forward to finding out how the next kill would be dictated, and it was all morbidly troubling.

After a few seconds of fanfare, the firework display disappeared and the paper scroll appeared, except that time, our task was revealed at the bottom.

ATTRACTION #5
Hundreds of dragons churn the waters. Find them and find your clue.
Answer: Zong Zi
Task: Order Chinese takeout.
Upload

"Another riddle?" Kang stood up straight and planted both of his hands on his hips. "This is stupid. What kind of killer goes through all this trouble to kill a person? They could walk out of their home and end the life of the first person they see if they want."

"I'm with Detective Kang on this one, Abby. It's not making a whole lot of sense."

I understood how they could be frustrated. The department had spent major bucks on a surveillance operation only to walk away with a rice snack and another riddle. Even I felt doubt creep into my head, but I quickly gave it the boot as I recalled the crime scenes of our other victims. "Look, guys, I know it seems like this is getting us nowhere, but step back and look at the entire picture. Consider our other victims and how they have met their deaths. All of the crime scenes connect back to this game play."

"Or maybe we wanted them to and made the connections work," Kang suggested.

I turned to him. "You of all people should recognize that's not true. The last objective was also indirect: 'Leave someone's heart in San Francisco.' We just need to apply a little killer instinct to this one."

"Say we do come to an agreeable answer as to what this means. What then?" Reilly asked.

"We stage the scene and submit the photos. It's the

only way to get to the person behind all of this."

"Chinese takeout!" Kang threw his arms up in the air. "How much more nebulous can that be?"

Kang continued his rant but I had already tuned him out and focused back on the statement in front of me. *Order Chinese takeout. Literal or not? Hmmm… I wonder if… that's it!* "Hey, listen up. This isn't a riddle. We're the ones turning it into a riddle when it shouldn't be."

"What do you mean?" Reilly's eyebrows shot upward, widening his eyes.

"This is, and has always been, about killing. This is the time when the killer does what they do. They only need to link their kill to that phrase. There is no right or wrong way to do it. It's about showmanship at this point. This is where the staging comes from. It's now about how entertaining or clever can they make their kill."

Kang's head bounced around as he pondered.

"The simplest form of delivering is to kill a Chinese person. But do you get points for that? Is that enough to seal the deal? Is it too obvious? If so, how could a killer add some pizzazz to that?"

Reilly sat up. "Chop up the body and deliver it in a large takeout container."

Kang and I both looked at Reilly at the same moment.

"What? I'm riffing here."

"That's exactly what we need to be doing—coming up with a bunch of ideas until we hit *the* one."

"How do we know if we hit *the* one?"

"We'll know."

Everyone quickly got on the same page, and our killer brainstorm session progressed at a fast rate. Within twenty minutes, we had written down fifteen possible ideas for our kill. I really didn't think the Carlsons spent much time thinking about their execution. I honestly believed they probably settled on the first or second doable idea they came up with. The Carlsons weren't the type to agonize over their methods. They were all about the excitement of the thrill kill, not a ritual they needed to complete. Though, I began to understand why they were attracted to this game play and why they would go through the trouble rather than, as Kang put it, "walk outside and kill the first person they see." The riddles and the creative execution multiplied the thrill for them.

Chapter 55

Our idea, given the situation, was simple and didn't require a bunch of resources—something we thought the Carlsons could easily pull off. We simplified Reilly's idea of chopping up a body and placing it in a five-foot-tall replica of a Chinese takeout container by settling on a moped used to make deliveries. On the back of the bikes were large warming containers. Our idea was to park one of those delivery bikes in Portsmouth Square, a popular, one-block park between Kearny and Grant, and inside the delivery container would be the head of a Chinese person—fake, of course.

With our idea solidified, we focused on the logistics. It basically sounded easy, but where do you get a fake head that looks real? We hired a special effects artist in L.A.: Monte Jenkins. He had spent years at Stan Winston's Studios and had been instrumental in creating the velociraptor in *Jurassic Park*, but now, he worked for himself.

Our SFX guy stressed that he needed at least two days to deliver the finished prop. "Hey, you're lucky I have a head I can refurbish, or else you'd be looking at week, minimum," he said over the speakerphone. He also insisted we fly him up to SF so he could apply the finishing touches with pig's blood. "It's a must for authenticity, and it needs to be applied at the time of the killing so the blood coagulates the way it should."

I didn't know what was more surprising: the level of detail that guy applied to his work or the fact that he knew so much about decomposition of a human body.

Taking a cue from the Carlsons, we decided to plant the bike in the park in the early morning. We'd snap some pictures, then let the situation unfolded as it normally would. Eventually, as the park filled with people, someone would discover the head, and SFPD would be called. FBI would of course show up as well, and we would run through the motions of processing the crime scene as if it were real.

We moved as fast as we could without overlooking minute details. We believed our success relied on pulling off a believable crime scene. If the person viewing the photos didn't believe them, we ran the risk of losing our momentum or, worse, the mastermind of this game. One of those details was what restaurant name to use on the delivery container.

"Why does the restaurant need to be real?" I asked Kang.

"Well, what if this guy has knowledge of the restaurants in Chinatown? He would know it was fake."

He had a point. But what restaurant would allow us to

fake-kill one of their employees? The answer was the Dynasty Inn. The owner was Kang's second cousin, who immediately volunteered his restaurant as the decoy.

"So your cousin has no qualms about doing this?"

"No, actually, he thinks it'll generate business." Kang pointed at his head and twirled his finger around in a circle. "His delivery guys use the mopeds with the hot food containers on them, so it's perfect for our needs."

Eventually, we settled on a story that someone had stolen the moped from the restaurant, and the head wasn't from an employee of the restaurant. That bit of news disappointed Kang's cousin. With the restaurant situation settled and our timing locked into place for Sunday morning, all we needed was our head.

Chapter 56

With Operation Takeout only a few days away, I decided to remain at home and take it easy. The back and forth with the office had hampered my thigh's recovery a bit. A few days of rest would do wonders. To keep myself busy, I continued to poke around through the Carlsons' information. With all that we had learned in the last few days, I had been eager to see if there was more to be discovered.

The exact logic that had led the Carlsons from riddle to answer to task for each attraction interested me. Even with all we had learned, I could not pinpoint how the Carlsons had obtained the answers to the riddles. I could guess the logic behind the riddle, but that was it.

Even our search for the answer to the fifth riddle was a crapshoot; we'd had no idea what we were looking for or how we would obtain it. Maybe that's the point. The riddle provided just enough information for someone to discover the answer but not enough information for others to know. Anybody trying to pinpoint how we got our answer based on the cryptic information in the game would never have deduced that we had to mention the name of the game to a

Qu Yan character while taking a picture with him at the Dragon Boat Festival.

I slouched a few inches down in my chair and folded my arms across my chest. The more I tried to understand the workings of the game, the more I realized how much thought had actually been put into masking its real intentions.

As I flipped through the riddles, one thing stood out: we didn't know the locations the Carlsons had visited in the past with the exception of the fortune cookie company. Even if someone did come to the conclusion that we had gone to the boat races, there would be nothing for them to attend. It was an event, not a location.

I picked up the phone and dialed Kang. "Meet me at the corner of Grant and Washington."

"What's going on in Chinatown?"

"Hopefully some good fortune we can use."

Chapter 57

Kang was busy snacking on a rice cake and used his eyebrows to acknowledge me. He motioned for me to take a bag out of his hand while he swallowed. Inside was another rice cake.

"Go ahead. I bought it for you," he managed to say between bites.

I grabbed the bag, plucked the rice cake from it and took a bite. Perfectly sweet with the right amount of sticky—I nodded my approval as I chewed.

Kang's head bounced up and down along with mine. "Good stuff, huh? I get them from the Dim Sum shop over on Jackson. They make the best cake in my opinion. So why are we here?"

"Follow me," I said as I popped the remaining piece into my mouth. I led him west on Washington to Ross Alley.

"The Fortune Cookie Company is here," Kang stated.

I brought Kang up to speed on my thoughts about how the Fortune Cookie Company was an actual location and the Dragon Boat Festival had been an event. I thought we might glean some information from it. He agreed but pointed out that we weren't in character.

"We don't want to be the Carlsons. If somebody at the factory gave them the answer they needed, that person would have knowledge of what they looked like."

Kang's face drooped.

"What?"

"If that's true, then they already know what the Carlsons look like and might know that the couple at Treasure Island wasn't them."

"I realize that, but that's the situation we're in. Plus, we don't know if the Carlsons were wearing their disguises when they came here. It's too late for a do-over now. Let's keep plowing ahead. Today we're normal tourists checking out how fortune cookies are made."

"Easy for you to say. You're dressed in jeans and a hoodie. I'm in a suit."

"No one twisted your arm this morning when you dressed." I spun around and headed into the alley.

"We'll pretend we don't know each other," he called out behind me.

"I can do that."

The day was early, so there wasn't much of crowd—which was great since the cookie factory wasn't that big. I maneuvered my way inside, leaving Kang outside to stretch his neck over the crowd for a look.

I pushed through, right up to the rope that marked the end of the public area, roughly an eight-foot by eight-foot space, and found myself standing next to a French couple. The wife stood poised in front of a girl making cookies while her husband took her picture. An older Chinese gentleman stood nearby and collected money from other eager tourists wanting pictures. I couldn't help but overhear one woman whispering to her friend.

"That Chinese woman is making fortune cookies," she said. "Just like that… folding a small square of dough. Ain't that something?"

What? Baking? You never seen someone bake cookies? I rolled my eyes as I let out a breath. Once they had their pictures, I positioned myself closer to the man collecting the money. With the general public having limited access inside the factory and he the only person available to talk to, the Carlsons must have interacted with him.

"How's business?" I asked.

He smiled and nodded.

I grabbed a bag of freshly baked fortune cookies from a nearby shelf. "How much?" I asked.

He held up his four fingers.

I knew the riddle for this location, *Good fortune comes in many different shapes*, but I wasn't sure if blurting it out was the right thing, since it had already been solved. I opted for a variation of it first. "Do you make fortune cookies in different shapes?"

He smiled.

Well, that went nowhere. Let's try direct. "Good

fortune comes in many different shapes, I hear."

Still, he stared at me with his smile and said nothing.

I finally mentioned the name of the game. *Maybe it's the same for every riddle.* Same response. Since my tiny self took up valuable real estate and the old man wasn't responding, I vacated my spot and threaded my way back to Kang.

"So what did I miss? Did you talk to the old guy?" Kang asked.

"I did." I told him what I had said and that I hadn't received an answer. "You think maybe we have it wrong, that the Carlsons never came here?"

"Nah." He shook his head and shoved both hands into his pants pockets. "This has got to be the right place. The only other local fortune cookie manufacturer is in Los Angeles. I'm guessing something was set up here for the password retrieval, like a special fortune cookie or maybe even a person in costume like at the boat race. Once the password is retrieved, maybe that special whatever-it-is disappears."

"Yeah, probably." I tapped my foot against the pavement.

"Something's bothering you," Kang said.

"There's something about that old man that's not sitting right with me, but I can't figure it out. Come on," I said, turning on my heels, "let's get out of here. We have an early call tomorrow."

◇◇◇

The old Chinese man called one of his workers to the front to collect money while he disappeared behind a door in the back of the factory. Inside the small office were two young men counting stacks of money. He spoke to them in Chinese, and they immediately stood up and exited the room. He then made a call on his mobile phone.

"I find couple again."

"Where?"

"At shop. I have them followed."

"Good."

The old man hung up the phone and sat in a chair near a desk. He let out a long, slow breath as he dabbed his forehead with a handkerchief. He leaned back and let his body relax. He had redeemed himself and felt positive that he was in a better position with Quai Chan. At the dragon boat races, his job had been to deliver the password to the Carlsons. In fact, it had been his job to deliver all the passwords. When Jing Woo, the boss of Chinatown, told him to follow the strange couple that day, he had been unable to locate them. This did not sit well with Jing, and Quai made it very clear that he had three days to rectify the situation.

The old man lifted his shirt to reveal his torso wrapped tightly in bandages. His ribs were still tender, and the wound across his abdomen had begun to heal. He lowered his shirt and let out another long breath. Good fortune does come in many different shapes.

Chapter 58

Kang, Monte and I arrived at Portsmouth Square in an unmarked van a little after three thirty on Sunday morning. We had our disguises on in case we were seen by a passerby or somehow by the mastermind. Monte was in the back making the final touches to the prosthetic head. "You almost done?" I asked.

"Yeah. Staging a crime scene—it's so exciting."

"You're not staging anything."

Monte stopped and looked up at me. "What? Why can't I help?"

I shrugged and wondered why I needed to explain myself. "Because I said so."

That night, a crescent moon coupled with heavy fog blessed us with the perfect cover to do what we needed. In the back of the van, we had the moped from Kang's cousin's restaurant, complete with decapitated head in place. Monte had added the bloody touches on the drive to the square. I must admit; the damn thing looked more lifelike than I had imagined it would.

We parked and waited inside the van for a few minutes, surveying the area. The plan was to stage the scene, snap some pictures, and get out of there. We anticipated that the entire operation would take us roughly fifteen minutes.

Kang rolled the bike out of the back of the vehicle down a small, portable ramp. Our target was the center of the square where a lamppost cast a soft light. We spent another ten minutes documenting with pictures and video.

"How long should we wait before uploading our evidence to the app?" Kang asked.

"If the real Carlsons had done this, they would still be reveling in the glow of the kill. I know we're both eager, but maybe it's better to wait a day."

◇◇◇

From out of the shadows, Quai Chan emerged, invisible to the naked eye due to his daily wear of a black Kung Fu suit. The eyes and ears of Chinatown had alerted him to the couple's arrival in the square. He arrived in time to watch the couple roll a moped out of their vehicle and park it under a lamppost. He knew from the descriptions given him by Lee, the owner of the Fortune Cookie Company, that this was the right couple. *Maybe he will live*, Quai thought.

He waved his hand as if he were motioning someone. He was. Four dark figures emerged from the shadows and spread out around the square. Within a few seconds, Quai and his men had surrounded the couple as they took pictures of the bike.

A second later, a white male exited the van, and approached the couple and started taking pictures. The woman immediately pointed at the van, her arm stiff like an arrow. She used her other arm to turn him around and push him back toward it.

Quai didn't need to see more. He motioned to his men, and all at once, they rose from their hiding spots, a mere fifteen feet away. They had long wooden tubes pressed tightly against their lips. A few seconds later, the three individuals fell to the pavement, unconscious.

Quai's men quickly moved the bodies back into the van and drove away as he watched the rear lights fade into the grasp of the gray. Quai stood from his crouched position and clasped his hands together, pushing them out, palm first, to create a rippling of crackles from his knuckles before making his way down to the motorbike.

He noted the restaurant and what was in the container but gave no visible reaction to seeing a bloody head. It was impossible to tell if he was fooled.

Chapter 59

Kang woke first. He blinked until his eyesight grew clear. Surprisingly, his first observation wasn't what his eyes saw but what his arms felt—a lack of movement. He looked down and saw rope strapped tightly across his waist, tying him to a wooden chair that was bolted crudely to the cement floor. His arms were pulled behind his back and fastened together at his wrists. Kang noticed a bit of slack in the rope and immediately began to work on it. He also realized his weapon was missing, and so were his keys and wallet. His disguise had been completely removed except for a bit of glue on the tip of his nose that had held the prosthetic down. *They know who we are.*

Those were the first of a series of dire observations but certainly not the last that Kang would make in the next few minutes.

To his left sat Monte, the SFX guy. He was tied down in a chair with armrests, his hands tightly secured to each one. His head swayed from side to side as he mumbled quietly to himself. Sitting to his right was Abby. She too had been stripped of her disguise and, he assumed, her weapon as well. Her chin rested against her chest, and her hair had fallen forward, covering most of her face. He could barely hear her shallow breaths, which was a relief, because upon sight, she looked dead.

Above him, a lone bulb dangled from a jerry-rigged electrical hookup. Every few minutes or so, the light would flicker. The room had no windows, only a wooden door leading out. Aside from the chairs the three were sitting on, the space was bare. The walls were constructed from small, red bricks, which gave Kang some encouraging information. *We're still in Chinatown.* However, the chill in the room told him they were most likely below grade. *An old basement, perhaps?*

Coughing from Monte grabbed Kang's attention. "Monte," he said, "you okay?"

He swung his head toward the direction of Kang's voice. "Yeah. My head hurts, though. Why am I tied? Where are we?" His words gained speed, and he spoke louder. He started to tug on his arms.

"Monte, I need you to remain calm. Look at me!"

Monte focused back on Kang. Heavy breaths escaped his hanging mouth, and the pits of his T-shirt had darkened.

"Everything will be okay. We'll get out of this. But in the meantime, I need you to remain calm." Kang kept his voice steady and his emotions in check. If he showed any sign of worry, he knew he would lose Monte.

"Why are we here? What's wrong with Agent Kane?" he asked, looking past Kang.

"She's fine. We were all knocked unconscious."

Kang then turned his attention to his partner. "Abby," he called out, but she didn't respond. He tried once more but louder. "Abby!"

Her head swung toward him.

"Abby, it's Kyle. Can you hear me?"

She mumbled and could barely open her eyes.

"I think we were drugged, maybe with some sort of anesthetic agent. Looks like she got the worst of it," Kang said.

"Is help on the way?" Monte asked.

"Help is on the way," Kang lied. "Now listen closely. At some point, we will face our captors, and when we do, I need you to remain calm. Let me do all the talking and do not, under any circumstances, engage them. Is that understood?"

Monte nodded.

Kang looked at the man from head to toe. He was either one degree away from losing it or on the verge of shock. Neither outcome was ideal.

"Do you know where we are?" Monte's words barely slipped out over his lips.

"I believe we're still in Chinatown. That brick," Kang motioned with his head to the wall, "is common in most of the older buildings, but I think we're in a basement."

"We're *underground?*"

"Monte, what did I just say about remaining calm?"

"Sorry."

"A lot of the restaurants and stores have underground storage units." Kang had been in a couple. It was also rumored that a network of tunnels existed under Chinatown, but Kang had never found any evidence of it. Even though he was a full-blooded Chinese man, he wasn't privy to the secret workings of Chinatown. Only its residents understood fully what went on in its confines.

It also didn't help that he was a cop. Chinatown had always policed and punished their own. That's how it was and always had been. It had helped to shelter the first wave of immigrants from the dangers of the city and the corruptions of the government. Cops were not to be trusted. And sadly, Kang was well aware of that.

Chapter 60

Back on the surface, a slew of law enforcement personnel had descended on Portsmouth Square. Reilly and his team were already fake-inspecting the crime scene when he realized that a half hour had passed since he had arrived. His intent was to do a walk-around and leave, but without the agent in charge of the case on site, that wasn't possible.

He called to no one in particular, "Anybody seen Agent Kane?"

"She hasn't shown, sir," answered a passing agent.

Reilly dialed Abby on his cell phone but got her voicemail. *Shit! Where are you? This is supposed to be your operation.* He walked over to one of the SFPD uniforms on perimeter duty. "Do you know if Detective Kang has shown up or is on his way?"

"Not that I know of, sir. I can put a call in to dispatch, and they can try to reach him."

"Thanks."

Reilly walked back to where the bike was parked. The forensics team was busy dusting the bike and photographing the surrounding area. The fake head was still inside the container, though now, in the light, Reilly could tell that it was a prop. He flipped the lid closed right as he felt a tap on his shoulder.

"Abby, it's about time…"

"Sorry, wrong agent." Agent Tracy House stood before him.

"Oh, I thought you were… What are you doing here?"

"Abby filled me in on the plan. I came by to see how real the crime scene looked. I'm impressed."

"Well, I'm not. Abby is MIA. She's supposed to be here overseeing this charade."

"If you need help, I can step in."

"Thanks, Agent. I would appreciate it."

House motioned with her head to a pack of journalists standing outside the taped off area. "Looks like someone needs to give a fake update to the media."

Reilly shook his head and clenched his jaw before heading over to feed the pool of reporters.

House walked over to the bike and took a peek inside the container when a uniformed officer tapped her on her shoulder.

"Sorry to disturb you, but that other agent," he said, pointing to Reilly, "asked me to check on the whereabouts of Detective Kang. I wanted to say that dispatch had no luck in reaching him. I also wanted to mention that the van he requisitioned wasn't returned. He didn't ask me to check on that, but I did—"

"Wait, what do you mean it wasn't returned?"

"It should have been returned early this morning, but it wasn't. I thought that was worth mentioning."

"Thanks. It is." The wheels in her head began to spin while her stomach grew hollow. Something wasn't right. House pulled out her phone and dialed Abby as she made her way over to Reilly. There wasn't any answer.

"Special Agent Reilly," she called out, interrupting his spiel to the journalists, "you're needed at the crime scene."

"That's all for now. We'll let you know when we have more information."

As soon as they were out of earshot from the reporters, Reilly whispered from the corner of his mouth, "Thanks for saving me there."

"Sir, I think we have a problem. An SFPD officer has just informed me that the van Detective Kang requisitioned to bring the bike here was never returned this morning."

"Shit!" Reilly grabbed another passing agent. "Agent Burns, you familiar with the effects guy we flew up here?"

"Yeah, I helped coordinate his travel plans."

"Good. I want you to find out if he is in his hotel room, immediately."

"I don't understand," House said. "Why are you checking on the guy who made the head?"

"Because he tagged along with them last night to finish prepping the head."

Reilly took a deep breath as he looked over the scene. Abby had asked if there should be backup, but they had both come to the conclusion that the operation was simple enough that they didn't need any. *I should have known better.*

"Were they supposed to check in after the drop?"

"Only if for some reason they were unable to complete it," Reilly answered. "I should have sent a team to watch them."

Agent Burns reappeared as he was getting off his mobile.

"You have an answer for me?"

"The room was empty, and the bed didn't appear to have been slept in."

"Agent House, round up every available agent on site and meet me back here."

A few minutes later, House returned with six other agents. Of the bunch, she looked the most concerned and rightfully so. To her, Abby was more than just a coworker. Reilly reached over and gave her shoulder a comforting squeeze. "Hey, you didn't put Abby on this case; I did. I don't want you blaming yourself, okay?"

House nodded as she worked to swallow the lump that had begun to lodge itself in the bottom of her throat.

"Listen up. We have a situation where one of our own, a detective with the SFPD and a civilian have gone missing." Reilly informed them of the details he had learned only minutes earlier. "I want a search perimeter established, starting right here in this square and branching out. Also, let's get an APB on the van they used and have SFPD and the Highway Patrol monitor the roads and bridges out of the city. I want—"

Reilly stopped and lifted his right foot. Beneath his shoe, he saw a thin, metal projectile about three inches long with red fletching at the end for stabilization.

"What the hell…?"

"If I'm not mistaken," House said as she bent down and picked up the object, "that looks like a tranquilizer dart."

"Let's get whatever is on the tip of it analyzed and hope we're not too late."

Chapter 61

Kang was staring ahead, contemplating their options, when a noise from Abby grabbed his attention. "Abby," he called out. She opened her eyes for a brief second before closing them. He called out once more. This time, her eyes remained open, but her lids were heavy. "Over here. It's me, Kyle."

Abby flopped her head toward him again. "Kyle… What's going on?" she slurred.

He noticed a thin trail of dried blood on her neck, partially covered by her hair. It only confirmed his earlier suspicions about them being drugged. *A tranquilizer gun?* It had to be. He didn't recall hearing a noise or seeing anyone. One minute, he had focused on Abby as she tried to get Monte back into the van, and the next thing he knew, he had woken up tied to a chair.

While Kang and Monte appeared to be recovering from the effects of the drug, Abby was having a much harder time. She appeared woozy and spoke sporadically without making much sense.

Kang didn't like their chances of survival and needed to quickly tilt the odds in their favor. He had been diligently working on loosening the knot that secured the rope around his wrists and had made significant progress. *Just get one hand free. That's it.*

Ten minutes had passed before he heard the scuffle of shoes outside the door and a key sliding into the lock. A beat later, the wooden door creaked open, and in walked three Chinese men. One was noticeably smaller than the others, but the intensity of his stare told Kang he was the leader. They were all dressed in black Kung Fu attire. The two tall men each had a sword strapped to their back, and one held a laptop under his arm.

The small man stepped forward to within a few feet of Kang. He had a wry smile. "Detective, how are you feeling?"

"Why are you holding us hostage?"

The man spread his feet apart and cupped his hands in front of him. "Why do you ask a question you already know the answer to?"

Kang's brow narrowed. "Who are you?"

The grin on the short man grew wider as he looked back briefly at his companions. "He wants to know who I am." His followers chuckled. "I am the Black Mantis."

"So you are Quai Chan. I've been wanting to meet you for a very long time."

"Well, Detective Kang, your wish has been granted." Quai began to pace the room slowly, methodically. "That show you put on in the square—very clever. What was its purpose?"

Kang remained quiet. The more he allowed the man to talk, the more he would learn what they knew and what they wanted.

"Your tongue is tied? I thought it was only your hands." More laughter. He then snapped a finger, and the man holding the laptop moved forward. He flipped it open and tapped at the keyboard before turning it around.

"I have live footage for you." Quai pointed at the screen. The video showed a woman reporting on the very crime that he and Abby had staged earlier that morning. Kang took note of two things right away: the time stamp on the video—a little after eight in the morning—and the fact that the laptop had a Wi-Fi connection. The room they were in either wasn't far from ground level or they were on ground level. Hundreds of tourists could be walking around just outside that door. That gave Kang hope.

"They found a head," Quai continued, "the head you left this morning. You remember doing that?"

Kang looked at Monte. He had followed his orders and kept his mouth shut. He also did one better and avoided eye contact by keeping his head down.

"What is it you want?" Kang asked.

"Why did you put a head in a delivery container and leave it in our beautiful park—a park that men, women and children enjoy on a daily basis? Why would you do that? What prompted you? Did you want to scare people? I think you would have scared the children but not the men and women. That head wasn't very good. Next time, find yourself a better looking head."

His laughing triggered more chuckles from the other two men. It also triggered a response from Monte.

"What do you mean find a better looking head? That head is extremely lifelike."

"Monte!" Kang barked.

Quai turned his attention to Monte. "I thought you were sleeping, but now, I realize you were too afraid to look at me."

"You don't know what you're talking about."

"I do know what I'm talking about. And that head is a piece of shit."

Monte shook his head and looked away but not before muttering an audible "Fuck you."

Kang couldn't believe his ears.

Quai's eyebrows dipped before he reached behind his back and removed a pair of sais, spinning them around in each hand. The light from the bulb above flashed off the polished metal. Kang hadn't noticed the weapon on Quai when he had first entered the room, but he quickly saw that the tips were sharpened into deadly points. Before he could utter a word to calm Quai, he brought both arms down, driving the steel shafts into the back of Monte's hands.

No!

Monte threw his head back and let go a long,

screeching cry before peeking back at his now pinned hands. Blood seeped from his wounds and dripped from the arms of the chair. His eyes grew wide. His jaw fell open, allowing a strand of saliva to stretch from his mouth.

He let out another cry. The brick wall multiplied its volume. Kang thought the worst had passed until Quai turned to one of his men, removed the larger sword from its sheath and spun around, all in one fell swoop.

Suddenly, Monte went quiet. His legs shot straight out, remaining rigid. Everything moved so quickly; Kang felt one step behind the action. Quai raised the sword and placed it against the side of Monte's head.

Monte's legs relaxed and dropped back to the ground. Kang suddenly knew why he was so calm. Tiny, red streams began to pour down the side of his neck. Quai then tapped Monte's head with the blade, and Kang watched it fall from its perch and hit the floor with a thud—a clean cut.

Chapter 62

Back in the square, the command center for the fake crime scene had quickly been repurposed for a real crime. House and Reilly gathered around a small map of Chinatown.

"What makes you so sure they're still in Chinatown?" Reilly asked.

"The game is played in the city, and a lot of it ties back to Chinatown. I can't say for sure, but if we have to go on a hunch, that's a pretty good one. Clearly, their cover was blown. How? When? Most likely back at Treasure Island. Plus, all the crimes took place in the city, with the exception of the Taylor girl found on Mount Tamalpais."

"Okay, I'm biting, but let me ask you one thing: why didn't they make a move on our decoys at Treasure Island? Why wait?"

"I think what happened speaks as your answer. Even we didn't know they were missing since three thirty this morning. Whoever is behind this is smart and calculating. They bided their time, and it paid off."

"Still, it makes no sense to abduct an FBI agent, a detective with the SFPD, a civilian and hold them as potential hostages. What did they have to gain? They could have disabled the app, rendering it useless instead," Reilly pointed out.

"That's what worries me," House said. She rested her hands on her hips. "That seems like the best solution, but we're not necessarily dealing with sound individuals here. The app was the only live connection we had to whomever was behind it. There's more to it and we're not seeing it."

"You think they're…"

"What, dead?" House shrugged and picked at her fingernails—a nervous habit. "Well, I can't see them wanting any sort of exchange out of it. My best guess is that they wanted to find out what Abby and Kyle knew about the app."

House squinted in the sun that had started to poke through the clouds. She and Reilly both knew what that meant. Either they would be performing a rescue operation or a recovery. And they were running out of time for a rescue.

House's phone rang.

"House here. I see… Yes... And the effects?... Was that all? ...Okay."

Reilly eyed House, looking for an answer.

"That was the lab. They found traces of xylazine on the dart. It's a horse tranquillizer, but drug addicts use it to get high. It turns people into walking zombies, barely mobile and semi-conscious. A large dose can kill a person."

"How long does it last?"

"Two to three hours, maybe longer. Depends on the dosage."

"That bought us some time. They can't question them in that state."

"Since they were able to stage the crime scene, they were probably apprehended shortly after. Maybe at four?"

Reilly nodded. "Sounds about right. They could have been in a position to talk by seven this morning." He looked down at this watch. "It's eight thirty. They might still be alive."

"Sir, I think we're better off concentrating all our efforts within the Chinatown area. It's our best chance."

Reilly took a moment to think over House's suggestion. "Okay. Redirect every man we have available and the SFPD to Chinatown, but leave Highway Patrol at the road blocks."

"Got it," she said before taking off.

Reilly let out a soft breath. *Man, I hope you're right.*

Chapter 63

Quai and his men left shortly after decapitating Monte. The stale air in the room quickly acquired a metallic overture. A pool of blood surrounded his chair, some of it inching its way closer to Kang's left foot.

By then, Abby could talk, though sometimes incoherently. She didn't look to have complete control of her body, and fell in and out of her catatonic state, but at least she was experiencing periods of normalcy. However, she did seem to be aware of their situation, as Kang had done his best to explain to her what had happened.

With Quai gone, he made gains on loosening the knot, ignoring the burn from the rope that rubbed his wrists raw. He was close to freeing his hands.

Once again, Kang heard shuffling outside the door and a key inside the lock. He knew who to expect. The door swung open, and Quai stood there, alone.

Dumb move, asshole. Kang was a stone. His body language implied nothing and his facial expression remained flat.

Quai shook his head as he slowly walked toward Kang. "Your friend here talked too much and met his fate. What do you think will happen to you for not answering me?"

Kang couldn't resist. "You and Chinatown are not above the law."

The man pointed at his chest in wonderment. "I see you many times in Chinatown. Why you don't come for me if I am not above the law?"

He knows me from before? How?

"You're wondering how I know you? I know everything that happens here."

Keep deflecting the conversation. Buy yourself time, Kang told himself. "I didn't know you were such a big fan." Kang flashed a smile, his words pleasant. "When this is all done, I'll send you an autographed photo."

Quai threw his head back and let out a bellowing laugh. When he regained his composure, he pointed at Kang. "You a very funny man. It's good to have a sense of humor, even in a situation like this."

Right then, the door opened, and another man entered, pushing a metal cart that had a number of surgical and carpentry tools on it.

"I wondered when you would resort to the old cliché of using torture," Kang mocked. "I mean, don't all evil men do this, failing to get what they want from their captors through thoughtful discussion? It's like a bad action movie taking place right before my eyes."

Again, the small man allowed himself to succumb to laughter—a staccato shrill this time that started on a high note and ended with a few coughs. The man with the cart joined in, nervous at first, wanting to be sure his boss found the joke funny. He then positioned the cart between Kang and Abby.

"Ah, your agent friend is coherent."

Kang looked to his left and saw Abby staring at the man. She blinked a lot but she looked to have her senses back. Maybe she had shaken off the remaining effects of the drug.

"We almost killed her up at the park. She's much smaller than I had anticipated," he said, shaking his head. He walked over to Abby. "I thought she was the leader, but it turns out you are the one who does the talking."

Kang smiled. *You don't know Abby.*

Quai stared into Abby's eyes. "Anybody home? Hello?" He turned back to Kang. "I think we lost her again."

Abby's eyes were half closed, and Kang's hopes faded a bit. He feared she might never recover. "Leave her alone."

The man smiled at Kang before turning back to Abby. He reached for the top button on her blouse and unbuttoned it. He continued with the second, and then the third. The smile on his face grew as he pushed the material back, revealing a lacy, black bra. He slipped the strap off her shoulder and pushed her bra down, exposing her left breast. He groped it with his hand, pulling and pinching her nipple. "Now why would I want to leave her alone when I am free to play with her?"

"You bastard!" Kang spat.

"What? What are you going to do? Nothing. I can fuck her, and all you will do is call me names." He then yanked the other side of her bra down and fondled both breasts. Her head swayed slightly from side to side. Her eyes were barely open. Moans slipped out from between her lips. He looked back at Kang. "I think she likes it." Abby let out a louder moan, gaining Quai's attention once more. He leaned in close, inches from Abby's face.

Big mistake.

Chapter 64

Quick and unexpected always favors the instigator.

When Quai turned back to face Abby, the Black Mantis got more than a cheap thrill. Abby's forehead slammed into the bridge of his nose, pulverizing the fragile bone. It was the thump that could be heard clear across the room. Quai pulled his head back and wailed in agony. Kang saw a glimpse of what was left of his nose after Abby's forehead had destroyed it. Quai grasped at his face. Blood poured from between his fingers. He stumbled backward until his back hit the wall.

Kang seized the opportunity and yanked his right hand free from the rope. Still in a seated position, he grabbed an ice pick from the metal cart and drove it into the chest of the guard caught looking at Quai—a man without orders. Kang didn't wait for a reaction and moved to free himself. He planted both feet on the ground and pushed back, straightening his body. The loud crack of wood splintering pierced the quiet room as the chair collapsed below his weight. Kang grabbed the rope, which was still tied around his waist and part of the chair, and shimmied the debris down his legs as he worked to get it to his feet.

With his man down, Quai shook off the effects of Abby's head-butt and moved toward Kang. Quai struck with multiple blows aimed at the tall man's chest. The first fist hit its mark, but Kang was able to deflect the other blows. Still, Quai continued his flurry of strikes to various parts of Kang's upper torso and head. Free of the rope, Kang looked for an opportunity to retaliate.

Quai dropped down for a leg sweep, but Kang timed a jump and delivered a kick straight to Quai's head, sending him onto his back. Quai flipped back to his feet and assumed a defensive stance. Even with his face painted red and his broken nose forcing him to breathe from his mouth, Quai smiled. "You learn Kung Fu at the academy?"

He then shifted his body weight to his rear leg, leaving his front leg flexed forward with the toe resting lightly on the floor. He brought both hands up to a guard position, and his fists assumed a hook formation. Kang knew this style of Kung Fu—the Northern Praying Mantis: fast and continuous strikes focused on vital parts of the body.

Watch out for the elbow, Kang told himself. He raised his arms out in front, moving the full weight of his body to his rear leg and leaving his forward leg gently resting on its heel. Kang's favorite style was *Hei Hu Quan* or Black Tiger Fist—perhaps the best match for his opponent.

Kang tightened both fists. A beat later, he attacked, delivering five tiger palms that penetrated Quai's defense five times.

On the sixth, Quai hooked outwards with his left hand, deflecting Kang's last right-handed punch, and created a turning force that opened up Kang's entire right side to an easy attack. He struck Kang hard in the temple, nearly missing his target: the right eye.

Kang's momentum still had his body turning, so he embraced it and followed through, spinning completely around and delivering a reverse kick to the head of his opponent without much effect.

Kang moved into a bow stance and delivered more tiger palm strikes to stop Quai from advancing. Kang then circled his arms over his head in a wide arc and delivered a double claw attack to the left side of Quai's rib cage. Quai backed up, but Kang continued his approach and circled over his head again, delivering a claw attack to Quai's right rib cage on the right side. Both strikes had the force to crack bones—his intention.

◇◇◇

I had my father to thank for that move. "Your head can do more damage than your fist, Abby. It's the unexpected punch," he would always say. My reminiscing didn't last long. An epic brawl had erupted in front of me.

I was surprised to see that Kang was so well trained in martial arts. He battled the bloody mess I had created with a velocity I could barely keep up with: straight punches, forearm blocks, high kicks, it was if I were watching a late-night Kung Fu movie. I lost track of who connected and who got blocked until the man with no nose made a sweeping leg attack. Kang had anticipated a high kick and dropped down. He took a foot to the windpipe and immediately fell to one knee, making a throaty noise.

I struggled to free myself, but the bindings that held my hands were too tight. I was helpless as I watched his opponent move in for the kill.

Kang took a knee to his face that snapped his head back, followed by an arc of red and then his body.

Our captor stopped his advancement and laughed. "Your Kung Fu does not match your ego."

I had to do something. This guy was about to finish off my partner and my only hope of getting out of there alive. So I did the one thing I knew would get that man to focus on me; I opened my mouth.

"Hey, Shrimp Boy. Why don't you pick on someone closer to your size?" *Like me.*

Chapter 65

Fresh blood leaked from the man's nose, but it seemingly had no effect on him. I could see the muscles along his jaw line ripple with rage as his eyes settled on me. Calling him out was about as far as I had thought my plan through. *Now what?* I was out of ideas and out of time.

"Kyle," I yelled, as I struggled in my seated position, "now would be a good time to recover."

He moved toward me, forceful breaths spraying red from his mouth. His eyes were bloodshot. His body movement was stiff and ready to explode on me.

Then, like a rail-thin beacon of hope, Kang rose up behind him, blood smeared across his face. He reached around my attacker's neck with his left arm. There were strands of rope still knotted around Kang's wrist. He grabbed the other end of the rope with his right hand and yanked back, lifting the man off the ground. He dangled a good foot or so above the floor as Kang leaned farther back, pulling on the rope and driving it deeper into our attacker's neck. His legs flailed around, and his hands pulled on the rope as he choked. But I saw that the dying man had one last move—his only move. I yelled out to Kang, "Watch out for his head!"

Kang moved his head to the side in time to avoid a backward head-butt.

The man continued to struggle, and the rope cut deeper, allowing no air to enter, no sound to escape. The taut stretching of his pants from his air kicks was all I could hear. And then he stopped moving. Kang held his grip a few seconds longer before letting him drop to the ground with a soft thump.

Kang then bent at the waist and rested his palms on his knees. He greedily sucked in air like an intake valve before he slowly looked up at me. His mouth hung open, and blood coated the inside of his lips and tongue.

"This looks familiar," I said.

Kang stood up and untied me from the chair. That's when I noticed the headless man still strapped into his chair. "Don't tell me that's Monte."

Kang nodded before bending down and searching the man he had choked.

"Who is that?"

"His name is Quai Chan. He's the enforcer for Jing Woo, the man that runs Chinatown." Kang stood up empty-handed.

"The last thing I remembered was telling Monte to get back in the van."

"I think they hit us with tranquillizer darts." Kang moved Abby's hair, revealing the dried blood. "They caught you in the neck."

I reached up and felt my neck, now aware of a slight throbbing in the area. Kang lifted his shirt and showed me where the dart had struck him. I fixed my bra and quickly buttoned my blouse back up.

"I have no idea what they used, but be glad it didn't end up killing us." He looked at the metal cart and picked up a long dagger. "Grab something. We'll need help getting out of here."

I chose a hammer. "Where the hell are we, anyway?"

"We're still in Chinatown. The red brick is the giveaway. We might be underground, in a basement perhaps. I've heard rumors of an underground network of tunnels."

"Tunnels? Under Chinatown?"

"Come on," he motioned. "Let's move."

He put his head against the wooden door and listened. "Sounds quiet." He cracked the door a few inches and peeked out before opening it all the way. We exited the room and entered a hallway. The walls and floor were cement, and there were bulbs lighting every few feet.

"Looks like the rumors are true. Which way?" I asked. Both directions looked identical.

Kang shrugged. "Hell if I know. The grade in this direction seems to angle up." He pointed. "Maybe this is the way out."

We walked ten or fifteen feet, Kang leading the way,

before a doorway on the left side of the hall came into view. He placed his ear against the door and listened but heard nothing. He turned the doorknob slowly. It was unlocked. He quietly pushed it open to reveal another small room, except the floor was covered with mattresses, and there were seven or eight girls sleeping in various states of undress. At least they looked asleep. Kang closed the door. "We'll have to send help for them later."

We continued down the dimly lit hall until we came upon another door on the right. Before opening it, Kang took the same precautions as before. This time, it didn't work. Inside the room were three goons packaging marijuana into small bags. They sprang from their seats and came at us. Kang tried to shut the door, but the pull from the other direction was too great and his hand slipped off the knob. Within seconds, the three men had attacked us in the hall. Kang plunged his knife into the neck of the first guy out of the room and tossed the gurgling man off to the side, ready to defend against the second.

The third man slipped by and came right at me with his arm cocked, ready to explode. I ducked, causing him to miss, but his momentum sent his body into me, knocking me to the ground. He tripped, landing a few feet away. I flipped over to my knees and stood up quicker than he did. Not necessarily wanting to kill this guy, I spun the tool around and punched the handle into his chest. Oomph! He doubled over. I followed with an elbow to the back of his head and sent him to the ground unconscious. I turned in time to see Kang slam his guy into the wall face first, twice. He stopped moving and fell to the floor.

I looked at the guy with the knife sticking out of his neck. I still couldn't believe that Kang was responsible for that and the dead body in the holding room. Killing a man in hand-to-hand combat is about as up close and personal as it gets.

"Come on; we need to hurry. Surely the noise will have alerted more men," Kang said as he pulled the knife out of the dead man's neck. We hurried as fast as we could. I kept waiting for more men to appear, wondering if I would have to use the other half of the hammer. We made a right and a left.

"There, up ahead." Kang pointed at a door and we ran toward it. He yanked on the knob but it was locked. "Damn!"

"Move," I said. "This knob looks pretty old."

I hammered away at it. After the fourth swing, it broke off. I hacked at the area where the latch held the door in its frame. Two strikes and the old wood split apart. Kang backed up and kicked the door off its hinges, revealing a storage room.

We made our way past shelves of dry food, large cans of soy sauce, plastic containers of seasonings, jugs of cooking oil, and more. Toward the back, we saw a wooden ladder leading up to a pair of metal doors. Kang grabbed the hammer from my hand and struck the doors repeatedly. I thought for sure more goons would show up any minute.

But then the metal doors creaked, and a beat later, they opened. Staring down at us were three very confused cooks.

Chapter 66

For the second time in one month, I found myself in the hospital, except this time I was forced to spend the night for observation. The toxicity test confirmed traces of xylazine in our systems. My levels were higher than what they found in Kang and in Monte's remains.

"They probably injected the same amount in all of you, but with your weight and size, the drug had a much more aggressive affect on your body," the doctor had told me earlier. "You're lucky you didn't die. That stuff is meant to knock out a horse, not humans."

Over to my left, lying in another bed, was Kang. He was out cold but in stable condition. Reilly had ordered that we be put in the same room and an officer be stationed outside for our safety and to keep us from leaving. We both had IVs stuck in our arms to replenish our fluids, the hospital's way of keeping a leash on us—they didn't want us bolting prematurely either. I don't blame them. I wanted out of that sterile room with its fluorescent lighting. I kept the lights off and used the small table lamps instead.

I watched the subtle rise and fall of Kang's chest and listened to his gentle breaths. He seemed peaceful in his bed. It was hard to imagine that, hours ago, he had been a raging ball of testosterone, battling enemies to see to my safety. *Talk about a partner having your back.*

When I told the paramedic that I didn't need to go to the hospital, Kang insisted. He told me how I continued to flow in and out of my catatonic state. One second, I would be right behind him, following him down the hall; the next second, he would look back and find me standing still and swaying. I didn't believe him. I thought he was joking, but he insisted it was true. I had no recollection of it.

On the way to the hospital, I remember telling him about the room with the half-naked women and the other one with the three men who attacked us. "I took one of them out."

"Yes, you did," he answered in a neutral tone. "But what you're not remembering is the group of men who came up on us in that hallway and attacked you from behind, knocking you to the ground."

My brow narrowed.

"You don't remember that, do you?"

It wasn't until the doctor confirmed what Kang had said that I bought into his story. "It's a known side effect with addicts who use xylazine. They tend to go in and out of consciousness even though they're awake. It probably happened to all three of you but your effects simply lasted longer."

I had to wonder what else had happened that I couldn't

remember.

Once we were alone in our hospital room, I interrogated Kang for all the details. He started by filling me in on what took place from the moment he regained full consciousness until we appeared in the kitchen of a Chinese restaurant. According to Kang, there was one other thing I didn't recall.

"I threw myself at you?"

"See, that's why I didn't want to tell you. I knew you would get embarrassed."

I sucked in a deep breath. "I'm not embarrassed, because I know it didn't happen."

"Do you? You heard what the doc said earlier."

"You're messing with me."

"Don't worry. It didn't bother me. I have that effect on women, especially when I rescue them."

I pressed my lips tightly together as my face turned various shades of red. He had officially embarrassed me.

Kang looked at me from his bed. "It's okay. I don't mind being your hero," he said before laughing and rolling over to his side.

I didn't want to encourage him, but I couldn't keep myself from laughing. As I lay quietly, I started looking at Kang differently. I knew he was still the same jokey guy I had worked with for the last month, but somehow, seeing him through the lens of an action hero changed things for me. Suddenly, he was a strong, take-charge guy who defended me from evil men and ensured my safety. He had become my knight in shining armor. I mean, what kind of gal wouldn't want a guy like that coming to her rescue? I couldn't help but feel like I had developed, how would I say this, a mild crush on the guy. *Me and Kang? Nah.* I tried to repress the feelings, but they lingered.

As I lay there trying to understand my newfound feelings, the door to our room squeaked open, and in walked Agent House.

"Hey there, Special Agent."

I smiled at my friend, happy that she had come to see me. "What are you talking about?"

"Rumor has it they're promoting you."

I waved off House's remark. "I'm not interested. More responsibility means more work. I already have plenty to deal with."

House removed a Thermos of hot water from her bag and placed it on the table next to me along with a familiar little tin.

"You didn't."

"I did," she said as she poured some hot water into a cup. "Swung by your house, and your Po Po gave me some of your tea. Speaking of, she hasn't told the kids yet about what really happened. They think you're at work. Do you know what you're going to say?"

The kids were always the toughest part about my job. I thought it would be easier as they grew older. It's not.

Maybe when they're eighteen I can tell them the whole story. "Hmmm, I'm not sure. The truth I guess."

House squeezed my hand gently and smiled before looking over at Kang. "How's he doing?"

"Fine. He's sleeping."

"You got lucky with him. I hear he's some sort of Kung Fu master and that he dropped a guy with one finger."

"Boy, the rumor mill is in full churn, huh?"

"Oh, yeah, and everyone is loving it. Wanna hear more?"

"No, thanks. I've had my fill of drama."

A devilish smile grew on House's face as she leaned toward me, a giggle escaping her lips. "I watched you from outside the window before coming in," she said. "You were staring at him."

"Shhh!" I said, my voice barely audible. "He might be listening."

"So it is true; you did call him your hero," she singsonged.

"It's not, and I didn't." My cheeks burned, and I could barely make eye contact with her.

"Why are you so embarrassed?" she continued in a hushed tone. "He's a good-looking guy."

"It's not like that. Our relationship is completely professional."

"Relationships change."

"This one doesn't."

"Why not? The case is pretty much over."

"Where does it stand?"

"Good question. Quai Chan and his goons, had they survived, would have faced a long list of charges ranging from murder to kidnapping and assaulting a federal agent."

"What about the tunnels?"

"A search of the tunnels garnered us a few more members from the local Triad gang, and we confiscated a large stash of marijuana and illegal fireworks."

"And the girls?"

"They're from China—underage and trafficked into the country. We turned them over to ICE's Victim Assistance Program. Other than that, just bodies left from your rampage."

"Mine? Try Hercules'." I motioned toward Kang with my head.

"Nonetheless, Forensics has a long day ahead of them."

"Kang mentioned a guy named Jing Woo."

"Boy, you do need a briefing." House looked down at her watch before lowering her voice. "In three hours, Reilly plans on hitting Jing. We got a tip that he holds court at a tong over on Waverly Avenue. Reilly's dropping the hammer, using two full tactical teams. I feel sorry for anybody in the building when they strike."

"I feel out of the loop."

"You should be. You're in a hospital. Look, not a lot of people know about the Jing hit, not even SFPD. Reilly didn't want anything leaked. There is enough incriminating evidence in those tunnels to tie to Jing, app aside. I'm sure there's more to be found at Jing's place. It's about time we cleaned house in Chinatown. SFPD has let that place police itself way too long."

House motioned over to Kang with her head. "Isn't there some festival in Chinatown this weekend?" The playfulness in her voice had returned.

"I think so."

"Ask if he's going. Tell him you are. You guys can hang out, it won't feel like a real date, and you can kind of see how it feels without any pressure."

I stole a look at Kang before turning back to House with a big grin on my face.

"See? I knew you liked him," she said, laughing.

"That's a really good idea."

"What's a good idea?" Kang said, interrupting our planning session.

Chapter 67

I froze, and while my heart leaped out of my chest and hid somewhere under the bed. *How long had he been listening?* I whacked House on the arm, urging her to say something. She shook her head violently. Suddenly, the talkative one had rigor mortis of the mouth.

He rolled over to face us.

"You're up," I managed with as much normalcy as I could muster. "Uh, I was telling Tracy about that festival in Chinatown."

"Oh, yeah, the music festival. I plan on going."

"Maybe we can meet up."

"Yeah, that would be great—granted, if they let us out of here. Text me when you two get there."

"I can't go," Tracy blurted sharply. "I already have plans. Sorry, but Abby, you should go. It sounds fun."

Man, the acting in this Girl Likes Boy skit is so bad. No way he buys off on it.

"Okay. Abby, looks like you're stuck with me."

Okay, he did.

Just as I was about to suggest a time, the devil appeared, and it had a squeaky voice.

"Kyle!"

Into our room walked a thin, tall, high-heeled, Gucci-purse-carrying, pearl-necklace-and-jade-bracelet wearing, plum-lipstick-pouting, hand-towel-as-a-skirt-sashaying, fair-skinned, Asian beauty with a stuffed teddy bear holding a "Get Well Soon!" balloon.

She shuffled in with tiny steps as she shimmied her braless breasts under what had to be the sheerest blouse ever invented in the history of mankind. "I'm so sad to see you here," she whined as her eyelashes batted hard and long enough to produce sustainable wind energy. "How's my wovey dovey? Is my waby feewing better?"

She then made kissing sounds and had the bear kiss Kang all over his face. And damn it if he wasn't eating the act up. Kang was in La La Land, laughing and giggling with that woman as she snuggled up to him. It wasn't until House cleared her throat that the two broke apart from their over-the-top, puke-inducing public display of affection.

Kang lifted his arm, pointing past this woman. "Suzi, this is Agent Tracy House and Agent Abby Kane. Abby is my partner on the Cotton Candy case."

Suzi turned to us and flashed a plastic smile that lasted one-point-three seconds before flatlining. She extended her hand. "Hi. I'm Suzi Zhang, Kyle's girlfriend."

Chapter 68

Jing Woo never saw it coming.

That's what happens to a man who lives above everyone: he believes he's untouchable. Even moments before his door was blown open, Jing ruled as if he were an aristocrat with faithful subjects. Not in a million days or nights would he ever have thought the end would come the way it did. But it had.

The reign of the most powerful man in all of Chinatown had ended. But that's not all Jing was known for. He was also Chinatown's biggest private contributor of monetary donations and a highly respected community organizer, at least from a distance. He was responsible for a dozen or so after-school programs for Chinese children, improvements to Portsmouth Square, numerous Chinese cultural expansion events, and an array of beautifying projects all throughout the Chinatown area. He had even helped subsidize the Chinatown Community Development Center, whose primary responsibility was providing affordable housing to Chinese immigrants. For all intents and purposes, Jing Woo was a hero in the community.

But it was a mask of illusion, because all of this good

came at a steep price.

Fear was how Jing Woo ruled. And his grasp on Chinatown was tight and impenetrable, even by SFPD. He made millions though the trafficking of opium, firearms, women, and even fireworks. He ran the massage parlors as well as the underground Mahjong games. Every business in Chinatown paid tribute, or they had no business being in business.

For years, Jing saw yearly increases in revenue; there was nothing he couldn't smuggle in or out of Chinatown. For every dollar he invested into the community, he made one thousand back. It was a no-brainer to be the people's Robin Hood. Who would want to take down the people's hero?

Jing Woo soon found out.

Chapter 69

As promised, the hospital discharged Kang and me the following day with orders to take the next couple of days off. I was all for it, especially after hearing about the Jing Woo raid. All the key players were dead. We would have preferred to see them have their day in court and spend the rest of their lives in prison, but the dead thing worked for us.

My family was my only focus when I returned home. I even pulled Ryan and Lucy out of school and awarded them a four-day weekend, which they loved. We had a grand time. We ordered movies on-demand, ate bowls of popcorn, and played multiple rounds of Go Fish.

A few months earlier, I'd signed Lucy up for dance classes to help her get over her shyness. It worked. She put on four five-minute shows for the family, complete with costume changes. We also helped Po Po with the cooking, which she tried to stop even though we knew she appreciated it. When we picnicked in Washington Square, we borrowed one of the dogs from Fanelli's Deli, Fino, my favorite, and took her with us. Ryan and I continued our discussions on Bruce Lee and martial arts in general. I brought in two masseuses for the family. It was the only time the house remained quiet.

And of course, we resumed Dim Sum Sunday. Po Po was able to see her friends again, Ryan got, not one, but two boxes of snappers, and Lucy was pleased with her new stash of Hello Kitty stickers. Everybody was happy, and I was emotionally content.

With Operation Family Time in progress, I never did make it to the Chinatown festival to meet up with Kang. I was over it. My feelings were the result of what I had originally thought them to be in the hospital—a super hero crush—a common phenomenon associated with people who are rescued by someone of the opposite sex. Plus, at the hospital, it was clear to me how much Kang liked his new toy and the teddy bear she had brought.

By the time Sunday night arrived, we were all beat. Po Po and the kids had gone to bed early, leaving me alone to enjoy a relaxing soak in a bathtub I don't use nearly enough. Afterward, I headed up to my office to check my email; I had stayed offline for four days thanks to a missing cell phone I had yet to replace. *A quick peek couldn't hurt.*

I didn't see anything that couldn't wait until Monday morning, until I saw the email from Kang that contained photos from the staged crime scene. I hadn't realized he had emailed them while we were still there.

Curious, I clicked on the email and was surprised at how well the photos had come out, considering my experience with Kang's photography at Treasure Island. Seeing the pictures reminded me that we never did upload them to find out what would happen next.

As usual, my curiosity got the best of me. I still had the Carlsons' hard drive loaded on my laptop, so I booted it up and clicked on the game. After the familiar intro played out and the headers and map appeared, I clicked on the fifth Attraction, and the paper scroll unraveled, revealing how far we had gotten. The cursor blinked in the empty field titled upload.

Well, why not? The worst that could happen is nothing, right?

I selected two pictures and hit the upload button. A few seconds later, the swirling circle disappeared and the phrase, "Upload complete. Thank you," replaced it.

Hmmm, interesting.

From what we had learned so far, each time the Carlsons completed a task, it unlocked the next Attraction. *So what happens when all the Attractions are completed?*

A second later, a chime sounded and the word "Congratulations" floated across the screen, followed by a note. "You have successfully completed the chase in San Francisco. Click the plane ticket for your next challenge."

I clicked on the animated plane ticket, and it swooshed back and forth across the screen, erasing everything before disappearing. A new map of the world then appeared. This time, there was a new trajectory line connecting San

Francisco with Bangkok, Thailand. Also, the five San Francisco Attractions were gone and replaced with five Bangkok Attractions.

I couldn't believe what I was looking at. The game was continuing. San Francisco was just another stop. Then my eyes spotted the word, "Leaderboard." I had never seen it before. I clicked on it and watched the Attraction heading minimize, and in its place, a leaderboard appeared. There were twenty-five teams on the board. A large arrow pointed at the fourth position, Team Carlson.

Don't tell me...

The map had also changed. It no longer only showed the three waypoints representing the Carlsons' travels. There were a number of arced lines connecting many of the major cities all over the world. And each waypoint was color coordinated to a team on the leaderboard.

No, this can't be. Other teams! Global!

My chest tightened instantly, erasing everything my relaxing bath had given me. A prickling sensation appeared along my arms and spread out across the rest of my body as my mind processed the information in front of me.

A talk bubble appeared over France. It read, "Team Annihilate has completed the second Paris Attraction."

Is it updating in real time? Suddenly another talk bubble appeared over Northern California. That one read, "Team Carlson has completed the chase in San Francisco."

Nooooo! I shook my head. I didn't want to believe, and

yet I had no other choice. There was no denying what I had uncovered. Chasing Chinatown wasn't just a game for the Carlsons; it was a game for multiple killers all around the world. Innocent people were being slaughtered so that some a-hole could be entertained. How many had suffered so far? How many more were to come? I knew right then that our investigation wasn't over. It was only the beginning.

◇◇◇

Russian Hill is book one in the three part Chasing Chinatown series. Stay tuned for the next installment, Lumpini Park. Abby and Kyle are faced with stopping a deadly global game, and the only way to do it is to move up the leaderboard themselves. For a preview, look at the next page.

Lumpini Park

The heat index that day was ninety-four degrees Fahrenheit. A fluke? Hardly. Every now and then, San Francisco becomes a hot, sticky mess—something Special Agent Reilly would discover in less than forty minutes.

The assault team consisted of twelve men from the FBI Special Weapons and Tactical Teams packed into two modified, civilian vans. Reilly and four other agents followed in a black SUV.

Waverly Place was their destination, a small street in Chinatown about fifty yards long and lined with tongs and temples. A van sandwiched each end of the street, and the two tactical teams exited and approach the tong on foot.

The street was unusually quiet for that time of day. A blessing? More like a sign. A hushed murmur of Chinese was all they could hear as they approached the small crowd of residents that had gathered outside the tong.

Team One was ordered to clear the crowd of looky-loos while Team Two, Reilly's team, moved into position to breach the front door—only the lead man reported that the door was already open.

By the time Reilly and his men entered the tong, salty streams were seeping into the collar of his shirt. The Kevlar vest he had on didn't help matters, but what really hit him hard, hard enough to stop him in his tracks, was the thick smell of death.

Reilly had found the red sticky to go with the red hot.

Two feet into the tong lay a headless man. Reilly sidestepped the crimson pool that had fanned out from the severed neck. The edges had already coagulated into a gel dam, preventing further spreading. He thought of searching the man for identification but changed his mind. He'd have to step into the sticky to get close enough. He stood, looked around and shook his head at the splatter that now spotted the whitewashed walls. *What the hell happened here?*

He could hear the tactical team on the upper floors shouting, "Clear!" faster than expected. That told him one thing—no resistance. *More bodies.*

He was right.

What he had originally thought was the buzzing of an electrical current turned out to be an assault by another team associated with death: flies. Reilly let out a breath and turned to the bottom of the blood-stained stairs. *Lead the way, my buzzing friends.*

After passing the second decapitated man, he gave up trying to avoid the blood. It's like walking in mud; eventually, you say, "Screw it," and give in, because what's the point? The entire shoe would need cleaning anyway.

Reilly had seen a lot during his twenty years with the Bureau. Death didn't bother him, but headless humans did. He'd counted nine so far, more than enough to make him shiver under his heavy vest.

He had never understood the thought process behind choosing decapitation over the simplicity of a gun. A firearm provided distance. Decapitation was close and personal. All he could conclude was that a person who reveled in this manner of dispatching people put absolutely no value on life. How could they? It's traumatic to see the aftermath let alone watch it take place. Reilly couldn't imagine what it was like to be the executioner.

He continued up the stairs, keeping his thoughts to himself. The assault team had already cleared the top floor and was on their way back down.

"No threats. The building is clear, sir," said the team leader. "Our job here is done. I'll leave six men outside the building until SFPD can set up a contained perimeter."

Reilly nodded.

The team leader took another step but stopped and grabbed Reilly by the arm. "It's bad in there." He motioned to what remained of a shattered door, which was barely hanging by its hinges.

Reilly's intelligence team had told him the top floor was where Jing Woo held court. From the look on the team leader's face, he had a pretty good idea that questioning the elusive leader would be a no-go. He stepped through the doorway, careful not to spear his arm with a splinter.

The room was still lit by, his count, fifteen candles of varying heights. He didn't see the body right away, his eyes needing a moment to adjust to the lower light levels. But once they did, it was unavoidable.

In the middle of the room, lying on his back on top of a small, teak table, was Jing. His head, both arms, and legs from the knees down hung off the edges. The robe was undone, revealing his grisly death. He had been opened from sternum to pubic bone.

Reilly took a step forward, unsure whether the shadows from the candle lighting were deceiving his eyes. They weren't. Jing had been gutted. All that was left was an empty cavity. Reilly looked at the floor, careful of where he stepped, and moved around to the other side of the table, where he discovered Jing's innards, completely intact and left to rot.

Later, when medical examiner Timothy Green weighed in, he said, "He was alive when they removed his organs. It was fast, precise, and I believe he felt every bit of it." Green also reported high levels of amphetamines in Jing's body. "Most likely used to keep him from passing out during the procedure."

It was obvious to Reilly that someone wanted Jing more than he did. Was it to punish him for the disorder that had taken place on his watch? Had they wanted to silence him? Who knew? This was a first for law enforcement in

San Francisco. Never had the walls of Chinatown been breached. They had moved into uncharted waters, and no one knew what to expect from the vacuum created by Jing's death. All they could do was hope for the best

A Note From Ty Hutchinson

Thank you for reading RUSSIAN HILL. If you're a fan of Abby Kane, spread the word to friends, family, book clubs and reader groups online. You can also help get the word out by leaving a review. If you do leave one, send me an email with the link. Or if you just want to tell me something, email me anyway. I love hearing from readers. I can be reached at thutchinson@me.com.

Better yet, sign up for my Super Secret Newsletter and receive "First Look" content. Be in the know about my future releases and what I'm up to. There will even be opportunities to win free books and whatever else I can think of. Oh, and I promise not to spam you with unnecessary crap or share your email address. Sign up now at http://eepurl.com/zKJHz.

There's a lot of procedure in the FBI, and I don't always stay true to it. If I leave something out or change the way things are done, it's because I don't think it helps the story. A dear friend of the family is a retired FBI agent, and that person does a pretty good job of keeping me in check, both verbally and with eye rolls. But in the end, I write what makes the story better, and that's the way it is. After all, this is fiction.

I tend to hang out in these places. Stop by.
Blog: http://tyhutchinson.wordpress.com/
Facebook: http://www.facebook.com/tyhutchinson.author

The Novels of Ty Hutchinson

Abby Kane FBI Thrillers
Corktown
Tenderloin
Russian Hill (CC Trilogy #1)
Lumpini Park (CC Trilogy #2)

Darby Stansfield Thrillers
Chop Suey
Stroganov
Loco Moco

Other Thrilling Novels
The Perfect Plan
The St. Petersburg Confession

14 18 36 48
53, 71, 98, 100   103
108, 121 - crop leg,
122, 137, 143, 162, 176, 179,
180, -crop - 195, 196-crop -
201 206, 207 208, 213
(222) 223   227, 230
243, 252, 267, 266,
265, 274, 278, 280,
281,
R-200 211, 215 233
248